W9-AWQ-569

A POWERFUL POTION

The crowd waited as Sophie pretended to feel the love potion coursing through her body. Slowly, she turned to Ian. They had rehearsed that Sophie would put her arms around his neck and give him a simple close-mouthed kiss. But Sophie had something else in mind.

She walked deliberately toward him, female power surging through her veins. She felt as though she could do anything. The world was hers. And he would be, too. At first, Ian did not understand her intent, but his eyes widened with surprise as she reached up and pulled his head down for a kiss.

This, Ian realized, was not what they had rehearsed....

Other *Leisure* books by Zoe Archer:

LADY X'S COWBOY

Love in a Bottle

ZOE ARCHER

LEISURE BOOKS NEW YORK CITY

To Zack,
who always believed.

A LEISURE BOOK®

December 2006

Published by

Dorchester Publishing Co., Inc.
200 Madison Avenue
New York, NY 10016

ISBN 0-8439-5738-7

Visit us on the web at www.dorchesterpub.com.

"The trees shake their leaves and whisper pleasingly; the birds agree with all sorts of lovely songs; and the whole vegetable kingdom releases a lovely aroma. The insects fly about in the air, and perch here and there like ornaments... A person would have to be a stone not to be revitalized by all these things."

—Carl von Linné (Linnaeus) (1707–1778)
Diaeta Naturalis 1733

No matter how fast you run,
your shadow more than keeps up.
Sometimes, it's in front.

Only full, overhead sun
diminishes your shadow.

But that shadow has been serving you!
What hurts you, blesses you.
Darkness is your candle.
Your boundaries are your quest.
—Jelaluddin Rumi (1207–1273)
From "Enough Words?" *Kulliyat-e Shams*

Chapter One

Wiltshire, England
1763

It was the most beautiful fungus Sophie had ever seen.

She would never have described herself as a person normally interested in fungi. Either one was pro-fungus or anti-fungus, as far as she had observed. Usually Sophie's concentration was solely centered on plants, with her specialty being flowering plants, but she knew enough about the realm of fungi to recognize a rare specimen when she saw one. If she were able to obtain a sample of the fly agaric mushroom long before any of the area's other botanists, it would be quite a feather in her cap. Or would it be a mushroom cap in her feather? Sophie did not dawdle on the details. She wanted the mushroom. That would show them.

She finally gave up hope of examining it from a respectable distance, since it was carefully hiding itself under a fallen tree green with moss. Sophie set down her sketch pad and pencils, removed her broad straw hat, and began to do what she had not done since the first of her twenty-three years.

She crawled.

Her blasted panniers made the work difficult, and she was likely muddying up her gown, yet she did not care when such a beautiful and extraordinary specimen as the fly agaric mushroom presented itself like a shy scarlet princess waiting in the woods to be courted.

Sophie chided herself as she carefully edged closer, over the bracken and tender forest-floor plants. If she wanted to be taken seriously as a botanist, she would have to give up such fanciful notions as fungi princesses and focus on clear, logical observation. Men might have the luxury to indulge in pretty comparisons. No one questioned a man's right to dabble in the sciences. Yet women were an entirely different matter. Any false move on Sophie's part would only prove that whatever interest women had in the study of plants should be limited solely to the planning of gardens.

Gardens, ha! Sophie almost snorted aloud. She was much happier here, in the wilds of nature, far from the judging eyes of social custom.

She inched toward the fly agaric—such a dreadful name for such a beautiful specimen—unconcerned that she likely looked ridiculous and undignified. Her mother would succumb to the vapors if she ever saw her daughter eagerly reaching toward a mushroom, all alone in the middle of the woods. Yet that was exactly why Sophie was *not* traveling with her mother. Vapors were quite a nuisance when there was research to be done.

2

Almost there. Sophie carefully noted the fly agaric's stem structure, its identifying bright red cap with white scales, the number and definition of the gills under its cap, its oddly solitary position, the pair of black shiny boots standing right next to it.

With a startled yelp, Sophie leapt back, landing on her rump in a flurry of skirts.

A man stood in front of her, wearing said boots, soft doeskin breeches, a fine but plain dark blue waistcoat, and a bottle-green coat. Then she looked at his face and lost all interest in his clothing.

Taken together, the various parts of this man made up a pleasant whole. An *extremely* pleasant whole. Though Sophie was on the ground, she could plainly see that the man was rather tall. His legs were long and lean, and he filled out the shoulders of his coat in a way that clearly bespoke a level of fitness unlike any other man Sophie had ever met. And his face . . . Sophie was not given to dreamy interludes sighing over heroes in romantic novels—yet here was a man to make a woman sigh. His rich brown hair was pulled back into a queue, and his eyes were a shade lighter than his hair. He had strong, even features. But what made her stomach contract in a strange and pleasant way was his smile.

She didn't know men could have such beautiful, charming smiles, full of wit and mischief, and yet be so completely masculine. This man proved her wrong. There was nothing calculated about his smile, no empty gesture of friendship or politeness. No, this stranger, whoever he was, truly seemed to enjoy life, as though it were a merry gift that kept unfolding in surprising and delightful ways. He exuded a particularly male charm, an awareness of himself and his effect on others that was not cocky or obnoxious, but rather a natural extension of the pleasure he found in the world. He made her want to smile, too. So she did.

"I would be most flattered by your smile, my lady," the man said with a chuckle, "save for the fact that you were smiling in exactly the same way at a mushroom not moments before."

Sophie felt deflated. Her face must have shown as much, because the mysterious gentleman immediately stepped forward—carefully over the mushroom—and offered her his hand.

"My apologies, my lady. I have been teasing you when, like a churl, I have left you sitting on the ground."

She regarded his outstretched hand. It was large and beautifully formed, with long square fingers. Though the stranger spoke like a gentleman, his hand was more work-roughened than that of other men she knew, except the gardener at home. This man had a fascinating hand. She felt as though she could study it all day, learn its secrets.

"And now you are applying your excellent observational skills to my hand," the man said, his voice interrupting her scrutiny. Sophie's eyes flew to his face, mortified, but he was not at all offended. "Again, you flatter me. Please allow me the honor of helping you to your feet."

Sophie slid her muddied hand into his. An immediate deep thrum shot through her when their flesh touched, like a plucked string on a viola.

Silently, he pulled her up with almost no effort on his part, until she was standing squarely on the ground. She rubbed the bridge of her nose with the tip of her finger, hiding behind a habitual gesture to find inner equilibrium. Then she remembered her mother's constant remonstrance against such a vulgar gesture and quickly clasped her hands in front of her.

He made her feel a bit off, this stranger, uncertain in a way she wasn't used to. And she thought, for just a moment, that she set his balance off, too.

The stranger was once again smiling. Yet Sophie could detect that he had retreated somehow, that there was a part of him that had erected a façade and used it as a shield. Against what? she wondered. Her? It seemed impossible. What threat could she pose to anyone, let alone a young and handsome man?

"Permit me the honor of introducing myself," he said, bowing smoothly as if they were in a drawing room and not a forest glade. "Ian Blackpool, my lady."

Sophie curtsied, an automatic response. The gesture seemed particularly odd out here in the woods of Wiltshire, far from human habitation and custom. "Sophie Andrews," she answered.

His eyebrows arched playfully as he pressed his hand to his chest like a courtier. "Ah, the fair nymph of the woods speaks at last. I was beginning to despair of ever hearing your dulcet voice. You continue to heap tributes upon me."

Frowning, Sophie backed up. She did not like being spoken to in such a fashion, as though she were an empty-headed miss who could be charmed with easy flattery. She had received enough of that kind of attention to last her a lifetime, and had resolved never to endure it again. Although Mr. Blackpool was certainly one of the most handsome men she had ever met, her sense of pride demanded that she treat him no differently than she would anyone else offering up meaningless, patronizing compliments. Out in the field, she wanted life unhindered by pretense, to create the world as she wished it—as though she were Prospero and this stranger Caliban.

Taking up her hat and sketch pad, she walked as close as she could to the fly agaric mushroom. "A pleasure meeting you," she said quickly, sitting down on the fallen tree. She ignored the vibration of awareness that moved through her as she passed him. "Good day."

She opened her sketchbook and, after fishing ink and pen from her pockets, began to draw the mushroom. She bent over her work, looking up only to observe her subject and shutting Ian Blackpool out of her line of vision. Instead of responding to her unsubtle hint, he sat right next to her. Surprised, Sophie had to rein in her impulse to jump up and spill her ink. For a man she had just met, he certainly had a way of ruining her composure.

"I've offended you, Miss Andrews," he said, appearing troubled.

"Not a bit, Mr. Blackpool. *Good day.*" She resumed sketching, her hand flying across the page and the nib of the pen scratching loudly in her meaningful silence. Yet Ian Blackpool did not move from his seat beside her.

"I can see that I have," he insisted. "There's no use denying it. Your face is quite pink."

As if on command, her cheeks flushed. Sophie couldn't remember the last time someone had made her blush with emotion. Mr. Blackpool grew more discomfiting by the second. She opened her mouth to dismiss him, but he cut her off.

"If you wish me good day again," he said dryly, "I will have to—"

"Have to what?" Sophie interjected hotly. "Give me a spanking?"

He grinned wolfishly. "That idea has merit."

Sophie set down her pen in astonishment. "I believe you are one of the most bizarre men I have ever met."

"You flatter me."

"I do not," Sophie insisted hotly. "I don't believe in flattery. And," she added, gazing at him pointedly, "I don't like it when people give me extravagant compliments."

"So," he said, "I did offend you."

"Yes," Sophie admitted.

"By complimenting you."

"When you say it like that, it sounds ridiculous."

"Not a bit," he said, echoing her earlier words.

Sophie trailed her fingers along the petals of a wood anemone as she sought to explain herself. "Compliments are handed out to women like sweets are given to children in order to keep them quiet until dinner. People, men especially, think that if they heap all manner of flowery words on a woman, they won't actually have to talk to her, that she will be pacified with the verbal equivalent of a sweet."

"Something tasty and filling but ultimately unhealthful," Mr. Blackpool concluded.

Sophie nodded. "Exactly. I've had a bellyful of flattery and now my stomach hurts."

"What is the tonic for such indigestion of the soul?" he asked with a gentle smile. He plucked a blade of grass and began to chew it thoughtfully.

He wasn't making fun of her. He honestly wanted to know how to help. "Talk to me like a *person*, not a woman," she replied. "Don't let my gender prove an obstacle to real conversation. Let us exchange ideas and philosophies. They are the meat on which I would much rather feed, not empty sweets."

He nodded contemplatively, looking at her with a newly realized respect. She liked seeing it, from him especially.

"You speak good sense," he said with a nod. "I would wish the same for myself." He shifted his weight, brushing his shoulder against hers as he did so. Sophie again felt that strange strumming awareness resonate through her body. If anything, the sensation had grown more intense. Shyly, Sophie cradled her sketch pad closer to her chest, as though trying to shelter herself. She did not want her gender to influence her behavior, but she became aware of how alone she was with this attractive man, the size difference between them, and the warm curiosity of his brown eyes. She felt as though she should go, but she was reluctant to part company with Mr. Blackpool now that they had settled their dispute. Prospero did not want to leave the island.

"Perhaps," she said, struggling with her awareness of him, "I was being rather waspish just a moment ago."

"On the contrary, you've every right to speak your mind." He contemplated the fly agaric mushroom. "Your interest in this red fellow has something to do with your dislike of being patronized, I'd wager."

Her eyes widened at his perceptive statement as she nodded. Straightening her spine, she announced with self-conscious pride, "I am a botanist."

He tipped his head respectfully. "A noble calling."

"I think so," she said, waiting for his disapproval. Surely it would come, as it had with so many before him. She continued to wait, but it did not arrive.

"Yet your friends and family don't agree," he said instead. Ian Blackpool seemed a most singular man.

His understanding of her predicament sent a rush of gratitude through her, and prompted a release of pent-up frustration. "A woman has no place in botany, they say." Distracted, she stood and began to pace. "Especially a woman of *breeding*," Sophie added, the word becoming a vile insult. "They would rather see me mindlessly tinkering in a garden, planning rose beds and topiary, than making real scientific discoveries, actually contributing something to the world." She stopped pacing and brushed the loosened strands of hair from her face. Forcing herself to be calm, she added, "I'm not being quite fair. My family wishes me well, but they know that there are few venues open to a woman in the sciences. None, actually."

Mr. Blackpool rose and came to stand a few feet away from her. He gave her a long, assessing look that made her flush deeply. "And how do your sweethearts feel about your botanical pursuits?" he asked.

"Sweethearts?" Sophie echoed as her mouth dried.

His smile was lazy and intimate. "Surely a pretty young woman such as yourself has sweethearts," he said. "Trust me, love, that I am not giving you an empty compliment." He reached out and gently brushed the bridge of her nose, where she had accidentally smudged some dirt. Sophie watched his gesture, completely hypnotized by its masculine sensuality.

"I've had suitors before." She cleared her throat. "None that would qualify as sweethearts, exactly."

"What did these suitors think of your passion?" he asked warmly, rubbing his fingers together as though recalling the feel of her skin beneath them. At her blank look, Mr. Blackpool explained, "Your passion for botany."

Sophie felt as if she was playing a game where she did not know the rules. Mr. Blackpool not only knew the rules, he was cheating. Yet she was determined to prevail, prove that she was capable of managing herself in all things, not merely the scientific. "They proved to be even less understanding than my parents," she said, tipping up her chin. "After my next birthday, I shall be an official hopeless case, completely unmarriageable."

He abruptly stepped back and laughed casually, though to Sophie the laugh sounded strained. She got the impression that she had trumped him but did not feel particularly pleased about it. "I never mentioned marriage," he said with an abstracted grin. "Only sweethearts and suitors."

He had done it again, that barrier he put up when their hands had touched. Sophie did not consider herself an unusually sensitive individual, yet she found that Mr. Blackpool's strange dance between intimacy and distance unsettled her. Even more unsettling was her awareness of his feelings—an almost complete stranger. Ever since they had made contact, she had found herself aware of him. *Very* aware.

"I have established that I shall never marry," she said with resolve. "It seems as though no man wants a botanist for a wife."

"You're quite serious about botany, to give up hopes of a husband and family in order to pursue it." He crossed his arms over his broad chest, taking her in.

Sophie thought about the children she would never have, the long years of solitude with no one such as Mr. Blackpool to grow old with, and the fact that her sacrifice for science might never be recognized because of her gender. It was cruel. A sharp longing and sadness pierced her, thinking of it. But she loved her work with the kind of ardor she supposed most people felt for their sweethearts.

Sophie once read that Queen Elizabeth considered herself married to England, so strong was her determination to have complete control over herself and her country. Sophie had decided she would take botany as her husband for the very same reasons. She had to continue her scientific pursuits. She would not relinquish her rights to herself. And if the nights were long and her bed lonely, and the love of a man for a woman something she only read about in novels, it would have to be enough, knowing her work waited for her every morning. "I am quite serious," she replied gravely.

He nodded with equal solemnity and held out his hand. "May I look at your work?"

She hesitated, her hands wrapped around the binding of her sketchbook. Only a few people had ever seen her botanical drawings—her Uncle Alforth, and a fellow botanist she corresponded with in France under the name "Andrew Sophey"—but never an unknown man. Sophie was proud of her work, spending nearly all her waking time devoted to it, but she felt as though she were exposing a very personal part of herself to Mr. Blackpool.

She wanted his good opinion. Yet she also knew that she would have to harden herself to criticism if she wanted to make any headway as a botanist. If he didn't like her work, she would survive; she would become better for it.

"Of course," she answered, handing him the folio.

What followed were some of the most harrowing moments of Sophie's life. She stood at Ian Blackpool's shoulder and watched him leaf through the accumulation of her past year spent in the field, studying flowering plants until her eyes were sore, her fingers cramped, and her mother cried that her youngest daughter would never find a husband.

Each page was devoted to a single plant, with carefully detailed drawings and Sophie's tiny notes filling all available space. When she'd had the luxury, Sophie had used watercolors to get the most accurate depiction of the plant, but most of the work was in black ink. Even now, watching Mr. Blackpool silently examine her sketches, Sophie was overcome by her devotion to this science, and how much she loved learning about the growing things of the earth.

He looked at each page, his brow furrowed but his appearance unreadable. He even examined her sketch of the fly agaric mushroom, created a few minutes earlier. At last, he carefully closed the cover and turned over the book. The intimate sight of her sketchbook clasped in his hands made Sophie's stomach do a little flip, as though he held the living embodiment of her soul. She tried to keep her own face blank as she waited for his response.

"I have never, ever seen anything so . . ." he said, and stopped, casting about for the right word.

Mentally, Sophie filled in the blank for him: Dreadful. Ridiculous. Absurd. A hundred disparaging adjectives crowded her mind.

"Amazing."

Her hand flew to her mouth in surprise.

Reopening the sketchbook, Ian Blackpool began to flip randomly to different pages, respect and wonder evident in his expression. "The detail is incredible," he said, indicating various sketches. "The way in which you've captured the root structure and described how it works—it's remarkable. You clearly know an extraordinary amount about what makes plants grow." Their gazes met over the open book, holding fast with the intensity of his admiration.

"Do you really think so?" Sophie asked, breathless with happiness. Her pleasure in his pleasure was so powerful, she did not quite know what to do with herself. Before he could answer her question, she continued in a giddy rush, "I've read just about everything, Theophrastus's *Inquiry into Plants*, Tournefort's *Institutiones rei herbariae*, and, of course, all of Linnaeus. I'm a fervent believer in his classification system. I didn't bring my herbarium with me today, but I've organized it exactly as Linnaeus describes in the *Philosophia botanica*. But I've been thinking that—" Sophie stopped, realizing that she was chattering on like a ninny. She laughed a little at herself. "I'm unused to having someone to talk to about botany," she explained. "Uncle Alforth tries to look interested, but he just wants to encourage me. I can see his eyes glaze over whenever I start nattering on about fructification or some such nonsense."

"Clearly, it isn't nonsense," Ian Blackpool said, his mouth quirked wryly. "You have a great talent for botany. It would be a terrible shame if you didn't continue in your work."

Sophie ducked her head, shy under his genuine appreciation. It felt better than any other compliment she had ever received. "Thank you." Her eyes dropped down, traveling over his lean form with a frank appreciation she had never experienced. She noticed for the first time that stalks of wild plants were poking out of his pockets. "You've been collecting some samples of your own," she exclaimed with delight, happy to return to a subject she knew well. "Dog violet and primrose and burdock. Are you also a botanist?" Sophie's heart began to speed up at the prospect of finding a kindred spirit, especially one so handsome.

He glanced down at his pockets, seeming to have forgotten about their contents. "No, not at all," he said with a rueful smile as Sophie felt a twinge of disappointment. "Merely a dabbler in the realm of healing herbs. I was looking for specimens myself when I came across you in the depths of your research."

"Have you read Gerard's *Herbal*?" asked Sophie.

"I'm mostly using folk wisdom as my guide." He handed back the sketchbook, and Sophie took secret pleasure from feeling the echo of his body heat in the leather cover. "What's a young woman doing unaccompanied in the middle of nowhere?" he asked suddenly. "You could meet with all kinds of nefarious characters out here. Me, for example. How do you know I'm not some villainous kidnapper who abducts young women and makes them his love slaves?" He leered menacingly.

A nervous giggle escaped Sophie. "Of course you aren't," she said, then added half-fearfully, half-hopefully, "are you?"

"No," he said with a hint of regret, "but I could be. Scientific endeavors aside, shouldn't you have some kind of chaperone or guardian with you? A father, a brother?"

She looked guilty. "Uncle Alforth. I left him sleeping at the inn at Little Chipping. He doesn't know I've gone out. But," she protested in her defense, "we're going home tomorrow, so I've only got the rest of to-day to finish my survey of local plants." Sophie opened her sketchbook again to study her drawing of the fly agaric mushroom and was surprised to find it so vividly rendered. She had only spent minutes drawing it, and yet somehow she had been motivated to sketch it with an astonishing passion.

"And how is your survey progressing?"

"Very well," Sophie said, beaming at Ian Black-pool's continued interest. "Uncle Alforth took me on special holiday to visit the Chelsea Physic Garden. I spent several days there."

Mr. Blackpool looked surprised. "I didn't know it was open to the public."

"Uncle Alforth knows Philip Miller, the curator. Mr. Miller even gave me a copy of *The Gardener's Dictionary,* though I'm not a gardener. He said he wished his sons were as fascinated by plants as I."

Almost under his breath, Ian Blackpool said quietly, "*You* are quite fascinating."

Sophie found herself blushing again. She still was not comfortable receiving praise, particularly from this man, and returned the conversation to safer subjects. "I hope to go to the new gardens at Kew on our next trip. I hear that they are going to be the grandest botanical garden in the country."

Sensing her discomfort, he followed her down the more comfortable path. "Do you travel with your uncle often?"

"Whenever Mother allows. I hope her good favor lasts the rest of the summer. There is so much more I'd like to see before autumn sets in. Also, I was thinking— What's that?" she asked, hearing a musical chime.

He pulled a pocket watch from his waistcoat and consulted its dial. "The striking of the hour," he explained.

"Good God!" Sophie cried. "What time is it?"

"Five o'clock."

If Sophie's mother had been around, she would have collapsed after hearing her youngest daughter curse roundly. Fortunately, Mrs. Carolyn Andrews was nowhere in the vicinity, and Sophie was left to curse as she pleased. Which she did, though she wasn't at all pleased. She was quite frantic.

"I had no idea so much time had passed," Sophie said miserably, snapping her sketchbook shut and gathering her hat. "Uncle Alforth has probably awakened by now and will be in a dead panic if I'm not at the inn. He promised my mother to keep a better eye on me."

"Clearly he takes his duties seriously," said Mr. Blackpool dryly.

Sophie shot him a look that said his sarcasm was not appreciated. She began to rush back toward the main road and the village of Little Chipping, where she and her uncle were staying. She had not taken three steps before she turned, hastening back toward Mr. Blackpool.

"It has been wonderful meeting you," she said breathlessly. "I'm sorry we cannot continue our conversation. I enjoyed it immensely."

"Likewise," he said. Taking her hand, he bowed over it and pressed a kiss to her knuckles.

She was aware only of the marvel of his lips against her skin; everything else fell away in a focus of sensation. Her eyes widened. The only time she had ever experienced a similar feeling was when she encountered a rare plant specimen, but even that seemed a pale echo of what she experienced now. Other men made the gesture empty, a courtly relic that usually irritated her. Not Ian Blackpool. A wealth of promise lay behind the touching of his mouth to her hand. "It has been an extreme pleasure, Miss Sophie Andrews."

It was a promise that would never be fulfilled. Sophie gazed at him for several moments, trying to memorize every plane of his gorgeous face and the image of this handsome, strong gentleman truly looking as though he enjoyed talking with her about the one subject most dear to her heart. If only she could stay. But Uncle Alforth, who was so good to her, was waiting.

Casting one last longing glance at Ian Blackpool, Sophie dashed off through the woods. Even if she remained a spinster, she would always have the memory of this afternoon.

It was not until she was nearly halfway to the village that she realized she knew very little about her companion in the woods. She had been so excited by the prospect of meeting someone genuinely interested in her work, she'd neglected to learn anything about him. Where he came from, if he was a gentleman of leisure or a man of business, and if he *was* a man of business, what kind. His clothes were of good quality, though a trifle worn, and he carried a slightly dented pocket watch with a gold case. Contradictions.

Perhaps it was best this way, so her memory would not be tarnished by the mundane world. Ian Blackpool could forever remain her paragon of a real man.

He watched her disappear through the trees, the retreating dream of a woman of the forest. He wanted to follow her, discover where she hid herself, learn more about this strange hybrid rose called Sophie Andrews.

Such a typically English name for such an atypical woman. Ian had traveled enough, seen enough, to no longer find anything shocking or surprising. A female botanist, though, was a first. He'd met many women who dealt in herbals, who knew the medicinal value of plants as well as they knew their own children. Yet none of these women, for all their knowledge, were truly interested in the *why* of the plants they employed so skillfully.

Sophie was. She was a woman who sought the *why* of plants with such passion that the air around her all but vibrated with it. *Why* was a difficult question to ask; it made things more complicated, but that seemed to urge her on. Ian himself chased his own *why*, the thing that brought him back to England after so long an absence. Perhaps their common pursuit had been the thing that drew Ian to Sophie, the same way she had been so incredibly excited when he had praised her work.

Her botanical sketches were praiseworthy, but Ian's interest in Miss Sophie Andrews went beyond her dedication to her work. She was as pretty and unexpected as a wildflower on the heath. Her honey-colored hair willfully fluttered out of its pins and framed her oval face. Some might call the shade of her eyes hazel, but to Ian, they were as many-hued and complex as the growing earth, shifting tones of green and brown that changed to reflect her fascinating moods. She had a full mouth, an un-English mouth that defied convention as much as the scattering of golden freckles across her nose and cheeks.

Ian did not understand the female aversion to freckles. They made a man wonder where else on her body such delicious markings could be found. Sophie had been wearing a demure gown, a scarf tucked into its low bodice as befitting a day dress, but that did not stop Ian from picturing her slim form in all its glory, dusted with caramel freckles from top to toe.

Damn English social convention that kept him from making good on his fantasies! India had shown him how much his fellow countrymen kept their natural impulses tightly reined. Now that he was back, now that he had met such a tempting creature as Sophie, he wished he could let those impulses carry the both of them toward fulfillment.

The only fulfillment he would be seeking now would be a good, hot meal and someplace to sleep. He was weary of the narrow, hard bed in his caravan, and tired of bread, cheese, and apples. The lust for adventure he'd shown at twenty-four was not the same desire for comfort he now felt at thirty-one. Ian consulted his purse. What he found there made his heart sink. His supply of coin had dwindled to nearly nothing. There was no hope for it. He would have to work tonight.

"Damn," he cursed aloud. He'd forgotten to ask the name of the inn where Sophie was staying. There were three inns in the village, and he did not want to run the risk of seeing her again. It would look too suspicious if he inquired about the guests' names before getting to work. He could set up in the village green and avoid her completely. Yet Ian had already walked through Little Chipping and seen that its citizens tended to congregate around taprooms.

He had a strong desire to see Sophie again, but he

knew it would be a bad idea. He was dangerous to Sophie Andrews. He had felt it every time they touched, every time their conversation grew intimate. Naturally, he had distanced himself whenever that threat arose. Even if she believed her work came first, she was still a lovely girl with a thirst for life. She had the ability to give her heart. Ian could never do the same.

Chapter Two

Sophie was out of breath by the time she reached the White Hart Inn. She had forgotten how far she had wandered from the village of Little Chipping, and after walking sedately for half an hour with no sign of the village, gave up all semblance of decorum and ran the distance back. She ignored the curious stares of those she passed as she neared the village. Uncle Alforth was a patient, tolerant, and loveable soul, and Sophie had no desire to worry him unnecessarily. At least she was wearing her most comfortable stays. Passing out by the side of the road would not help her predicament.

Barely inside the door of the inn, Sophie was about to bound up the stairs to check on him when his familiar jovial voice rang out from the taproom.

"And here's my dear niece, back from her wanderings at last. Over here, my child!"

Contrite, Sophie made her way toward her uncle. Merely seeing him again after her short absence made her smile. He was ensconced at a table near a window and surrounded by the friendly, drink-flushed faces of guests and locals availing themselves of the inn's fine ale—no doubt paid for by Alforth. He loved company and usually bought rounds for whomever would join him for a session of storytelling and merrymaking. For that reason, he was always quite popular.

More than his willingness to buy a stranger a drink, Alforth attracted new friends because of his open and cheerful nature. Every joke was hilarious, every tale fascinating, and everyone possessed a heart as kind and forgiving as his own. Lately, he'd been happier in the taproom of the local pub or inn than at the numerous card parties, fetes, and assemblies that filled her family's social calendar.

The love between Sophie and her parents was dutiful and dictated by responsibility. She was the youngest daughter, with elder sisters Helena and Imogene married and younger brother Henry away at Oxford. Sophie was treated by her mother and father as a fond afterthought, which she did not mind, since that left her to pursue her own activities without too much intervention. Her parents were presences felt mostly at mealtimes, when everyone gathered together. Sophie might sometimes yearn for more affection from her mother, or more interest from her father, but she was generally satisfied with the course of their relationship.

Yet Sophie loved Uncle Alforth fiercely, protectively. He was her mother's younger brother, a lifelong bachelor, but he was one of her best friends, and she knew that he would say the same of her. The months he stayed at Cabot Park with Sophie's parents were always the happiest for her. Alforth gave presents and sweets to each of his nieces and his nephew, but Sophie was clearly his favorite, and he supplied her with a never-ending stream of books about plants, new folios for her sketches, even a tiny magnifying contraption by Anton Leeuwnhoek. Sophie's mother would *tut-tut* Alforth, saying that he was spoiling the girl in many ways, but the gifts advancing her knowledge did not cease.

Even if the presents stopped, Sophie would love Alforth just as strongly as she did now. She had never met such a beautiful soul, and hoped that if she ever did find a man she could marry, he would resemble even the palest echo of her Uncle A.

"You had me quite worried, Sophie," he chided as she came nearer, though his tone was mild. He was a small man, sturdy in stature, with a lined face that bespoke years of laughter. At home he scorned wearing a wig, but gave in to convention when out in the world, favoring a simple bob one, though Sophie's mother insisted he looked like a tradesman. She could tell now that he itched to take it off.

"I apologize, Uncle. I went out looking for samples and lost track of time." One of Alforth's new friends offered her a seat and she gratefully took it, worn out from her long walk.

"If you will excuse us, gentlemen," Alforth said with a grin, "I'd like to spend some time alone with my niece."

Alforth's guests slowly filed past him, offering thanks for their drinks and his company. He said farewell to each of the men by name, one by one, until he and Sophie were alone. A serving girl took Sophie's order for tea, and then Alforth fixed his niece with a look of tender concern.

"You gave me a start when I woke and you were

23

nowhere to be found," he said softly, patting her hand. "After all, I did promise your mother to see after your welfare during our journey. More than that, *I* worry about you."

"I'm so very sorry," Sophie said. She rubbed at her nose, repentant, then smiled her thanks as the serving girl brought her tea. "I never meant to be gone so long. Besides," she added, brightening, "as you can see, I am perfectly fine. Better than fine. Excellent. I did not meet with any disreputable scoundrels. In fact, I met a very nice young gentleman, and we talked about botany for a good long while." She found herself blushing just thinking about Ian Blackpool, and tried to hide the telltale flush from her uncle by bringing her teacup close to her face.

Alforth tipped his chair back in a way his sister would never allow as he considered his niece. Eyes twinkling, he asked, "And was this gentleman the reason why you were late returning from your sample-hunting?"

Sophie nodded, gazing into her amber tea rather than meet the too-knowing gaze of her uncle.

"Tell me more about your young swain," he said mischievously.

"Uncle A!" cried Sophie, setting down her teacup with a clatter. "Mr. Blackpool is certainly *not* my 'swain.' He's . . . merely interested in plants, as I am. Though he is not, unfortunately, a fellow botanist, we had much to talk about."

"So I wagered by your blushing cheeks."

Sophie frowned, yet she knew Alforth was merely teasing and joined in his laughter.

"Yes, I admit it, he was a very handsome fellow and I was sorry to say good-bye to him. But not because he was handsome," she added. "I found him . . . intriguing. I showed him my sketches."

Alforth's eyebrows rose in surprise, knowing that his niece was very particular in the selection of people allowed to view her work. The fact that Sophie showed this unknown man her botanical illustrations spoke much more deeply about her feelings for him than anything she had said or probably would say. Alforth wondered what kind of man had so charmed his reticent niece; a man she met at random while collecting plant samples. Though Alforth was concerned about Sophie's safety, he knew she possessed common sense and wisdom beyond her years and gender. Clearly, her mysterious man had affected her deeply, even though she had only been gone a few hours.

"And I managed to do a little work, too, as we talked," Sophie added, opening her sketchbook to the last completed page for his inspection.

He took the folio from her and had to restrain himself from exclaiming out loud. She had drawn some kind of mushroom with speckles on its cap with a few notations around it. The quality of her work was, as usual, very good, but Alforth noticed there was something different about this drawing, a new quality her other sketches lacked. There was a visible passion in the drawing, each line vibrating with life and . . . yes . . . sensuality. Alforth felt his own face begin to redden, as though he were gazing upon something very private. He glanced up at Sophie. She seemed to have no idea about the erotic nature of her drawing. Dear heavens, not so long ago she was but a child in leading strings and now . . . ?

Alforth was about to ask her a question that would likely embarrass them both, but he had to be sure she was untouched in every way. Before he could speak, however, Sophie shot out of her chair and pointed out the window.

"Uncle A, look!" she said excitedly. "There's the man I was speaking of."

Turning in his seat, Alforth gazed out the window of the taproom, which looked out onto the main street of the village. Sure enough, an extremely good-looking young man was standing in the middle of the road next to a painted caravan wagon. A crowd had begun to gather around him.

"What a strange cart," Sophie murmured. "I wonder what he's doing next to it."

Alforth began to get a very bad feeling.

Using his cane, he got to his feet and ambled over toward the window to get a better view. What he saw made his heart sink.

"Oh, Soph," he said sadly. "Perhaps we had better go upstairs and dine in our rooms this evening."

There was no answer. Turning, he saw that Sophie had quit the taproom. A flash of silk out of the corner of his eye made Alforth realize that his well-intentioned efforts to protect his niece had come to nothing.

She was already in the street, joining the crowd.

Ian fit the last boards into place for his portable stage. He tested it with his boot a few times to make sure it wouldn't give way under his weight. Thus far it hadn't, but there could always be a first time. Stepping back, he surveyed the platform arranged in front of his painted caravan and was satisfied with what he saw.

A crowd was already beginning to form and he hadn't even spoken yet. Little Chipping was far

enough away from a major town so that his appearance attracted attention. There were plenty of people
in his profession who stayed in London, scorning the
muddied byways of England for the muddied urban
streets, but Ian liked life on the road and in these
small villages better. Londoners were jaded, quick to
dismiss men like him for the next novelty on the next
corner. Village life was slower, and newcomers were a
welcome distraction from the usual monotony. His
best customers were in little towns like this one,
where the populace had enough knowledge of the
outside world to leave off their suspicions, but craved
something different. Villages had their dangers, too.
He'd been run out of a few towns for offending the
citizens' sensibilities, but those occasions were rare,
and Ian's horse was fast.

Looking at the painted wagon, Ian felt a perverse
sense of pride. He'd done the decorations himself,
having learned a few things about painting in India
and Persia, and the brightly colored figures never
failed to attract attention. The paintings were sugges-
tive but never obscene. He didn't want to get chased
out of town. Even so, he was particularly pleased with
his illustration of the sloe-eyed Indian princess, smiling beguilingly while holding a dainty flower between
her slender fingers. Tasteful seduction.

His mind flickered back to Sophie Andrews. She'd
been dogging his thoughts all afternoon, ever since
vanishing into the forest. Yes, she was something of a
novelty—a woman actively pursuing botanical science was bound to stick out in his mind. And she was
uncommonly pretty. That full, rosy mouth and the
sweet compactness of her slender form promised
many new, untasted pleasures. In all his travels, Ian

had met pretty women with unusual interests before. Yet Sophie Andrews possessed such a nimble intellect, a lightness of spirit combined with a sense of gravity, and a natural sensuality that intrigued Ian beyond mere curiosity. She was intrigued by him, as well. She had too open a temperament to hide her feelings.

He was not the man she thought he was, in more ways than she realized. As much as she fascinated him, he had to stay away. Ian had given up the life of a gentleman, though he was not without principles. Still, if only he could see her again . . .

He would not let his thoughts turn dark. Dark thoughts meant a poor performance. As he finished setting up, Ian kept to himself, despite the growing crowd of onlookers asking loud rhetorical questions. "Who's that man?" "What's *that* a picture of?" "What's he got in that wagon?" He liked to maintain an atmosphere of mystery for as long as possible. An excited hum was building, and he decided that he had better get to work before the sun set.

He stepped onto the platform. The crowd immediately hushed. A woman quieted her fussing baby. The children running in the street stopped and sat on the ground. An old man coughed into his handkerchief. Ian looked over the faces turned toward him like sunflowers, seeing a myriad of expressions looking back at him—eager, dubious, speculative, a few young women and some not-so-young women clearly showing a carnal interest in his masculine charms—and felt the familiar rush of excitement that filled him whenever he took to the stage. Pity that being an actor was considered a demeaning profession. It was heady, being the object of so much attention.

"Friends," he said, projecting his voice so that

everyone could hear, "I stand before you as a world traveler. A man who has seen many wondrous sights, including the famed perfumed gardens of Arabia and the jeweled palaces of India. Before my very eyes, I have witnessed the artful alchemists of pashas turn the basest of metals into gold, so every surface shone a thousand times brighter than the sun. In Constantinople, I watched, amazed, as one physician returned a man from the dead."

"Impossible!" a middle-aged man cried.

Ian smiled to himself. People responded as if on cue, and he could always anticipate their responses. In fact, he expected it. He turned and addressed the man.

"It is not impossible, my friend. It is very possible. There are marvels from the East you cannot envision in your most fantastic dreams. Believe me, I was as skeptical as you, before I became witness to these incredible feats." He began to pace the length of the small stage, gesturing dramatically. "And though these faraway lands presented themselves as veritable paradises on earth, I knew that I could not remain away from my countrymen and deny them access to the wonders that I know. At the risk of my own life, I returned home to bring to you good people today something so prized, so rare and precious, it is kept in a locked iron room in a rajah's castle, guarded by seven man-eating tigers, twenty eunuchs armed with scimitars, and fifty bow-wielding warrior princesses who would sooner kill a man than show him any mercy. The scribe who wrote down this secret was immediately put to death so he could not share his prize with any other man."

Lowering his voice so the crowd had to lean in close to hear him, Ian continued, "*I* am the only man other than the rajah to learn this secret. How it came into my possession is another story for another day. But today," he said, shaking his head with wonderment, "oh, today, my friends, your life is about to become a thousand times more glorious than you could have ever imagined."

The crowd held its collective breath as Ian stepped back and straightened to his full height, preparing to launch into the most important part of his routine. He was a tall man and used his height to his advantage, enabling him to see far into the mass of people now thronged around his stage. He liked to make eye contact with as many bystanders as possible in order to make them feel personally involved with his presentation. He did so now, peering sharply into many unknown faces, gazing into many unknown eyes. Blue, brown, green, hazel.

One familiar pair of hazel eyes at the very back of the crowd caught his attention.

Ian had to keep himself from cursing when he spotted the very unhappy eyes of Miss Sophie Andrews staring back at him with undisguised shock and growing anger. He'd hoped this wouldn't happen. He could almost hear her illusions shattering in the hushed anticipation of the crowd. He damned himself for being the cause. For a brief moment, he contemplated ending his performance, packing his caravan, and riding out of Little Chipping. But that would solve nothing. The damage was done. He had to continue. It felt like punishment, but perhaps it was a punishment he deserved.

Tearing his gaze from hers, Ian continued. "Love," he said hoarsely. He cleared his throat and went on. "Love is the greatest mystery the world has ever known. Ever since man has put pen to paper, he has written about the awesome, unknown thing we call love. What makes a man waste away for a woman when this same woman finds the man to be repugnant?"

"The pox!" shouted a ruddy-faced farmer.

The crowd burst into laughter, and Ian joined them, but weakly. Ordinarily, this was his favorite part of the performance, but he had lost his stomach for it. He glanced quickly at Sophie and saw that an older, bewigged gentleman stood beside her, squeezing her shoulder sympathetically, his gaze never leaving her stricken face. The uncle, if Ian remembered correctly.

"You are thinking too commonly, my friend." Ian forced his concentration back to his routine. "Love is as elusive as it is rare. Happy is the man or woman who finds it, for they know they have found a treasure more precious than all the wealth of kings and emperors. And once it is attained, who can say whether it is a true love or one that evaporates? How many wives, how many husbands, grow weary of their spouses as the years pass? I daresay, my friends, too many."

Ian saw that many in the audience were exchanging furtive glances with each other, assessing the men and women who stood beside them, trying to judge who among them knew a lasting love. Sophie crossed her arms over her chest and tilted her chin up in defiance. If she felt shame, she was not bowing to it. Other women might have run away in embarrassment, yet she was facing him. He admired her bravery.

"Love," Ian repeated, throwing his arms wide. "We all want to taste its vintage, but nothing guarantees we ever will. Nothing—except this!" With a flourish, he reached inside his coat and produced a small amber bottle, stoppered with wax. He felt the collective gasp of the crowd, a vacuum of air that tugged lightly on his clothes.

"This, my friends, is the greatest secret mankind has ever known finally revealed, stolen from an Indian rajah and transported to England across pirate-infested seas. And now I have brought it here to you good people of Little Chipping. This," he said in triumph, "is *love in a bottle*."

A spontaneous round of applause rose from the crowd as everyone confirmed with their neighbors that they had never before witnessed such an amazing spectacle. Sophie was not clapping.

"You may be asking yourselves, how can this man put love in a bottle? Is it not ephemeral, the strange alchemy that cannot be defined, cannot be bottled? No, my friends. I have taken the rajah's secret and created the exact substance that generates love in men and women. One sip from this bottle and you will know the glorious pleasures of love." Ian gestured toward a gangly boy on the cusp on manhood, who flushed deeply to be singled out. "One drink will make the callow youth feel the soul-deep wonders of eternal devotion." Turning, Ian held out his hand to indicate an old man, bent over his cane and trembling with age. "One taste of this potion will make the elderly patriarch gambol in a second springtime of desire. Yes, this bottle is humble, but it holds within its glassy walls the most transcendent joy mankind has ever known. Love."

Did he imagine Sophie's snort of disgust?

"What's in that bottle?" asked the old man, pointing with his crude cane.

"A good question, my venerable friend," Ian said. "I cannot tell you precisely, for it is a dangerous business to create the formula. But I can say that the secret lies in the fertile creations of the earth, the commingling of plants and herbs. I have combined roots and spices from India and Arabia—the rajah's original recipe—and improved it with the flowering bounty of England's native plants to produce this: Blackpool's Amorous Elixir."

"Lies," said a woman in the back. "He's speaking lies."

Though the woman had not raised her voice, the entire crowd turned to look at her as though she had shouted at the top of her lungs. Ian looked, too. He'd had his share of naysayers before, loud and bullying people who would hector and hassle, men and women alike. Yet he had never been called a liar before, in all his time spent on the road. He wondered who would say such an unpleasant thing here, before this large group.

Sophie Andrews.

She stepped forward as the crowd parted, ignoring her uncle, who tugged on her sleeve. The roiling emotions that had played across her face had coalesced into righteous anger, twin spots of bright heat forming in her cheeks.

"Madam," Ian said levelly, "I am not lying."

"You are not speaking the truth," she countered. "That is lying, in my estimation."

The crowd murmured to themselves, intrigued by this new development. Speculation arose as to whether or not the young woman was part of the act, but many expressed doubt that an obvious gentlewoman would participate in something so base as a traveling patent show. She did not fit the part of the zany or Merry Andrew, for where was her harlequin jacket? Where were her amusing tricks and tumblings as she shilled for her master? No, this lady was not part of the act, and it thrilled the crowd to their core.

"Sophie—" her uncle murmured, again reaching for her arm.

"I must, Uncle A," she answered, her voice low. Taking several more steps forward, Sophie faced Ian Blackpool and the gathered assembly. Her whole body trembled. She had never spoken so publicly before, yet she had never been more moved to do so. Sophie had never known such disappointment, such a sense of betrayal, and she was furious with Ian Blackpool in a way she could barely articulate.

"Plants are the greatest gift Mother Nature has given humanity," she said, "and those who study them dedicate themselves to understanding this sacred science. You debase them both by trumpeting false virtues in the marketplace like a fishmonger."

"I glorify them by bringing the bounty of their riches to the populace," he answered.

Sophie's laugh was sharp and brief. "Plants can do many things, but they cannot make someone love."

He gazed at her steadily, but she would not blink. She saw the considering look in his eye as he assessed her. Sophie almost imagined she saw contrition in his stare and dismissed it as idle fancy. No man who misled young women into thinking they were gentlemen when in fact they were the exact opposite could be apologetic. It was contrary to their nature.

Sure enough, he broke the contact of their eyes and gestured beside him on the stage. "You are a skeptic, madam. I invite you to see for yourself."

She wondered if he meant to punish her for her outburst, but rational thought had fled and she took the stage beside Ian Blackpool. Sophie had to prove him wrong, let the crowd know that he was not who he pretended to be. She felt, righteously, that she had to protect their innocence since hers had been destroyed. Yet when she stood upon the platform, dozens of pairs of eyes fastened onto her, and she stepped back instinctively from their force, unused to so much scrutiny. She felt the reassuring hand of Mr. Blackpool on her back and nearly smiled in gratitude before she recalled that she was furious with him.

He presented the bottle to her and the crowd. "Blackpool's Amorous Elixir is a miraculous distillation of many varieties of roots, plants, and herbs. You say that plants cannot make a person love, but we have only to consult the great learned men of history to realize that plants have been used in the promotion of love since time began."

"Most of those men believed the earth was flat and the moon made of cheese," Sophie countered.

The crowd laughed, and a thrill of triumph shot through her.

"Plants are made up of chemicals bound together," she continued with gaining confidence. "They can produce fine medicine to heal the sick when used properly. They can create reactions in the human body. But love," she went on, turning to face Ian Blackpool with her hand on her heart, "goes beyond the flesh and is the realm of the soul. It cannot come from plants. It is absolutely impossible."

"As impossible as a female botanist?" he asked, but his voice was so quiet only she heard.

Sophie flushed, hearing her situation thrown back at her. "Impossible," she repeated.

"There is only one way to find out." He held out the bottle.

She stared at it for a long time. The crowd had fallen completely silent, watching her contemplate the bottle. Her uncle had jostled his way to the front. His eyes were sympathetic and dark, and she realized that she had severely compromised herself as soon as she stepped onto Ian Blackpool's stage. Sophie looked at the man in question. She wanted to find him repulsive, see his good looks only as an oily façade for his true self, but damn him and damn her, he looked as charming and handsome as he had back in the woods. She wanted to leap off the stage and run back into the forest, hide herself in the past, where she could believe gorgeous gentlemen simply appeared from the trees and honestly cared about her work.

That time had vanished forever. She could not go back, and she had only herself to blame for creating such illusions.

This bottle was the future, where no illusions existed.

"Sophie," her uncle said softly, "you don't have to do this."

"I do," she answered.

She uncorked the bottle, sniffed it, and drank it in one gulp. In her haste, she swallowed hard and found herself coughing for a moment. The liquid tasted of roses and other flowers, but it did not taste of love.

Sophie was about to turn back to the crowd to make her pronouncement but then lost her ability to speak. Ian Blackpool had swooped down on her, pulling her into his arms for a kiss. At first, her arms stayed pinned to her sides, both from the strength of his embrace and her shock. Her mouth compressed itself into a line as she felt his lips over hers. It was a theatrical kiss, meant to be seen. She struggled against him, pressing her palms against the lean hardness of his chest. But he only gripped her tighter.

Blood roared in her ears. The crowd receded from her consciousness as the kiss began to change. It grew softer, more speculative. Suitors had kissed Sophie before, yet none of them had held the wealth of meaning or sensation as Ian Blackpool's kiss did. He had a mobile mouth, surprisingly soft, supple lips that began to slowly nibble at her own until they parted for him. He tasted of tobacco and mystery. Her hands started to slide up the front of his waistcoat.

"Sophie!" her uncle cried.

"That's it, lass!" shouted a woman.

Sophie stepped back, blinking in confusion. She raised her hand to her mouth and gazed at the crowd, thinking in her daze that they had somehow vanished and then reappeared. Leers and catcalls met her eyes. Glancing over at Ian Blackpool, she saw a similar dazed expression on his face, as though he had completely disappeared into another world inside his mind. His hands were raised, as if he were still holding her.

Oh, God, Sophie thought. He'd been holding her in front of all these people. *Kissing her.* And worse, she'd kissed him back.

"Does it work, girl? Are you in love?" a man hooted.

It had all been part of the show. A plan to sell bottles of perfumed water.

Ian Blackpool began to collect himself. He shook his head and looked at her.

Her hand began to rise. Time collapsed on itself. Her body felt as though it had turned to clockwork, all gears and grinding mechanics. And so she moved like a windup doll, her palm outstretched. She slapped him. Hard.

"You're nothing but a worthless mountebank," Sophie said, her voice choked with tears.

In an instant, she had jumped off the stage and run into the inn.

Alforth fixed Ian with a deadly glare. "You had better clear out of here tonight, boy," he snarled, jabbing toward Ian with his cane, "or you will find yourself unfit for *any* kind of love." With that, he stalked after his niece.

Ian resisted the urge to gingerly touch his face where Sophie Andrews had slapped him. He knew he must be glowing red from the force of her blow. He deserved it, and worse.

Someone coughed. Ian remembered that he was both not alone and also in the middle of his performance. He'd come this far in his damnation; he wasn't about to turn back.

He gave the crowd a big smile. "Well, friends," he said with a grin, "you can't expect it to work right away."

Ian joined the crowd in their laughter, but he felt as though he had broken his own heart.

Chapter Three

Staring out the window of the carriage, Sophie realized she was glad to be going home. Homesickness was an unfamiliar sensation. Usually, when she and Alforth were returning to Gloucestershire, she felt a heavy weight settle upon her, knowing that familial expectations awaited her, as did the censorious looks her mother would give her at the dinner table when Sophie accidentally forgot to remove her muddied apron. Sophie almost always forgot to remove it, since she was often in the middle of working when the summons to dinner arrived. Consequently, there were many disapproving looks from her mother and much heavy sighing from her father. They loved her, but she knew in their eyes she was a disappointment.

Yet right now, she longed for the comforts of her snug library at the back of the house, with all her books and equipment lining the walls and covering her desk like a warm embrace. She had the childish urge to hide herself away in there, far from the eyes of the world following the dreadful scene of last night.

Even thinking about it now made Sophie want to curl into a little ball. She had exposed herself to public ridicule because of Ian Blackpool. If only she had gone back into the inn with Alforth and eaten her evening meal quietly in their rooms, instead of screeching like a virago before a hundred curious eyes.

After fleeing Ian Blackpool, Sophie had spent the evening pacing her room. No matter how she had tried, she simply could not sit still. Every nerve in her body felt alight, trembling and susceptible to every sound, every tiny current of air moving over her responsive skin like a gale. Even the sensation of her hair brushing the back of her neck had made her quiver with awareness. It must have been the elixir, she determined. Most likely it contained some kind of rudimentary stimulant, easy enough to obtain from a few select plants.

Certainly Sophie's peculiar feelings were not the result of Ian Blackpool's kiss.

"Are you all right, my dear?"

"What's that, Uncle?" She turned and gazed at his concerned, kindly face across from her.

"You groaned, Sophie. Is your stomach giving you trouble? You ate no breakfast this morning, and no dinner last night."

She shook her head. "My stomach is fine."

He nodded in understanding. "Something else pains you, I'd wager. Your pride, perhaps?" When she did not answer, Alforth heaved a sigh. "I fear I have failed you, dear Sophie."

"Uncle A, no!" she cried, grabbing his hands.

"It's true," he said sadly. "I should have exercised my discretion. I never should have let you go out alone yesterday. And when I saw that man, that

40

Blackpool fellow, outside the inn, I knew immediately who he was, what he was."

"A mountebank," Sophie said bitterly.

"Yes. The worst sort of rogue, selling potions to the unsuspecting people of England. And to insult you like that in public!" Alforth's expression became outraged. "I should have skewered him on the spot. In my youth, I was known as a ferocious duelist."

"Is that so?" Sophie asked her tender-hearted uncle.

"Perhaps not," conceded Alforth. "But if it weren't for my knee, that scoundrel would have been pleading for his mama." Alforth eyed the offending joint with distaste, the relic of a brief flirtation with life as an officer of His Majesty's Army. It was clear he was most disgusted with himself. He rested his chin on his cane, gazing at his niece with regret. "I lament that as your guardian on this trip, I was a complete fiasco. Carolyn will never let us go traveling together again."

"No," Sophie said unhappily, resting her head in her hands.

"Soph," her uncle said slowly, "perhaps it would be for the best if we do not mention the incident last night to Carolyn."

"You mean lie?" she asked, raising her eyebrows as she lifted her head.

"Not lie, exactly. Rather, an omission of certain events."

"Is that something you are used to doing?"

Alforth smiled wryly. "My little Soph, if you only knew how many events I have neglected to tell your mother, you would topple your dear old uncle from his pedestal."

"But it is not a very *tall* pedestal, my dear old uncle. The fall shall not harm you."

"What a hoyden you are!" Alforth smiled.

"I must be," she concurred, "since I think your plan is a sound one. We won't tell Mother. And I shall tumble from the pedestal with you."

He laughed, but saw that Sophie had lapsed back into her melancholic reverie. "You really liked him, didn't you?" he asked gently.

Sophie did not trust herself to speak, so she only nodded. At last, she whispered, "I thought he was different from everyone else." Rubbing her nose, she added, "Perhaps *too* different. Oh, Uncle A, what a great fool I am, letting my injured feelings for a charlatan lead me into disgrace."

"You're not a fool," he chided. "Merely young. Though the two terms are often found together."

"I thought I was smarter than that," she said. "Mayhap that is pride, too. But, goodness, the number of books I've read! I can speak French, Latin, Greek, and German."

"And Italian," Alforth added.

"Yes, Italian, too. I'm positive I know as much as Henry at Oxford—more, even, since he can't name more than ten plays by Shakespeare. So why, with all the wisdom of the philosophers behind me, did I make such an error in judgment with Mr. Ian Blackpool?" Her pulse began to accelerate by merely speaking his name, annoying her greatly.

Alforth considered her question. "Though he is a great scoundrel, Blackpool had a point yesterday. The workings of the human heart are most mysterious. All the books and scholarly pursuits in the world cannot protect one on the twisting pathway toward love."

"Love! I never mentioned anything of the sort," Sophie said quickly.

"Of course. Not love, but perhaps affection."

"Perhaps." Sophie looked at her uncle with interest. "You sound as though you have experience in this realm."

"A little," answered Alforth vaguely. When Sophie continued to gaze at him pointedly, he said, "When I was a bit older than you are now, I fell in love. Don't look so shocked, my dear. I was not always the rusted mechanism you see now. She and I made wonderful plans together for the future, but a month before the wedding, she caught a fever and died."

"Oh, Uncle A," she murmured sadly.

"I resolved to never forget Violet, and that is why, to your mother's dismay, I have remained a bachelor ever since."

Sophie gave her uncle's hand a squeeze. It amazed her that she could still learn things about Alforth, and amazed her even more that he could have kept something so important a secret for so long. The knowledge humbled and saddened her, understanding that there would always be a part of Alforth that she could never know, a part locked away just for him and the ill-starred Violet.

It was *that* kind of love that Ian Blackpool could never duplicate with his ludicrous elixir. No matter what he claimed, no herbal extractions, no plant essences, nothing would be able to mimic the deep, lifelong love that Uncle Alforth felt for his lost Violet. Sophie sadly realized she would never experience that kind of love, whether in real life or from a bottle. By choosing botany, she had chosen solitude.

"But come now," Alforth said in a hearty voice, breaking their reveries, "I have made us both melancholy at the end of a marvelous trip, which is a bad business. We have many things to look forward to when we get back. My new house is nearly finished, and I'll be able to visit much more often."

"How did you ever convince Father to let you build on his property?"

Alforth gave her a wink. "I think your mother was much more persuasive, especially when I gave her leave to stay at my house in London whenever she liked. An even trade, hmm?" He peered at her. "Still down at the mouth? I have just the thing that will cheer us up." He fumbled with one of his traveling cases, which he had insisted on bringing into the carriage. Curious, Sophie watched as he pulled out a paper-wrapped parcel and handed it to her.

"Open it, Soph," he urged when she hesitated.

Tearing at the paper, Sophie revealed a large, leather-bound volume. "*Flora anglica*, by William Hudson," she read aloud.

"Just published," Alforth added. "I picked it up when we were in London. I thought I would give it to you for your birthday, but it seems you need a bit of brightening up today."

She set down the book carefully beside her and threw her arms around her uncle. "You are much too good to me, Uncle A," she said, her voice thick with emotion.

He patted her tenderly on her back. "Not a bit of it, girl. You'll make me proud one day with your discoveries. You already do."

Sitting back, Sophie picked up the book. She vowed that she would, indeed, make her uncle proud of her botanical work. All nonsense with Ian Blackpool would be immediately forgotten and she would dedicate herself to her studies with a new fervor. If only she hadn't been distracted by Mr. Blackpool's presence yesterday, she would have been able to obtain an actual sample of the fly agaric mushroom, as she had originally intended, instead of just one little sketch.

She glanced out the window and, with her botanist's eye for detail, remembered that they were almost to the spot where she had met Ian Blackpool. Exactly where the rare mushroom waited for her.

"Can we stop the carriage?" she asked.

"Whyever for?"

"There's a sample I forgot to collect yesterday and we are almost upon it. Would you mind?"

"Surely not."

In a trice, Alforth had signaled the driver to stop. Sophie did not wait for help down, but leapt to the ground even before the wheels of the carriage had stopped turning. She had begun to head into the woods that bordered the road when her uncle's voice stopped her.

"I think I'll stay here, Sophie," he said. "The old knee is acting up. Let me send Driscoll with you."

"I'll only be a minute," she said. "Thank you, Uncle, and thank you, Driscoll. Just wait here for me."

The driver bowed. Alforth looked concerned, but with a little wave, Sophie headed into the forest.

Yes, she told herself as she walked, Ian Blackpool would be nothing more than an embarrassing memory. She would have to avoid the village of Little Chipping in the future, with no great loss. It was indeed fortunate that she had recollected herself in time to obtain a sample.

Treading carefully, Sophie retraced her steps from the day before into the sun-dappled clearing that sheltered her prized mushroom. She thought she would be able to find it quickly—it was bright red, after all—but to her dismay, the mushroom was nowhere in sight. Sophie quickly stepped forward. Perhaps she had been wrong about its location. But the clearing looked familiar. She had been there before. Baffled, she cast her gaze around the wooded enclosure. It had been growing right next to the fallen log, right where *he* had stood.

A frightening thought struck her: Someone else had gotten to the fly agaric mushroom.

"Looking for this?"

Whirling around, Sophie saw Ian Blackpool standing a few paces away, the brilliant crimson mushroom resting in his hand. He looked exactly the same as he had yesterday and, blast him, she had not exaggerated how wickedly handsome he was. And there was that devilish smile, intimate and knowing, tormenting her. She had a flash of the memory of his lips on hers.

Sophie compressed her mouth into a line. "Is it worth my time to ask you what you are doing here?"

He shrugged. "I think the answer is obvious."

"Enjoy your tête-à-tête with the mushroom because I have nothing to say to you." Sophie began to walk away, but his other hand shot out and grabbed her arm. Gazing down at his fingers, she said quietly, "Release me at once. My uncle is nearby, and he and our coachman will come in a trice if I should cry out."

"The old gent and the lanky fellow? Neither of them look to be in peak fighting form."

Sophie had no doubt that Ian Blackpool could pound both men into jelly with no effort on his part, and quailed to think that he might. "You won't hurt them, will you?" she asked, alarmed.

He looked appalled at the suggestion. "I may be a mountebank, but I'm no ruffian."

"And yet you're holding me against my will," she pointed out.

He released her immediately, though his hand hovered near her arm. Sophie contemplated making a dash for it, but, as if reading her thoughts, he said cheerfully, "I wouldn't advise it. I'm a fast runner, and you're wearing stays and panniers."

Mightily disgruntled, Sophie folded her arms across her chest. "So I am to be your prisoner?" she asked, raising her eyebrow. "Really, Mr. Blackpool, you amaze me with your many skills. Mountebank, gaoler. What's next? Dancing master? Bear-baiter?"

"You'd enjoy seeing my head bitten off by a bear, wouldn't you?" he asked lightly.

She smiled grimly. "*Enjoy* is too mild. *Relish,* perhaps, or maybe *delight in.*"

"Such bloodthirsty impulses from such a refined young woman." He shook his head in dismay. "It's shocking what's become of the better classes."

"If I have fallen low, I have you to thank for it," Sophie shot back.

For the first time, Ian Blackpool appeared somewhat contrite. "Ah, yes," he said, stepping back and contemplating the mushroom in his hand. "That's the reason why I've been waiting for you." He looked up at her, and Sophie was struck by the sincerity in his gaze. "I understand that I hurt you, Miss Andrews, and that's something I didn't mean to do." He reached out and dropped the mushroom into the pocket of her apron.

Sophie regarded him suspiciously. This man made his living deceiving others. She could be no different. "Are you apologizing?"

"Let's not be hasty," he said, putting up his hands. "*Apologizing* has such demeaning connotations."

"And yet yesterday you demeaned me. You demeaned the field of botany. You completely misrepresented the benefits of plants to those people, and you misrepresented yourself as someone who would have any knowledge of such things."

He nodded. "And the fact that you thought I was a gentleman and not a seller of elixirs has nothing to do with your anger now."

Sophie opened her mouth, then shut it again, finding no words to contradict him.

"If so, that was your assumption, Miss Andrews, not my deception."

Sophie flushed hotly. She could not explain how or why she felt so betrayed by him, but she did. He had seemed such a paragon when they had been alone in the woods, everything that she could have hoped for in a man—witty, intelligent, interested in her work, and more handsome than the finest *Quercus robur* specimen. Yet all her illusions had been shattered when she found that he was a common street performer, peddling botany like the latest fraudulent patent medicine. It seemed the harshest of ironies that the only man who'd ever shown true interest in her was a mountebank. Only Alforth knew the inner workings of her heart, but Sophie trusted her uncle. Ian Blackpool, however, could damage her irreparably.

"Nonsense," she snapped instead. "All my life I've wanted to be taken seriously for my work with plants, and here you are, bold as you please, lying for a living and taking everything I desire for granted." This was also the truth, and easier to speak than her more personal disappointments.

"You're right. It's not fair," he said quietly, surprising her again with his candor. "And for that I do apologize."

Sophie wasn't sure what to do. It was much easier for her to feel righteous anger than this confusing mix of emotions. When she tried to assign a clear definition to Ian Blackpool, he would defy her expectations. One moment, she could slap him. The next, he was the essence of a gentleman.

"And will you apologize for insulting me?" Sophie asked.

"How did I do that?"

"You know," she said through clenched teeth. "On stage . . . after I drank the elixir . . . what happened next." She felt beyond foolish, stammering like a sheltered miss, which, she realized, she was. Yet the chaste pecks her suitors sometimes gave her had not prepared her for Ian Blackpool's vocabulary of desire.

"You mean when I kissed you?" he asked, grinning broadly.

Sophie wanted to fold herself up in mortification. "Well . . . yes."

"I won't."

"What?" she cried.

He seemed to be enjoying her discomfort. "Though the venue left something to be desired, I won't apologize for kissing you," he said, his free hand on his hip. "I don't regret it at all. In fact," he added, his smile turning into something much more sensual and knowing, "I liked it quite a bit. And so did you."

Once again, Sophie lost her power to speak. When she was able to regain her voice, she declared hotly, "You've been drinking too many bottles of that potion." Before he could respond, she began to stalk back in the direction of the carriage. To her aggravation, he followed.

"Come now, Miss Andrews," he said merrily, striding easily beside her. "I seem to recall a high degree of participation from you when we kissed."

"Your memory is clearly faulty," she snapped. "And *we* did not kiss—you assaulted me."

"We could go back to Little Chipping and ask the villagers," suggested Ian. "I'm sure they would be happy to settle this dispute."

Sophie did not slow down, but did shoot him a look that indicated she would do nothing of the sort.

"Have you never been kissed before?" he asked.

"Of course I have," she retorted, but, seeing his smile, tried to repair the damage. "You know I have suitors, and they have all been perfect gentlemen."

"But not so gentlemanly that they did not try to steal a kiss now and then."

"Now and then," Sophie concurred. "Yet they showed good judgment as to the decision of *where* and *when* to bestow a token of affection. They did not treat me like a . . . like a strumpet!"

"Is that how you imagine I think of you?" he asked more gently. "As a strumpet?"

"Clearly you do, else you would never have insulted me that way. We have nothing more to talk about, and I will gladly part company with you forever."

Before he could answer, she stopped short behind some shrubbery, her attention fixed on her family's carriage in the road.

"I don't know those men," she murmured.

"Which men?" Ian Blackpool asked, coming to stand beside her.

Sophie pointed. Her uncle was standing outside the

carriage, conversing with four men on horseback. Another mounted man was talking with Driscoll near the horses. They appeared to be tradesmen, judging by the slightly threadbare quality of their clothes, and yet their horses were of the highest caliber. Still, they appeared friendly, and Uncle Alforth talked with them readily.

Sophie shrugged. "I suppose they are fellow travelers," she guessed. Turning to Ian, she continued, "I meant what I said. I'll take my leave of you now and join the company." She was going to take a step when Ian Blackpool gripped her arm tightly and pulled her back behind the shelter of the bushes.

"Why do you insist on manhandling me?" she asked, cross. Looking up at Ian's face, she saw that he stared intently at the men, his expression hard and wary.

"Don't go out there," he said in a low voice.

Something in his tone made her feel suddenly very small and a bit afraid. "Why not?"

In answer, he put his finger to his lips. Sophie followed his gaze back to the carriage and nearly screamed when the five men suddenly brandished pistols, turning them on her uncle and the driver.

Alforth immediately put his hands in the air, with Driscoll following suit. One of the highwaymen climbed on top of the carriage and began to throw the luggage into the road. Two of his compatriots dismounted, opened the baggage, and began tearing through the contents as the remaining men kept their pistols trained on their victims.

"Oi, Dan," a highwayman searching the bags called. He held up one of Sophie's gowns, showing it to one of the men still on horseback. "Look at this, and this." He also took up one of her botany books and eyed it with distaste. Seeing her clothing in the robber's hand made Sophie sick with rage and fear, the sense of violation overwhelming.

The mounted man, Dan, turned calculating eyes on Uncle Alforth. His face was a study in ruthlessness, stained dark with grime and stubble. His black hair was pulled into a stubby queue and one ear was pierced with a golden hoop. "Why you got ladies' clothes, gov'nor?" he asked coolly. "Is there another person in your party? A female person what likes books?"

Icy terror shot through Sophie as she prayed she would not be discovered in her hiding place. Ian Blackpool's fingers tightened on her arm as he began to pull her behind him, and she felt his whole body tense in preparation for a battle. He was going to protect her! She would have thought a man like him would have gladly handed her over to the bandits and bid them all a good day.

"I am traveling alone to my sister's," Alforth answered, his voice surprisingly steady. "The gowns and such are gifts for my niece."

"And the books?" asked Dan. "Surely they ain't for your niece."

At any other time, Sophie would have objected loudly to Dan's assumption, but clearly this was not the moment for advancing the cause of female learning.

"For my nephew, of course," Alforth explained smoothly. "He loves plants."

The highwaymen seemed satisfied with that response, and continued to pillage the bags, taking jewelry and anything else that caught their eye.

"We have to do something," Sophie hissed to Ian.

"I'd welcome your suggestions," he replied, his voice grim. "But they are five armed men, and the one pistol in my caravan won't serve much good against them."

"But surely they're going to shoot my uncle!"

He shook his head. "They won't."

"But—"

Ian silenced her with a look. "Let me think."

Once the luggage had been thoroughly plundered, the men all turned to Dan with a questioning look. "What now?" one asked.

Dan walked his horse over to where Alforth stood. Resting his arms on his thigh, he leaned over the saddle and gave Alforth a long, assessing look. Sophie's heart burst with pride as she saw her uncle face the highwayman bravely, showing no fear. If only she could help him!

"You look like a fellow what's got a comfortable living," Dan said after a pause. He rubbed his jaw absently. "Judging by these gifts for your niece and nephew, I'd say you're a generous fellow, too, with a generous family."

Alforth made no answer.

Addressing his men, Dan announced, "He'll do. Grab the trunks and tie 'em back onto the roof. Put the driver and the gent in the carriage. Pickton, you drive. Doyle and Fry, get in the carriage and keep an eye on our guests. Dean and I will ride. And get these here bags out of the road. We don't want no one finding this stuff and getting suspicious. Not yet."

The men scrambled to follow Dan's orders. They herded Alforth and Driscoll into the carriage with guns at their backs. Sophie noticed the quick, searching glance her uncle directed into the forest just before he was forced into the carriage. He was looking for her. She could see the concern on his face. She wanted desperately to cry out to him, let him know that she was safe, but that was impossible.

The coach drove on, with the bandit Pickton at the reins and two others inside, guarding Alforth and the driver. Dan and his henchman rode behind the carriage, leading their compatriots' horses. In an eerie echo of Alforth's actions, Dan cast a piercing gaze around the site, and Sophie could have sworn she felt his sharp black eyes on her even behind the shelter of the bushes. But he did not see her, and set his spurs to his horse. In moments, the road was clear, and everything that had transpired there but an awful memory.

Ian and Sophie waited in silence for several minutes before emerging from the woods to stand in the road. He peered up the way and announced darkly, "They're gone."

"Are they going to kill Uncle Alforth?" Sophie rasped.

"No," said Ian. "Killing his prisoner isn't his style."

"*Whose* style?"

"That man was Dark Dan McGannon, the notorious kidnapper. I thought it might be him and his gang when they were chatting so pleasantly with your uncle, and that's why I kept you back."

"Oh," Sophie said weakly. "Well . . . thank you." She blinked a few times, collecting herself. "Kidnapper," she repeated, as the idea dawned on her in full. "That means he'll be demanding a ransom. Which means we just have to pay him and he'll let Uncle A and Driscoll go free." She began to feel a bit more optimistic.

Ian looked grim, however. "He likes to collect the ransom, then sell his prisoners into indentured servitude. By the time you pay McGannon off, your uncle could be halfway to South America."

"Then we have to get the authorities!"

"There's no way the constabulary could arrive in time, and even if they did, they'd be little help. McGannon isn't a fool. He's a notorious kidnapper because he's good at it. Village law enforcement would be a joke to him."

Sophie felt desperate. "What do I do?"

Ian held out his hand and she took it without question. His touch reassured her beyond any words. "*We* are going to get your uncle back."

Chapter Four

Ian's greatest worry was not how he intended to reclaim Sophie's uncle from Dark Dan McGannon, though the criminal's reputation for brutality and clinical indifference toward his victims was widely known and often discussed. Those who tried to find and capture him met with little success—he was an elusive bastard who knew how to hide himself—and the ones who crossed his path usually didn't make it back alive.

Ian wasn't even much perturbed by the idea of following the kidnapper's cooling trail. What troubled him most of all was *why* he was doing this at all.

Flicking the reins of his horse, Ian glanced over at Sophie sitting beside him. They were following McGannon as fast as Ian's lone horse pulling a caravan could allow. Sophie had not spoken much since they had retrieved his wagon and set off in pursuit, a span of less than an hour. Her pale face and compressed lips revealed the depths of her concern over her uncle. She had good reason for her anxiety—McGannon had no qualms about killing his targets, and Sophie's bond with her uncle was strong. She loved the old man, loved him in a way that was entirely unselfish and unconditional. Of course she would want to help him.

Ian discovered he was a little jealous. Of the old man, *and* Sophie. That one could be the object of so much affection and the other could give it so freely mystified and enticed him. He didn't understand the way in which love could appear without summons, without awareness, as though it were a gift one could give oneself: the ability to love. He would have interrogated Sophie, tried to decipher what it was she felt, how she felt it, and why, but this was not the time for his own pursuit. He pushed those questions aside.

Yet the question that continued to dog Ian was, why was he risking his life for a man he barely knew, who, at their last meeting, threatened to damage his personal plumbing? And for a woman who had clearly expressed her dislike—no, disgust of him?

"It's getting near dusk," Sophie said, gripping the side of the wooden seat. "We'll lose them for certain."

"Don't worry," Ian assured her. "I've a feeling we've nearly found them."

She nodded, her eyes fixed intently ahead. Not once had she questioned his judgment in this matter, and her confidence and faith in him was humbling.

Perhaps *that* was what had Ian dashing across the countryside, chancing his own safety on an improbable rescue. Sophie Andrews had every reason to despise him, to mistrust him, for at every turn of their brief acquaintance, he'd proven himself to be a scoundrel and a knave. And yet she had been less surprised than Ian himself after announcing that he would help Alforth. She was a puzzler, this one, and maybe, Ian realized, the great enigma was not why he had agreed to help her, but why she had agreed to *let* him help her.

"Who are you, Sophie?" he asked aloud.

She turned surprised eyes to him. "What do you mean, who am I? I'm just Sophie, that's all."

He wondered, almost to himself, "Are you a gently bred young lady, sheltered behind the safety of books and plants?"

"Sheltered?" she repeated, frowning. "I am not. I've been to London and Bath, and," she added with a blush, "I've read *Tom Jones*."

Her idea of scandalous reading had him laughing. He had a well-thumbed copy of *Fanny Hill* somewhere. Perhaps he ought to lend it to her. "Maybe *sheltered* isn't quite the word. But you're facing a situation that would have most women, and some men, in a dead panic. And you're not panicking."

"On the outside, perhaps," she said with a tremulous smile. "Inside, I'm as twisted as orchid roots. There doesn't seem to be much point in histrionics, though. That won't help my uncle or Driscoll."

Ian shook his head. "You do intrigue me, Miss Andrews."

Abashed, she had no response, and continued to watch the road.

Well, Ian thought prosaically, he had always had a fine sense of curiosity. He presumed it was that inquisitiveness which had him pushing his horse to exhaustion shadowing one of England's most infamous criminals. Lord knew he had done some strange things in his thirty-one years. This little jaunt would be mundane in comparison.

"Up ahead," he said, pointing. "Where the tracks

lead off the road and through those woods. It's them. You can tell by the number of hoof prints."

"I don't see how they'll be able to drive the carriage over that rocky ground." A line of concentration formed between her brows as she surveyed the scene.

Ian found that as he steered his wagon off the road and into the wooded countryside, he, too, encountered a good deal of difficulty keeping the caravan from tipping over. The trees around them told a similar story—broken branches and churned-up earth indicated that the kidnappers could not maneuver the large, expensive carriage through the rough and densely wooded area.

"Oh, Lord," Sophie said, reaching out and grabbing his arm.

An unfortunate sight lay before them. The men driving the carriage had obviously lost control and the vehicle had tipped, smashing against several trees. Splintered polished wood lay in massive chunks on the ground, three of the wheels had come off, and one had even rolled a good deal away from the remains of the carriage. The door of the carriage hung open, revealing an empty interior. It was a chilling sight, resembling a giant animal carcass picked clean by scavengers.

Slowing the horse, Ian quickly got down from the driving seat and went to inspect the damage. He made several passes through the wreckage before returning to Sophie.

"I didn't see any signs of human injury," he said, swinging himself back up beside her. "The people inside the carriage were probably bruised a bit, but not hurt. And the team of horses ran away, though I don't know how far they'll get hitched together."

"But my uncle?"

Ian snapped the reins and his tired horse started forward at a more sedate pace. "He's fine," Ian assured her with more confidence than he felt. He decided not to tell her about the patches of blood dotting the upholstered squabs. "We're almost at Mc-Gannon's hideout."

"How can you tell?"

Indicating the trod-upon ground, Ian explained. "Your uncle and the coachman were put on horse-back with the other men. The deeper hoof prints show that the horse is carrying a heavier burden."

"Two men, instead of one."

"McGannon wouldn't tire his horses out unless he knew he was near to safety."

She seemed to agree with his logic. And then she finally voiced the concern that had been unspoken for the whole of the tense day. "And once we do find Mc-Gannon and my uncle, what shall we do then?"

"I have a plan."

Dark Dan McGannon was reported in the broadsheets to have an icy stare like the hand of death gripping his victims' souls. He was said to be the unwanted child of a Barbary pirate and an abducted Spanish princess—or maybe the bastard of a London whore. He ate the hearts of his unlucky captives. He kept three concubines from Nubia, draped in golden chains and nothing else. He stood seven feet tall in his boots.

But it was all rumor. He was just a man who was good at his job, which was kidnapping. Nothing else mattered to him.

He and his gang now settled themselves in their

hideout, a Roman ruin set deep in the woods. McGannon was proud of the location of his lair, and the greatest shame was that he could never share its particulars with anyone outside his gang. It had been a temple or meetinghouse of some sort more than a thousand years before. Now it was a collection of crumbling columns surrounding a leaf-strewn clearing. He and his men had at one point built a roof to cover part of the clearing, and under this shelter was a small set of furniture—two chairs, a table—as well as the more fragile items that had been stolen over the years. Paper goods, silk, a fur-lined velvet cloak. There were always down-at-heels tradesmen willing to buy such goods, trying to ape their betters through fine trimmings.

But he knew that the man he had kidnapped this morning was no fraud. He was the real thing—a gentry cove. McGannon had no breeding, but he could see it straightaway in others. That was what made him a good kidnapper.

He looked over at his new prisoners. Mister Alforth Morley, gentleman, and John Driscoll, coachman, were tied together and guarded by Pickton. The old man's eyes were glazed. He'd gotten a sizeable gash on his head when the carriage tipped.

McGannon scowled, thinking about it.

"Damn it, Pickton," he'd roared to his man after the accident, "I told you to slow down!"

"Sorry, sorry, Dan," Pickton had whimpered, crawling out from under the coach. He waited with clenched eyes for McGannon's fist, or even a bullet, but neither had come.

"You'll get no share of the booty," McGannon had said instead. Pickton looked so grateful, McGannon feared he might cry.

This was Dan's secret to success. He dealt fairly with his men. Other gang leaders might have beaten or even killed Pickton for his mistake, but that kind of behavior made men shifty. Loyal men went farther for you. McGannon needed them to go as far as they could. He'd told them to rob women, and they'd done it. They'd stolen from churches on his say-so. They were well-trained dogs at his command. Sometimes he had to piss on them once in a while to remind them he was head dog in the pack, and they took it without a word against him.

He had a good life, McGannon decided. The best.

Now he watched his boys, his pack of dogs, snuffing and picking over the stuff they had salvaged from the wrecked carriage. The only good thing that had come out of being a draper's son was the ability to scrawl his letters, so McGannon sat at the table, scribbling out the ransom note.

It had been a fine day's takings. A rich gaffer bearing fancy gifts for his niece and nephew—a finer pigeon couldn't have been plucked. At the table where McGannon sat, some of the books that had been taken from the trunks were spread out. Normally, the gang didn't bother with books. They didn't fetch much when it came time to fence them. But as McGannon flipped through the pages of one of the volumes, he knew these books would get a good price. Books about plants, with big pictures finely wrought, and lots of words in Latin. Some cracked gent with a bend toward the scientific would pay handsomely for these beauties. McGannon smiled thinking about it.

His smile faded when Doyle, on lookout, came striding into the ruin with his pistol trained on the backs of a gent and a dame walking before him with their hands held high.

"I found these two sneaking around the place, Dan," Doyle said, head jerking toward his captives. "Thought I ought to bring 'em to you."

McGannon nodded, slowly rising to his feet. He surveyed his new prisoners. They were both neatly turned out, the girl better off than the cove, and each bloomed with the fine health of those who had regular meals and soft places to sleep at night. The woman was a pretty little peach, sandy-haired and freckled, though McGannon's tastes ran to redheads with ripe melons ready for a fondle. He could get over his partiality quick enough, though, when he had this doxy on her back. Dan had no doubt she'd wind up there before the night was over.

As if reading his mind, the girl's eyes widened with alarm.

"We weren't 'sneaking around,'" the man said hotly. He seemed more at ease than his woman. McGannon felt he had the girl's story right, but the gent was a stumper. His clothes were plain but sharp, his accent fine, but his frame packed tight with muscle. McGannon didn't doubt this stranger could trounce any one of his men handily. It didn't add up. Fortunately, the gang were greater in number, armed, and ready to kill.

"If you weren't sneaking," McGannon asked, narrowing his eyes, "what *were* you doing out here? We ain't exactly off the main coach line." Pulling out his own pistol, he shoved its barrel roughly into the man's stomach, forcing a grunt of pain out of him. "Speak up! I'm growing hard of hearing in my old age."

The gent reached out and pushed the pistol aside

with the tips of his fingers, which surprised, amused, and irritated McGannon with the sheer guts of the gesture. "No need for threats. Our business here is legitimate."

"Don't know how legitimate he is, Dan," Doyle chimed in. He handed McGannon another gun, saying, "I found this on him when I did a search."

"I'd be an idiot if I didn't carry protection with me when traveling," the prisoner said dryly. "The broadsheets are full of nothing but rough men."

"You've met with some of the roughest," sneered Fry as he came forward. He turned to McGannon. "I'm tired of this bloke's nattering. Let's blow a hole in his head and amuse ourselves with the bawd."

Doyle and Dean laughed raucously in agreement.

The girl kept quiet, but edged closer to her companion, her face chalky. The man didn't look afraid. Instead, he seemed to grow angry.

McGannon silenced his men immediately with a wave of his hand. "We got plenty of time for that," he said, his voice low and calm. "I'm awful curious how Mister and Missus Pickthank, here, came to be in our peaceful corner of England."

"I'll explain," the man said, "once I go back to my caravan and get a few things."

"What in blazes are you yammering about?" demanded McGannon. He turned to Doyle for an explanation.

"They were leading some kind of gypsy wagon with pictures all over it," shrugged Doyle. "It's a little ways back."

McGannon smirked. This seemed to be growing more interesting by the moment. "Take the chap down to his wagon and let him fetch what he needs," he said after a moment. "We'll keep the drab with us to make sure he don't do anything rash."

He noted the small exchange of looks between the woman and the man. She was uncertain, but he calmed her, and she gave him a tiny nod. McGannon was curious but not alarmed. He had more man- and firepower than this bloke and slip of a female. He'd toy with them for a bit and then do just what Fry suggested. They'd kill the cove and screw the girl— maybe they'd kill her, too. Or maybe not. McGannon hadn't decided yet.

The cove in question turned a fierce gaze toward McGannon. "If you even touch her while I'm away, I'll kill you by inches."

The gang laughed raucously at the gent's threat. It seemed idle enough, but they knew there was a bit of truth in his words. He was dangerous, and not just because he was built like a racehorse. He had authority, a natural command of himself, that demanded respect. McGannon didn't like it, not at all. Should he be shot now? No; let the cove give them some entertainment first, and then McGannon would save the pleasure of putting a bullet in his noggin for later.

With a nod from McGannon, Doyle and the man left the enclosure.

A tight silence settled, with the gang openly ogling the girl and McGannon himself staring with wry speculation. The flames in the campfire popped. She shifted, looking like she belonged in a fancy drawing room, not a kidnappers' hideout. The contrast amused McGannon. He noticed that she gazed beyond the gang toward Pickton, standing watch over the captive gents in the back.

McGannon looked over his shoulder at the bound

captives, who stared back over their gags. "Them's our guests," he said with rough cheer. "We're making them quite comfortable, ain't we, boys?" The gang responded with hoots and jeers. "Just like we're gonna make you comfortable, sweetheart," he added with a wolfish grin. "I'm not averse to keeping morts around the camp, so long as they make themselves useful between the sheets. I've never knocked a woman of quality before, though. I've heard they were icy-cold in bed. We'll find out soon enough."

Not surprisingly, the chit didn't respond. She swallowed hard but boldly tipped up her chin. What a prize she was, McGannon smirked.

The leaves rustled. Doyle and the cove were back. In his hands, the gent carried a wooden box: some kind of apothecary's sample case. He looked over at the girl and, again at her nod, seemed satisfied. Without asking permission, he strode over to the table with the stolen books and set the case down.

"Gather around, gentlemen," he said. "I am about to show you the greatest invention the world has ever known."

Curious, the gang pressed forward, encircling the table. Even McGannon found himself grudgingly drawn toward the table. Their prisoner had a strange charm that was hard to resist, regardless of whether or not he was on the receiving end of a barking iron.

"This thing that I am about to reveal to you has been one of the best-kept secrets of the British monarchy for centuries. But after an exhaustive search, which I shall not bore you with today, I managed to come into possession of this secret, and now my assistant Daisy and I travel across this great country of ours giving this precious resource to the people. Take a good look, gentlemen, for you'll never see anything like this again."

With a flourish, the man unlocked the fastenings on the box to reveal its contents. None of the gang knew what to imagine, but they certainly were not expecting the sight exposed before them.

"Bottles," Dean said flatly.

"Not just any bottles," the woman interjected. Everyone swung their gazes to her in surprise, for it was the first time she had spoken, and she was not nearly as frightened as everyone had thought her to be.

"My assistant is right," the man said quickly. All eyes turned back to him. "These bottles contain a precious elixir. Anyone who drinks of it will be given the thing that all men desire."

"A foot-long cock?" Fry asked.

"You mean, you ain't got one?" Dean laughed.

"Shut up," snarled McGannon.

The gent laughed, too, unafraid of McGannon's threats. "That's another elixir for another day. But sex is fleeting, a few minutes' pleasure and then you're left with nothing. You're as alone as you were at the beginning."

The girl looked over at the man sharply, frowning.

"This potion gives you something much better, something men have been searching for since the days of . . ." He looked around, noted the crumbling Roman columns and plinths. "Since the days of this place. A long, long time ago." He held up one of the bottles, glimmering in the firelight. It looked magical in his hand. "Whoever takes this elixir will be given the strength of ten men."

"What's so marvelous about that?" demanded Fry.

The man smiled, an easy smile of camaraderie and

affection. "Think about it, friend: What could you do if you were as strong as a plow horse? What barriers would stand between you and the things you wanted? Nothing. The heaviest door would melt away beneath your fingertips like spiderwebs. The most cumbersome object, like a trunk filled with gold, would feel as light as a kitten in your hands. The possibilities are endless."

Stunned at this prospect, the gang began to mutter among themselves.

"A gang of five could have the muscle of fifty, with only five shares of the booty between them," the cove continued. "If, for example, you wanted to rob a coach, it would be as easy as tipping it over and shaking the contents out into the road, like emptying one's pockets."

"You mean," Fry asked excitedly, "the McGannon gang could become the most feared in the whole country?"

"Why stop there? Europe, or the entire world, would be at your command."

"There'd be no one stopping us," breathed Dean, a look of wonder on his face.

"None at all."

A happy reverie fell over the men, imagining all the destruction and mayhem they could inflict on an unsuspecting world.

"Bollocks," snapped McGannon, interrupting his gang's daydreaming. "There ain't no such potion that can make a man strong."

"I'll be happy to prove it to you." The gent reached into the case and pulled out more bottles so he held five. "I'll give you and your men each a free sample. Once you have experienced the might of Hercules, you'll thank me and bless whatever stars brought me and my assistant to your camp."

All of the men reached forward with eager hands, and even Pickton took a few steps away from his prisoners to get to the amazing potion, but McGannon stopped them.

"Hold on," he said with a snarl. His men, intimidated, backed up. McGannon came to stand scant inches from the gent, looking directly into his captive's eyes. It didn't please McGannon that his captive was a bit taller than he was, but size meant nothing.

The broadsheets were right about some things: McGannon's best weapon was his stare. He'd practiced it for years as a chub running through the streets of London, getting culled by any flash cove who preyed upon the green lads come down from the country. After months of empty pockets and an empty belly, McGannon knew he could never beat the streets using his fists or blade. Soon enough, he'd earned the name Dark Dan, not because of his black hair but the pitiless darkness of his eyes.

He stared at his captive, trying to break the man, get him to cow under his direct scrutiny. Few of McGannon's kidnap victims had ever been able to withstand the direct assault of his stare, tossing up whatever information he wanted with a bit of eye-to-eye contact. McGannon never had to raise his fists. When he eventually sold his prisoners into indentured servitude, they were always at the peak of health and fetched a much better price than if they had been beaten. It was another of his secrets to success.

McGannon looked deep into the light brown eyes of the man, this peddler of tonics, trying to find the lie.

He hadn't gotten to where he was in England's underworld by trusting, and he wasn't about to start now.

"You *sell* these bottles of nonsense, do you?" he demanded.

"I do, with the help of my assistant."

"Bollocks," McGannon repeated. "I see the clothes you two wear, the fancy manners you got. You expect me to believe fine gentry folk like yourself run around peddling potions out of your wagon?"

After a tense pause, the man hung his head. "Yes, you've found us out. We aren't exactly who we pretend to be."

The girl gasped, a nearly inaudible sound, but McGannon heard it. He felt the bitter surge of triumph.

"Then who are you?"

"My father is an apothecary in London—"

"Twaddle," McGannon snorted. "You're too posh to be an apothecary's son."

"I am," the man insisted. He continued, somewhat embarrassed, "He had . . . aspirations, and sent me to the finest schools so I could learn to pass as one of the gentry who frequented his shop."

"What about the girl?" McGannon asked, turning his piercing gaze toward the mort in question. She met his look without flinching.

Reaching out, the spruce fellow took her hand tenderly in his own. His heart in his eyes as he gazed at her, he explained, "She's the daughter of one of the gentry folk that would come into the shop. We met there, and began to rendezvous in secret. When I asked her father for her hand, he refused on the grounds that I was too low-born. So she and I ran away, and now I use the skills I learned in my father's

shop and improve upon them." He turned challeng-
ing eyes toward McGannon. "Satisfied?"

McGannon looked once more at the girl. He knew
she would be the ticket as to whether or not he was
being gulled. Were these queer birds really runaway
lovers selling elixirs, two figures out of some cheap
broadsheet ballad? She held her supposed darling's
hand with a blushing carnality, as though his touch
excited her through its illicit nature. Her bold hesi-
tancy, combined with a wariness offset with an open
trust of her lover, made McGannon begin to doubt his
doubt.

"All right," he said slowly. "We'll give your magic
drink a try. But I'd like a demonstration first."

The man looked riled. "What do you mean?"

"I want you to try it before we do. Show us what
your strength potion can do. And once I see that you
ain't trying to poison us, maybe we'll have a little
ourselves."

The gent shrugged. "Fine. Anything to make a cus-
tomer happy." He took one of the bottles and started
to bring it to his lips, but McGannon's grip on his
arm stopped him.

"Just a moment, if you please," he said, smirking.
"In case your potion works, I don't want you running
around my camp, smashing up the place. What happens when a mort drinks that stuff?"

"She becomes strong as well. Not as strong as a
man, of course, but certainly more than any other
woman."

McGannon plucked the bottle from the gent's hand
and, smiling darkly, strolled over to the chit. He could
see the pulse leap in her throat as he approached, but
she did not back down.

"Drink it, sweetheart," he said. His voice was a parody of good manners. When she hesitated for a bare moment, he repeated hotly, "Drink it."

With a quick movement, she snatched the bottle out of his hand. She popped the cork and, after glancing at her companion, drank the elixir in one gulp. Daintily, she wiped her mouth as she dropped the bottle into her pocket.

"You see?" said the man, coming forward. "Perfectly harmless."

"But does it work?" asked Fry. "Why should we try it if it don't work?"

The girl looked around the camp and, spotting something, began to walk away. She neared a large fallen log off to the side. It was a big old tree trunk, one that would take at least three men to lift, judging by its size. She walked around it for a few moments, considering it, and then, after wiping her hands on her apron, bent down as if to pick it up.

The men snorted and chuckled. Surely that lathy wench wasn't planning on picking up that log by herself. It would be . . .

"Impossible," Dean breathed, but it was true.

She had taken the log and lifted it. Not only was she carrying it herself, she was holding it over her head as though it weighed one stone and not ten. Even the tied-up prisoners being guarded by Pickton murmured in surprise through their gags. After a moment more, the girl set the log back down, dusted her hands off on her apron again, and walked back toward the assembled gang, a look of challenge on her face.

Now there was no stopping the men. They each grabbed bottles, even McGannon and Pickton, uncorked them, and drank them down in an instant.

"Tastes like pine needles," Dean said, rubbing his mouth with the back of his hand. "And something else, too. I don't know what."

"A special mixture of plant essences," the peddler said with a sudden smile. "You'll feel the effects in just a moment."

Doyle and Fry compared the size of their muscles, flexing and boasting to each other. McGannon regarded them with barely checked tolerance. He made sure to people his gang with street-savvy men who, at the end of the day, couldn't tell their asses from their elbows without his say-so. They were easy to manage and looked to him for guidance in nearly everything. But the qualities he prized also meant stomaching a certain amount of misbehavior on their part. McGannon himself had no time for such tricks. He wanted to see just how much strength this mysterious potion had given him.

Without a word, he stalked over to the fallen tree the woman had picked up moments earlier. In one quick movement, he lifted the log easily. McGannon found himself amazed for once.

"By God," he said, as his men laughed and cheered, "the stuff works." To prove his point, he threw the log into the air and caught it.

The sound of shattering wood filled the camp as the log snapped in two in his hands. At first, McGannon believed he'd truly broken a hefty piece of wood with only the strength of his fingers, but then he stared in shock and growing fury at the shattered log he held.

"Damn me, it's hollow!" he roared. He threw the tree remains toward the peddler and his assistant, and his men saw that, sure enough, the log that had at first looked solid was in fact eaten from the inside out by insects and was only a shell. Face contorted with rage, he snarled at the man, "You tricked us, you and your whore! I'll put you to bed with a shovel, you damned Faulkner!" More than anything, McGannon hated being taken for a fool. He would never be tricked. *Never*. He'd sworn that after those hard months in London, and kept fast to that rule.

"Ian, look out!" the woman screamed as McGannon drew his pistol. But queerly, the pistol felt heavy in his hand. Unbelievably heavy. In fact, his whole arm seemed to have turned to lead. As had his legs. And his head suddenly felt stuffed with batting. He couldn't hold the barking iron with the thick, unmoving sausages of his fingers. It dropped to the ground, but the sound it made as it hit the earth was muffled and far away.

Through his blurred vision, McGannon could only watch as each of his men swayed and stumbled on their feet. With clumsy movements, they tried to right themselves, reach for something, anything, to frustrate the strange stupor that was overcoming them.

"You . . . poisoned us . . ." he slurred, staggering toward the watery shadow of the man. He lurched, and fell to his knees.

"Not poisoned," corrected the man. "Once you wake up, you'll feel a bit sick, but you'll be yourself again in a day or two."

"Going to . . . kill . . ." McGannon mumbled, toppling forward. The rest of his threat was buried in the dirt as oblivion seeped over him. Before his vision blackened completely, he saw the face of the girl peering down at him. At least, he consoled himself as he fell into darkness, he had a good memory. He never forgot a face.

* * *

"Are they dead?" Sophie asked, leaning down over the still form of Dark Dan McGannon.

"I told him the truth," Ian answered, inspecting the insensible bodies of the gang. "When they finally do wake up, they'll feel awful, but at least they'll be alive."

"What a comfort."

Then Sophie did not spare the kidnappers any more attention as she ran toward her uncle, Ian following.

She pulled the gags off Alforth and the coachman as Ian used a knife to saw at their bindings. Throwing her arms around her uncle, she cried, "Oh, Uncle A, I'm so glad to see you. And you, too, Driscoll," she added. The coachman nodded gratefully. "You're hurt!" She dabbed at her uncle's forehead with her apron and was horrified to see his glazed eyes regard her with confusion.

"Is it you?" he asked, his voice thickened. "Is it Sophie?"

"It's Sophie." For the first time all day, she thought she might cry.

"Don't worry, my dear," Alforth said with a crooked smile. "It's only a scrape I got when the carriage tipped. But I am glad to see you, Soph," Alforth added. She could visibly see him gathering his wits, trying to piece together names and places. "And extraordinarily surprised. What on earth are you doing here? And how did you know that you could pick up that log? And why didn't you pass out, too? And who the devil are you, sir?" he demanded of Ian. The ropes at last fell away and the freed men rubbed at their wrists.

"You have many questions, which I'll be happy to

answer," Ian said, straightening. Shakily, Alforth and Driscoll did the same, with Sophie providing a supporting shoulder for her uncle and Ian assisting the coachman. "But first we've got to leave this place right now and find the nearest constabulary to arrest these men."

"Shouldn't we bind them first?" Sophie asked as she guided Alforth toward the entrance to the camp. "So they don't escape?"

Her uncle and the coachman rested as she and Ian found some rope and began tying up the kidnappers.

"Bind their wrists and ankles," Ian directed. "We don't want them getting free before the law arrives." Sophie followed his instructions, although her skill at knot-tying had never gotten beyond her second or third embroidery lesson. Her mother had given up teaching her when it became clear that she had no aptitude nor desire to embellish pillow cases. And Sophie kept getting mud on her needlework.

"I remember you," Alforth said, pointing at Ian. "You're that devil who was selling nostrums in Little Chipping. I should have your hide for insulting my niece."

"Uncle A," Sophie upbraided him, "Mr. Blackpool just saved your life."

Alforth blustered a bit, but conceded the point with a nod. "But you never should have come after us, Sophie. It was much too dangerous."

"Mr. Blackpool told me that Dan McGannon asks for ransoms and then sells his victims into servitude. We *had* to come after you. And on the way, he formulated this excellent plan for drugging the kidnappers."

Alforth held on to some residual anger toward Ian, however. "Even if you had a plan, you should not have brought my niece to such a horrible place as this. She could have been hurt, or worse."

"I realize that, sir," Ian said, looking grim. "But we were short on time, and I couldn't leave her by the side of the road. At the very least, I knew I could protect her if I was nearby."

Sophie blushed at his words, but no one noticed her reaction. Alforth was busy cobbling together something like an apology.

"You have something of a point, young man. Sensible thinking. Yes, perhaps so. Sophie's very important. Always put her first."

"But you drank the same potion, Miss Sophie," Driscoll said, interrupting the awkward moment. "Why aren't you dead asleep, too?"

"I put dhatura, an Indian plant, in the elixirs," explained Ian. "And we both drank a tincture of oxalis corniculata before we arrived here. It's the antidote."

"Was this your idea, Sophie?" Alforth asked.

"Not a bit. It was all Mr. Blackpool's doing."

A new look of admiration came into Alforth's expression as he regarded this strange man. He would have a lot of thinking to do on the way back to Gloucestershire.

"Now I have a question for Sophie," Ian asked, stepping over the tied-up bodies of the kidnappers. "How did you know about the log? It appeared completely solid."

"Simple botany," she replied with a pert smile. "A few clues let me know that it was nothing more than a husk. It was covered in a moss that grows only on bug droppings—so I knew that most of the tree had been eaten away."

Alforth watched as a similar look of admiration

filled the young man's eyes. "Well done, Miss Andrews," Ian Blackpool murmured.

"And well done to you, Mr. Blackpool," she responded.

Even though they were all in a kidnapper's hideout in the middle of the forest, with unconscious men all about them, Alforth got the impression that for his niece and the mountebank, the world grew very small at that moment, so that it only included them. He wasn't sure what to make of that.

"Perhaps we ought to go soon," Driscoll said. He colored at his bold recommendation, since he had never before addressed his employers in so familiar a manner. "If that's what you wish, Mr. Morley, Miss Sophie."

"That is an excellent idea," Sophie said, turning away from Ian. "But," she added, her expression darkening, "the carriage has been destroyed. How will we ever get all the way home? We cannot walk the distance."

"I believe I have a plan for that, too," Ian said with an enigmatic smile.

Chapter Five

"You'll find the men already subdued," Alforth said.

"Yes," Driscoll added. "They were given a potion—"

"—a sleeping drug—"

"—and they passed out—"

"Cold. Completely insensate."

"Certainly, thank you, you've told us as much twice already," the constable said, interrupting Alforth and Driscoll's excited narrative. For the past twenty minutes, they'd been giving the village law their depositions and detailed information as to where they could find Dark Dan and the McGannon gang. It hadn't taken long to explain the story, but, like all survivors of an ordeal, the ordeal itself began to pale in comparison to the pleasure of telling it.

"Uncle," Sophie said gently, "perhaps we ought to let Constable Euwer and his men go and get McGannon. We don't want them to escape."

"Quite right," Alforth agreed. "Thank you for

your help. Driscoll will give you our direction if you need to find us."

While the coachman took care of this final business, Ian stepped out from the nearby inn into the courtyard. "The last mail coach left at ten o'clock this evening," he told Sophie and Alforth. "There won't be another until tomorrow night. But the innkeeper told me they have a few rooms available."

"We were expected at Cabot Park this very night," Alforth said unhappily. "Caroline will be frantic at our prolonged absence. Perhaps we can hire a carriage."

Driscoll, having finished with the constable, was sent to inquire on the availability of a carriage, and came back with bad news.

"There's nothing to be found. Seems everyone's left town to attend an agricultural fair two villages over, taking their wagons, drays, and carriages with them."

Alforth and Sophie looked crestfallen. They knew Sophie's mother would be in a panic until they returned home. Even if they had wanted to stay at the inn, no one would get a decent night's sleep knowing Caroline Andrews would be lamenting their certain deaths.

"That settles it," Ian said. "I'm taking you home."

Alforth, Sophie, and Driscoll began to protest in unison, but Ian would not be argued with. "I'll bring my caravan around and get you back to Cabot Park."

He didn't wait for their chorus of thanks, but strode off toward the stables without another word.

"A very interesting young man you have there, Sophie," Alforth remarked once the man in question had disappeared.

"He is," she agreed. "But he isn't mine, Uncle A. He doesn't appear to belong to anyone."

"Quite peculiar. I can't help wondering . . ." Alforth murmured to himself.

Whatever Alforth was speculating about was cut short by the arrival of Ian leading his horse-drawn wagon into the courtyard. Sophie patted the mare's neck in encouragement, knowing the horse would have a long night ahead of her.

"There's room in the caravan itself," Ian said, throwing open the back door of the painted wagon. "Everyone can get some rest on the way."

Sophie, along with Alforth and Driscoll, peered into the interior of the caravan. Sophie hadn't had time to look at it before and was now more than a little intrigued to see where this young mountebank lived. It was a narrow space, neatly filled with the paraphernalia of a traveling peddler. Books and wooden boxes filled the shelves, and Sophie noted a small wardrobe and cot pushed against one of the walls. She was surprised by its orderliness and normalcy, somehow expecting that it would be cluttered and exotic with, perhaps, lewd pictures tacked up on the walls. It was a bit of a disappointment to see otherwise. She was pleased to note, however, a lovely and rich Indian cloth draped across the bed.

Her cheeks burned, knowing that every night he would lay his body down on that bed, close his eyes, and fall into the embrace of sleep. What would he look like asleep? He might snore, but she had a feeling he wouldn't. He probably didn't wear any nightclothes—they were an unnecessary expense for many, especially someone who lived out of a caravan. Ian would be completely naked under that embroidered blanket. It was such an intimate thought, Sophie wondered her face didn't burst into flame.

"There's, ah—" she began, but her voice was curiously dry. Clearing her throat, she continued, "There isn't enough room for all three of us back here. Uncle A, you and Driscoll get in and I'll ride in the front."

Both coachman and concerned uncle objected immediately, but Sophie would not give any quarter. "I insist," she said firmly, taking her uncle by the arm and guiding him into the caravan. "You both have had a dreadful day and need to try to sleep. We'll have Mother to answer to soon enough, and you'll need all the strength you can muster."

"What about you, miss?" Driscoll asked. He braced his hands on the door frame. "You must be worn out."

Sophie smiled. Truthfully, she answered, "Strangely enough, I feel rather sprightly. So don't worry about me and both of you *go to sleep*." She closed the door with a definitive click, blocking out any more protestations. Turning, Sophie nearly smacked right into Ian, standing directly behind her. She put up her hands to keep from bumping her nose against him, and found that her palms were braced against his broad chest. Oh, God, he felt so warm, the heat of him seeping through his clothing, and she could not mistake the smooth, tight planes of his muscles beneath her fingers. She wanted to spread her hands out, draw him in, learn his geography. But that was impossible.

"Ah, sorry," she muttered, jerking her hands back. "What are you smiling about?"

"You," he replied. "You command your uncle and coachman like a general. For a humble botanist, you've got a will of iron."

Sophie shrugged self-consciously. "We had best get

on the road," she said, steering the conversation toward more comfortable topics. "We won't reach Sevendowne until morning. It's the nearest village to Cabot Park," she explained.

He seemed to realize that she was ill at ease talking about herself, and so he let the matter drop. They both took their places on the bench of the wagon— Sophie accepting Ian's outstretched hand to help her up with a regal nod, a lady in spite of herself—and with a flick of the reins, they were headed on the road to home.

"What a beautiful night," she murmured, and it was true. A gentle warm breeze curled through the trees, filling the air with the sound of leaves shifting against each other. The bright waxing moon shone down upon the road and turned the sky a deep, velvety lavender.

"There are some plants that bloom only at night," she mused. "I've heard of a plant from the West Indies, the cereus, that unfolds like a giant white star and has the most wonderful perfume. I would love to see it."

"Perhaps you will."

She turned abruptly in her seat to contemplate Ian. "You said the drug we gave McGannon was Indian. Have you really been there?"

He nodded.

Sophie clasped her elbows and held her arms against her stomach, staring wistfully into the sky. "It must have been wonderful."

"Sometimes it was, and other times . . ." He shrugged.

"My brother gets a Grand Tour when he's finished

at university. I've never been farther than Ramsgate."
She sighed. "I wish I could travel wherever I wanted.
It seems heavenly. Just think of all the plants I could
study."

"Every place has its pleasures and its problems."

"Even England?" she asked with a smile in her
voice.

He glanced quickly over at her face, limned in
pearly light, a study in contrasts. The high planes of
her cheeks, the slender bridge of her nose, the ripe
fullness of her bottom lip, and even the tender length
of her neck, all grew luminous in the depths of night.
The hollow of her throat was a tempting indentation
in the darkness. He wanted to touch his fingertips
there, feel her pulse leap underneath him.

"England, too," he answered.

It would be a long ride, and a long night, if he continued to ogle the poor girl like a sailor on leave, so he
turned his attention back to the road.

"I had the innkeeper pack up some food," he said.
"There's a basket under the seat."

"Oh, bless you," Sophie breathed, reaching down
to retrieve the hamper. "I haven't had a bite to eat
since rolls and chocolate this morning." She laughed.
"Was it really this morning? Lord, it seems like a lifetime ago." Setting the basket on her lap, she pulled
out some small loaves of bread, cold sliced beef, a
wedge of good English cheese, and a flask of ale.
"This could be awkward. Let's see. Have you a
knife?"

He handed her the knife he kept sheathed in his boot.
She examined it for a moment, running her fingers over
the curved blade and the flared brass handle covered
with a hammered design of vines and leaves.

"How strange," she murmured.

"Something I picked up in my travels," he said, giving the knife no more than a glance. He had forgotten that objects like that would be remarkable to someone like her. "I got it years ago at a bazaar in Benares. For an extra few coins, I could have bought the knife-maker's daughter."

"You're joking!" Sophie cried with a laugh.

"You're right, I am joking," he admitted, laughing, too, at his own desire to shock her. "But I could have bought a fine goat."

Shaking her head and chuckling, Sophie bent to her task. In short order, she sliced the bread in half, put the meat and pieces of cheese on top, and placed the other half of the bread over all.

"I don't know what this is, but I think it will make eating everything a bit easier," she said, handing him one of the stuffed loaves.

"Very ingenious," he said. After taking a bite, he added, "And very delicious. This is a wonderful idea. You should take out a patent."

"Oh, no," she said between bites, "I'm perfectly satisfied with botany. I don't need to become an inventor."

"And are you?"

"Am I what?"

"Satisfied."

She regarded him steadily as she took a swallow of ale. "I've been pursuing an idea in my work for a long time, and even if I was able to prove my theory, I'm not certain what to do with the information. As a woman, no one will give credence to my findings. There's a man in France I correspond with who thinks my idea is quite intriguing, but he doesn't know I'm a female." She tried to sound nonchalant, but Ian could detect the frustration in her voice. "So, no, in answer to your question. I'm not satisfied; not completely."

She drank again from the flagon and handed it to Ian, having fallen silent to contemplate her own thoughts.

"That's one of the problems with England," he said, after taking a swallow of ale. "It's one of the most narrow-minded countries I've ever lived in. You should be allowed to make your ideas public, regardless of your sex."

"Thank you," she said. Something in her voice had Ian looking over sharply, and he could see even in the nebulous light that she was regarding him with a lot more admiration than he deserved. A warning bell sounded.

"Tell me about that theory you have," he said, trying to distract her.

Sophie roused. "It's really quite amazing. I'm looking for a flower—the peach-leaved bellflower. It isn't just any flower, you see. It's not native to Britain, and it's been known to colonize when it escapes the boundaries of a garden." Her hands had begun to dance as she described the unique flower, and if Ian had found her pretty before, now she positively glowed with beauty. Talking about her work did this; it lit her from within.

"Are they rare, these bellflowers?"

"A bit, but I'm not just studying the flower on its own. There have been scattered reports, unconfirmed, of the bellflower growing *right beside* sessile oak trees."

"And that's rare," he surmised, finding himself drawn still closer to her, to her passion.

Unaware of his sharpened interest, Sophie continued. "Unbelievably so. The composition of the soil for the oak and the kind of soil the bellflower needs are very different. It's a fantastic phenomenon. Two plants growing next to each other when all reason dictates they shouldn't. I've been looking for this singularity so I can document it." She turned fully to him, resting her hand on his arm as she said excitedly, "They should kill each other, but they don't."

"Why not?"

"It's about symbiosis—two organisms, each with the perfect complement to the other, so that neither could exist alone."

Ian was struck by this description. It sounded very familiar, for some reason. "Symbiosis," he murmured, testing the feel of the word. It had a pleasant sibilance that seemed to illustrate the very thing it defined; the joined relationship between two dissimilar creatures. It seemed to describe, through its tones, Sophie herself—sharp and curved at the same time. "I like the sound of that."

"I enjoy playing with the sounds of words in my head," she admitted. "That's why I like the Linnaean system so much—those beautiful embroidered names for all plants and animals. *Euphorbia dulcis*. That sounds much better than 'sweet spurge,' doesn't it?"

"Yes, much," he said with a laugh.

"But tell me about your work," she said, turning to him.

"You've already seen my work."

"Surely you can't just sell potions to country folk."

He fixed her with a direct, piercing look. He had to disabuse her of any notions that he might be more than he really was. She wanted him to be bigger, better, a hawker of potions who was also a gentleman with a higher calling. Such an illusion could be dangerous for them both. "That's exactly what I do, Sophie. I travel from village to village peddling love in a bottle to any naive soul willing to buy it. I take their money gladly and hope to never see them again. It's not a symbiotic relationship—it's parasitic."

"You're too hard on yourself," she answered, but her voice held uncertainty.

"I wouldn't be good at what I do if I had any illusions about myself. You described me perfectly before: nothing but a mountebank."

Sophie ducked her head, but she would not be dissuaded. Clenching her fists in her lap, she said, "I don't believe that. If you only sold elixirs, why did I find you in the woods the other day? Your pockets were full of plants. You were doing research," she concluded. "Admit it, you were."

He could put an end to the discussion right then. He could flatly deny her allegations, or try to charm or laugh her away from the subject altogether. He made his living through persuasion, after all. Surely one impressionable young woman would be easy enough to sway. Sophie, somehow, was different. He didn't want to manipulate her or gull her. Ian discovered something strange. He *liked* her. That in itself should have made him leery, but he found he couldn't ignore the respect he felt for her.

"I was doing some research," he said at last.

"I knew it!" she crowed, ridiculously pleased. "I knew there was more to you than some traveling charlatan. Tell me," she continued excitedly, "what kind of research? Cross-breeding plants? A new taxonomy? Or maybe a definitive study of the introduction of foreign plants?"

"Love."

She blinked owlishly. "Beg your pardon?"

"I study love."

Sophie stammered. "But . . . you can't . . . I mean, it's not possible—a person can't *study* love."

"Why not?" he asked with an arched eyebrow.

"Because, because," she sputtered, clearly disturbed by this idea, "because love isn't something that can be analyzed empirically. You *feel* love, here." She placed her hand over her heart, fascinating Ian with the image of her slender fingers brushing against the swell of her own breast. "It's not an object, or a scientific principle. It's an emotion."

"Is it?" He tore his gaze away from the temptation of her bosom. "Why do some people spend their whole lives alone? Don't they have feelings, too?"

"Of course they do."

"And why is it that a man can meet a woman who should be perfect for him in every way but feel nothing for her? Is it because he has no emotions?"

"Certainly not."

"Yet animals can spend their entire lives with one mate, and those plants you mentioned are linked with one another in order to survive. Some might call their relationships love."

Frowning, Sophie said, "But those are just animals with rudimentary brains. And plants—as much as I adore them, I know that they don't think or feel, not the way people or even animals do."

He shook his head. "No, I believe that the secret to love isn't wrapped up in the flowery phrases of poetry. It's not about two souls communing with each other, or," he searched for the right words, " 'Love looks not with the eyes, but with the mind—' "

" '—and therefore is winged Cupid painted blind,' " Sophie finished, appearing more disturbed. "It isn't? Then what *is* love?"

Ian held her gaze with his own. "Chemistry." Sophie began to protest, and he silenced her objections by continuing. "Why should two people link themselves together for their entire lives? Why should some marriages be happy while others be a misery? What makes a man see a woman walking down the street and suddenly decide he can't go on without her?"

"Love," she answered.

"It's a chemical reaction. Something in one person's chemistry reacts favorably to something in another person, and they interpret that interaction, that chemical reaction, as love. If the chemicals are not compatible, it's called hatred, or indifference. But it's all science, not emotion, that brings two people together or forces them apart. That's where the poets got it wrong." To himself he added, "That's where everyone gets it wrong."

"So you think you already know the secret to love," she said, rubbing her nose with her thumb distractedly.

"I wish I did." He sighed. "But somewhere in the veins of plants I'll find the answer, the chemical compounds that can make a person love."

"And then?"

He was taken aback by her question. "What?"

"Once you find those chemicals, once you learn what makes people love, what will you do then?"

Ian sat back and considered. He'd been pursuing his quest for eight years, traveling as far as India, North Africa, and Persia to find the answer to this one, all-consuming subject. He'd read libraries full of books in Sanskrit, Arabic, and Latin, and endlessly interviewed mystics and sages wherever he went. But he had never considered what would happen if he found the answer. It seemed ridiculous, absurd that this bookish English girl could have accurately honed in on the one flaw in his plan.

He laughed. "I don't know."

Sophie crossed her arms over her chest, irritated. "You are the most bizarre man I have ever met."

"I can't disagree with you," he said with a grin. His smile faded when he saw her hunch into herself, shivering. The temperature had dropped dramatically over the past hour. "You're cold."

She started to shake her head but abandoned the pretense when a paroxysm of trembling shook her body. "All my sh-shawls were in my trunks left at McGannon's hideout."

He quickly shucked his own coat and draped it over her shoulders. She was swallowed by the fabric, a small woman enveloped by the coat of a much larger man.

"Oh, no," she murmured, clutching the lapels tightly around her, "I couldn't."

Ian laughed again, amused by her warring impulses of good breeding and necessity. In response, he tucked the coat closer around her, feeling the strange and pleasant combination of the familiar wool surrounding her unfamiliar, feminine body. She wasn't very big at all, a sparrow of a woman, and he knew with absolute certainty that he would be able to span her waist with his hands. He also knew that once he had gotten his coat back, her fresh scent would linger in the fabric, combine with his own musk to create something new entirely. A stab of pure lust shot through him, and he flicked the reins to urge the horse on.

They fell into a companionable silence. Between the lulling sway of the caravan, the rhythmic clip-clop of the horse's hooves, and the long and frightening day, it wasn't long before Ian felt Sophie droop against his shoulder, fast asleep.

He looped his arm around her shoulders to keep her from slipping and, with a sigh, she snuggled close against him, one hand pressed against his chest. There was that scent—the clean, earthy smell of her that was a combination of grass and woman—and Ian was assailed with images of himself and Sophie, making love in the middle of a field, wearing nothing but sunshine and each other. Memories of their kiss combined with his fantasy until he was left with a confusing mix of longing and remembrance. Her mouth against his, the taste of her like apples, her satiny, freckled skin. She would be sweetly shy but responsive. There was an innate sensuality to her that he doubted she even knew about. He could show her. He knew a lot about sex. She was a smart girl, an apt pupil. The things they could do together . . .

Ian ground his teeth instead.

It was impossible, of course. But God, he wanted her.

Chemicals, he reminded himself. Nothing but chemicals. Lust and love were very different things, but what separated one from the other? A bit of fancy wordplay, some pretty illusions, and something else, something elusive. He knew the answer would reveal itself to him—eventually.

For now, he enjoyed Sophie's warm curves pressed against him, her delicate weight beneath his arm, as he drove along the country road, deeper into Gloucestershire. He'd never spent much time in this county, though friends of his would go to Cheltenham for the waters. He wondered if he would have met Sophie had he gone with them. No, she would have been too young, not yet out. Even if she had been old enough, she probably wouldn't have had much desire to mingle with society. Too much frivolity, not enough plants.

As his mind drifted, he felt Sophie start. She came awake with a sharp intake of breath, sitting bolt upright.

"Are you all right?" he asked, concerned.

She rubbed her hands over her face. "Yes," she murmured. "I think so. Just a bad dream about that horrible Dan McGannon. He was coming to get me, and he was going to sell me to an Indian rajah." She shivered, but not from the cold.

"You're safe now," Ian said. "Don't think about him anymore."

Sophie smiled gratefully, then became aware of Ian's arm around her shoulders. He thought she would shake him off or move away, but she stayed where she was.

"I didn't want you to fall," he found himself explaining, hating the apologetic note in his voice.

Sophie shrugged. "I don't mind. It's rather nice. Yes, I like it quite a bit."

He should have followed his instincts and removed his arm immediately, but he didn't. He continued to hold her. *Idiot.*

No, he didn't have much in the way of brains, but in the meantime, he would find some pleasure where he could. He settled for a compromise and changed the subject.

"Dan McGannon isn't so frightening," he said. "He wouldn't last a day in India."

"Do you think so?" she asked. "Is it very dangerous?"

"Between the tigers, the mosquitoes, and the Thugee, I'd say it's dangerous."

"Thugee?"

"They make McGannon look like a child on leading strings. They operate much like he does, actually, meeting travelers on the road and pretending to be travelers themselves."

"But they aren't."

"Once everyone is nice and comfortable, chatting away like old friends, the Thugee pull out their silk scarves and strangle everyone. Men, women, children, servants. Everyone." Ian smirked at himself, knowing he wasn't above telling a scary story to get a woman to sit closer. Sophie fell into his trap, jamming herself so tight against him, he almost lost his breath.

"That's awful!" she cried. "Are they thieves?"

"No, but they will take their victims' riches. They're devotees of the goddess Kali, the Destroyer, who demands human sacrifice as part of her worship."

"What a dreadful bunch," Sophie said with a dramatic shudder. "Imagine, making those poor people trust them and then betraying them. I couldn't stand being tricked like that."

"You wouldn't mind," he said wryly, "since you'd be dead."

She shot him a look. "I'd be dead *and* angry. I'd be a ghost and haunt them until they couldn't stand it anymore and begged for my forgiveness. Wretched beasts. I'd be much happier if they just popped out of the woods and killed me right off instead of misleading me."

Damn it, there was that alarm again. He was going

to have to part company with Sophie sooner rather than later, for both their sakes.

"I'll bear that in mind if I know anybody who wants to kill you," he said, comfortably shielding himself behind humor. "Save everyone a lot of aggravation."

"Thank you."

Ian smiled in the darkness, feeling the strangest sense of euphoria. Sophie Andrews could match him in the eccentricity department, and it delighted him, though it shouldn't. Impulsively, he leaned down and kissed the top of her head.

That shocked her. "Oh," she exclaimed, "I . . . well . . . hmm . . ." With stiff, awkward gestures, she disengaged herself from under his arm and sat, spine straight, a good foot and a half away. The bench wasn't very long, but she managed to perch on the very end. Ian's good mood plummeted.

The silence that stretched between them wasn't nearly as companionable as it had been earlier. They rode on, passing darkened villages and lowing cattle. Most of the villages in this part of the country were charming Tudor-style clusters of buildings, crossed with wooden beams, nestled against snug little hills and old trees. Neither spoke until the first pink rays of morning began to appear in the sky.

"That was Whittington," Sophie remarked softly as they left behind another sleeping town. "Sevendowne is a mile away. We'll be home soon."

Home. That meant they would take their leave of each other. Forever, most likely. Ian didn't want their final moments together to be unpleasant. Not when everything that had come before had been so . . . if not enjoyable, then exciting.

"Sophie, I—" he began.

"Hullo," said Alforth. He'd opened the small hatch that led from the inside of the caravan to the driving seat. "Have a pleasant night, did you? Didn't do anything scandalous, I hope." He winked broadly, but Ian could tell there was a threat couched beneath Alforth's bonhomie.

"Good morning, Uncle A," Sophie said. "Did you and Driscoll get some sleep?" Ian noticed her deft avoidance of his question.

"A bit, a bit," he answered. "Comfortable little wagon you've got here, Blackpool. We liked it quite a lot, didn't we, Driscoll?"

The coachman's long, ruddy face joined Alforth's in the open hatch. "Oh, yes. Thanks so much, Mr. Blackpool." Driscoll leaned over to Alforth and said in a stage whisper, "Tell them about the plan."

"The plan?" Alforth blinked in momentary confusion. "Oh, yes, the plan."

"What plan?" Sophie asked. "There's a plan? Why do you need a plan?"

"Well, you see, we were thinking, Driscoll and I, that is, we got to talking during the course of the journey, and, well . . ." Alforth said, curiously out of sorts.

"It's your parents, miss," Driscoll broke in, frustrated by Alforth's prevaricating. "We don't think they'd like Mr. Blackpool much."

Sophie pulled back, surprised. "But he saved your lives," she protested. "He defeated McGannon. He protected me. Of course they'll like him."

"No, they won't," Ian said. He kept his gaze on the road, unwilling to see the hurt and confusion in Sophie's eyes.

Driscoll continued. "He's a mountebank, miss. He

may be a fine, upstanding fellow who did us all a good turn, but it don't change the fact that he's a mountebank. Begging your pardon, Mr. Blackpool."

Ian waved off the insult, since it wasn't an insult at all, but the truth.

"Caroline is a good soul," Alforth added. "And Simon . . . well, he's a bit of an ass, but he means no harm. And they're both snobs. They would never admit a peddler to Cabot Park, no matter what noble service he had done for the family. They might even call in the magistrate. You know Caroline has a horror of gypsies."

"He's not a gypsy," Sophie insisted.

"But he drives a gypsy wagon, and to Caroline that's bad enough. She'll have him run off the property and out of Sevendowne."

"But it's not right!" Sophie cried.

"No, it isn't, my dear, but it's the way things are. That's why Driscoll and I have come up with a plan—to protect Mr. Blackpool. You'll do that, won't you?"

Sophie sent mutinous looks back and forth between Driscoll, Alforth, and even Ian. He realized that she was learning a harsh lesson, not only about her class but about her family. He'd done the same, and now it was her turn.

"All right," she conceded, glowering, "but I think the whole thing is rotten."

"Shall I explain the plan, or shall you?" Alforth asked Driscoll.

"Please, sir, go ahead."

"Will someone please explain the damned plan?" Ian growled.

Three pairs of surprised eyes turned toward him.

"Long night," he explained, feeling strangely angry and out of sorts.

Nobody questioned his excuse, however. And finally, after a bit more politesse, the plan was revealed. Everyone was pleased with it. Everyone, except Sophie. And Ian.

Chapter Six

Caroline Andrews at fifty-two was still considered by many to be the most handsome woman of her generation in all of Gloucestershire. Her blond hair had turned a distinguished shade of burnished silver, which she powdered to create the impression of unmitigated nobility. She was as slim as she had been at eighteen, when she had married Simon Andrews, and possessed an excellent sense of style abetted by the regular delivery of London's most popular fashion journals. Caroline often had the local gentry in for suppers and games of piquet and whist. To everyone of means within twenty miles of Sevendowne, she was an accomplished and stylish woman, with a husband as well-trained as a lapdog, and attractive, reserved children seen only at dinner parties and holidays. She liked things orderly, tasteful, and decorous. She hated chaos, noise, and untidiness—everything she had grown up with in Newcastle and now shunned with a vengeance.

This was most unfortunate, since her front drawing room was host to all three this morning.

Her brother, her daughter, and, Lord help her, the coachman, were all standing around her, talking at once, explaining in the most nerve-shattering voices how it was that they came to arrive home at Cabot Park a full twenty-four hours later than they had been expected. At six that morning, Caroline and Simon's sleepless vigil was interrupted by a message that their missing kin were waiting in the village. Their carriage was a loss that would have to be borne, but the family kept a second, the finer of the two, used for local travel, when impressing the neighbors was essential. This second carriage was sent to retrieve them immediately.

Caroline's relief to see Alforth and Sophie safe at home was now almost entirely replaced by the most severe megrim she had ever experienced. Everyone looked as though they had spent the night in a ditch—a clean ditch, but a ditch to be sure. Thank heavens it was too early for anyone to see them in such a state.

Baths had been suggested straight off, but everyone insisted they tell her their horrible tale before leaving her in peace.

And it was a horrible tale, growing worse by the minute.

"Kidnappers!" Caroline cried, falling back into her chair. Simon patted her hand and offered her a glass of restorative wine, but she waved it away. "How on earth did you manage to escape?"

"There was a man—" Alforth began.

"He was very handsome," added Sophie.

"But a *gentleman*," the coachman said, looking sharply at her.

"A handsome gentleman," Sophie agreed. "I was in

the woods collecting samples when the kidnappers came, but the gentleman found me and kept me safe."

"And the two of them followed our trail to the criminals' lair," continued Alforth. "Through cunning and guile—"

"*Gentlemanly* guile," insisted the coachman.

"Through the most genteel shrewdness, this gentleman managed to subdue the kidnappers and set us free," finished Alforth with a smile.

"Amazing," breathed Simon, still absently patting Caroline's hand. She snatched it back and pressed a handkerchief to her eyes.

"But how did you get to Sevendowne?" she asked, frowning. There was something about this story that did not seem quite right to her, though she could not say precisely what it was that bothered her.

Everyone exchanged glances that seemed to Caroline to be nervous and guilty. Eventually, Sophie spoke.

"He . . . ah . . . had a wagon," she said.

"A *gentlemanly* wagon," the coachman added weakly.

"He drove us all the way to Sevendowne and then he had to go . . . somewhere," Sophie continued. Aware of the vagueness of her response, she shrugged and rubbed her nose.

"Please, Sophie," Caroline snapped.

Sophie stopped rubbing her nose. She folded her hands together and looked at the floor. Caroline was immediately contrite, opening her arms to her daughter. Sophie was somewhat dusty from her night on the road, which made Caroline shudder, but she knew that, with everyone watching, she would make a poor example of a mother if she refused to touch her grimy daughter. Caroline wanted more than anything to be a fine example to whoever might be watching, even if it was only her brother, her husband, and, Lord save her, the coachman.

"Come here, my dear," she said.

Uncertain, Sophie took a tentative step forward, then stopped. She looked to her uncle for guidance, and he gave her a small motion of encouragement. The idea that her own child would find her mother's gesture of affection suspect annoyed Caroline, whose nerves were already frayed to the breaking point.

"I only mean to apologize and welcome you home," said Caroline crossly. "Can't a mother show her youngest daughter some parental sympathy?"

Sophie, sheepish, came forward and knelt in front of her mother. She was enveloped in the familiar perfume of verbena and lavender that both alarmed and soothed her, her mother's arms folding around her. Sophie was grateful for the cover she was being offered, since her face was flushed with the ineptitude of her lying. Her mother's slender, delicate hands stroked Sophie's hair, and her father gave her arm an encouraging squeeze.

"Poor girl," Caroline cooed. "Such a dreadful ordeal. Why not go upstairs, have a nice, long bath, and get some sleep?"

"I'm fine, Mother," insisted Sophie, although she could feel herself wilt.

Caroline gently but firmly pushed Sophie back so she could look her directly in the eye. "That's not a suggestion, Sophie. Go to your room right now and clean yourself. If you insist, come back down afterward. But please change your gown. You look like a stablehand."

With a nod, Sophie got to her feet and quietly left

the room. Before she closed the door, she heard her mother dismiss Driscoll.

"I have a few words for you, Alforth, which I must say in private," Caroline began.

Sophie would have lingered at the door, but there was no way to effectively eavesdrop without attracting attention. She drifted upstairs, figuring that whatever her parents and her uncle were discussing could not have much effect on her.

As she entered her suite of rooms, Sophie found her maid waiting for her with a filled tub. Her gown was removed and she bathed, grudgingly grateful for her mother's aversion to dirt of any kind. A day and night on the road chasing after kidnappers did not agree with hygiene. Scrubbing away, Sophie's thoughts drifted back toward Ian Blackpool. Their parting had been strange, oddly anticlimactic, considering everything they had been through together. For goodness sake, he had even kissed her twice—though one time had been on top of her head and didn't really count, but nevertheless, he *had* kissed her. She'd told him things about her work she had not discussed with any other person, and he'd told her about his strange theory of love.

How intimate their conversation had grown, as though they shared the confidence of people who had known each other for a long time. But they hadn't. Sophie had known Ian Blackpool all of three days. That was the length of their acquaintance, its beginning and end.

Rinsing out her hair, Sophie realized that despite the brevity of their relationship, she would miss him.

But they could never continue their association. Her mother was a squire's daughter and he was a mountebank, the son of Lord-knew-who. The idea of

Ian driving up in his gypsy wagon and playing cards in the green salon with the local vicar was ridiculous. Even Sophie knew that.

Still, she was sorry that they had parted company so stiffly, so formally, with a few strained words of thanks and him bowing over her hand. Alforth had insisted on giving him some money for his help, flatly refusing to listen to Ian's protests, but then realized too late that he hadn't any money to give. Neither did Sophie, or Driscoll. All their coin had been left behind in McGannon's hideout. Everyone had been embarrassed and unhappy. They watched Ian drive around the bend, disappearing from sight.

Clean and presentable, Sophie changed into a loose day gown and lay down upon the couch by her window. A soft morning breeze blew in through the open casement, bringing in the scents of the garden just beyond. She fully intended to go back downstairs and find out exactly what her parents and Alforth were discussing. She would go in just a moment, after she closed her eyes for a while to give them a little rest.

She fell asleep in an instant, and when she dreamed, she dreamed of potion bottles and knowing smiles.

The sun had turned her room golden with its dying rays when Sophie heard a gentle tapping at her door. She rubbed her eyes and sat up, calling in a sleep-fogged voice, "Come in."

Meredith, her maid, appeared with a tea tray. "Your mother asked that you take some refreshment, then join her in the green salon, miss."

"Thank you. Tell her I'll be down shortly." The maid bobbed and left the room as Sophie helped herself to a few cakes and a bracing cup of tea. Spreading a bit of Cook's strawberry jam on a muffin, Sophie idly wondered if Ian Blackpool had ever been a servant. Certainly he'd never had one himself, but he seemed so refined, he could have been a valet for a gentleman. The tidy condition of his caravan showed that he was used to cleaning up after himself and seeing to his own needs. Sophie had always had a nurse, and then an abigail. But she felt certain she could take care of herself if she had to.

She hoped Ian didn't think she was a pampered society girl. Even though she would never see him again, she wanted him to think of her with respect and, yes, fondness. As she thought of him.

Once she had finished her tea, Sophie dusted off the crumbs and went downstairs. Many of the servants were milling about, casting the strangest looks in her direction. A peculiar cold chill ran down her back as she saw Alforth, his face flushed and angry, leaving the green salon in a hurry. He was in such a rush, he bumped right into her, dropping his cane.

Sophie bent down and retrieved it for him. "Here you go, Uncle A," she said with a smile.

"Thank you, my dear," he said gruffly. Taking the cane, he suddenly appeared miserably unhappy. "Oh, Soph, I am so sorry."

"Whatever for?" she asked, alarmed.

"I have to . . . go." Saying nothing more, Alforth dashed off as quickly as his bad knee would allow.

Sophie wanted to follow him, but her mother's voice stopped her. "Is that you, Sophie?"

Bracing herself, she answered, "Yes, Mother," before she entered the room.

Her mother was ensconced in her favorite divan and her father stood, looking out the window at the front drive. Sophie did not think herself especially sensitive, but there was a palpable sense of tension in the room that made her swallow convulsively. Something definitely was wrong, and she longed to retreat into her study at the back of the house and take comfort in the taxonomy of Linnaeus.

"Close the door behind you, Sophie, and take a seat," her mother commanded decorously.

Wordlessly, Sophie did as she was told.

"Simon, if you please," Caroline added, and Sophie's father quickly left his place by the window to stand beside his wife. Sophie tried to smile in encouragement at her father, but he wasn't able to smile in return. As she sat there, Sophie realized that her father was beginning to grow old. His dark brown hair was threaded with white, and his eyes, so like her own, were surrounded by fine lines that showed how much he enjoyed his horse and hounds in the outdoors. His sixtieth birthday had been celebrated the month before, but he had busied himself with hosting shooting parties, and Sophie hadn't had much opportunity to give him her good wishes. Perhaps she ought to do so now, but, considering her mother's expression, it didn't seem like the best time.

"Did you have a good rest?" her mother asked politely.

"Yes, Mother. And a bath."

At this, her mother smiled. "Excellent. I hope you are recovered from your dreadful ordeal. I think my heart has only just now begun to stop hammering."

"I'm happy to hear you're better. And I feel quite well, thank you," Sophie answered.

Caroline nodded. "Good. We are glad to hear that."

Everyone took for granted the fact that Caroline

often spoke for both herself and her husband, including the husband himself.

Sophie was not used to spending so much time making small talk with her parents outside of the dining room and felt uneasy. She became aware of the ormolu clock ticking on the mantel, her father's feet shifting on the rug, and the growing impulse to rub her nose. Deciding it was best to get anything unpleasant out of the way as quickly as possible, she said, "Is there something you wanted to discuss, Mother? I'd like to get back to work as soon as possible. There were a number of plants I observed that I would like to record in my notebooks."

At this, her mother's lips thinned with displeasure. "That is precisely what your father and I would like to discuss with you. Let me ask you something first, Sophie: Do you think we have been good parents to you?"

The question caught Sophie completely by surprise. Despite some of the new fads in child-rearing, Caroline had never been interested in pursuing an equal and receptive relationship with her son and daughters. Her rules were law, not open to debate, and the only reason Sophie had been able to accomplish as much as she had in botany was due, in large part, to her undistinguished status as middle child and youngest daughter.

She decided it would be wisest to approach the question as cautiously as possible. "Of course I do," she said quickly, perhaps too quickly.

Her mother sighed loudly. "I fear, alas, that we have not. We have tried to do our best by you, but I feel that we have failed in our obligations."

"Not at all—"

"As your parents, we are supposed to do everything in our power to see to your best interests," Caroline went on, obviously delivering a speech she had prepared ahead of time, "and yet, in this, we have disappointed. We have allowed you to pursue an unhealthy obsession at the cost of your greater happiness, and our own happiness as well." She looked sharply up at her husband, giving him his cue.

Her father was not as accustomed to giving speeches, and whatever had been planned for him to say was now forgotten, with faltering, uncomfortable words tumbling out. "It's this whole botany business, Sophie," he said, shoving his hands in his pockets. "We thought, you being the youngest daughter, it wouldn't do you any harm to play with books and plants. You always loved plants," he added, musing to himself. "Running through the garden when you were a little mite, poking your fingers in the dirt, asking questions."

Caroline sensed that her husband was veering dangerously off course and cleared her throat loudly. He collected himself at once.

"We didn't think it would do you any wrong," Simon continued. "*I* didn't think so. What's the difference? I thought. Sophie's just a girl—it doesn't matter what she does with herself, so long as she finds a good husband to take care of her later."

"But you didn't, Sophie," her mother broke in. "Suitors came and went, and none of them would have you, even the most liberal-minded, and all because of your blasted botany."

Sophie's heart plummeted, recollecting the men who, having met her on one social occasion or another, would come calling with the hope of finding a suitable bride. Almost all of them had been pleasant enough, with a few exceptions that caused her to shudder even now, but once pleasantries had been exchanged, it was inevitable that she was asked about her hobbies. Most ladies cultivated a genteel way to fill their time—needlework, a spot of gardening, watercolors, or piano—anything but a real vocation that involved reason and work.

It didn't take long for the callers to find out the Truth About Sophie. With polite, strained smiles, they murmured something about being late or having to meet someone and dashed out the door, never to be heard from again except through a tersely written card left with the footman filled with further excuses.

It stung her pride a bit, and she felt that sting again now as her parents condemned the thing she loved most. She began to feel cold all over.

"I don't want a husband," Sophie protested, but she did not sound very sure of herself.

Caroline clicked her tongue. "Of course you want a husband. All women do. How else will you be taken care of? How will you feed and clothe yourself? Where will you find shelter, if not under your husband's roof?"

"You and Father . . ."

"We have places reserved in the family plot and will one day rest there. Then what will you do?"

"I always thought that Henry could take me in."

"Your brother will eventually have a wife and family of his own. Do you think he will take kindly to supporting his spinster sister, tottering about with her weeds and musty books? Or that his wife will allow such an imposition on her household?" Caroline snorted. "You'll be an embarrassment to them, an inconvenience. Is that what you want?"

Sophie's face flamed at her mother's harsh, realistic words. "No," she answered, her voice growing smaller.

"And then," Caroline continued, fully into her argument, "there was this whole wretched affair with the kidnappers."

Shooting out of her chair, Sophie exclaimed, "My work had nothing to do with that!"

"Didn't it?" Caroline asked. "You made the coachman stop so you could muck about in the dirt. While you were doing that, my poor brother was left waiting in the road, fit prey for any thief or scoundrel, and that's exactly what happened. He was set upon by kidnappers. If that other man hadn't come along to help you, I daresay both you and Alforth would be dead by now."

"The kidnappers could have found us even if I hadn't stopped the carriage," Sophie protested, but she was swamped by guilt. Perhaps it was true. Perhaps she had caused the ordeal with McGannon.

Her mother saw that her point had struck home and gave a small, bitter smile of triumph, though it was clear she did not enjoy the victory. "I have long protested the safety of your work, gallivanting alone through heaven knows where, subject to the whims of nature or, Lord help you, the whims of men."

"I could take a footman or stablehand with me," Sophie tried to reason, but her mother would not be dissuaded.

"That's almost as bad. No, Sophie, your father and I have decided that we have tolerated your mania for plants long enough. That time is at an end."

Sophie tried to push down the beginnings of hysteria. She felt as though a child she had been raising for more than ten years was being ripped away from her, taking her heart with it.

"What are you going to do?" she asked, stepping forward anxiously.

"It's all got to go," her father said with an apologetic shrug. "The books, the portfolios, the equipment."

"The dried weeds you press between sheets of paper," Caroline added. "All of it. We won't stand for it any longer, Sophie."

Sophie looked wildly from her mother to her father and back again. Blood pounded in her ears, the room dimmed. It was impossible. They couldn't take botany away from her, the only part of her life she prized, the one thing that gave her life meaning. Her soul was being stripped away like so much wallpaper, leaving an empty room. "No," she cried. "I won't let you."

Her mother laughed sharply. "Won't *let* us? We're your parents, child. We can do what we please."

"You'll have to go through me," Sophie shouted. She ran to the door and threw it open, startling the servants gathered there. They scurried away as she bolted down the hallway to the back of the house, back to her study, where her beloved books and all her research lay waiting for her.

But they were gone.

Sophie stood in the open doorway to her study—she always kept it locked and the key on her person—and found it completely bare. All the books had been taken down from the shelves, her desk cleared of papers, even the tiny plant samples she kept in little earthenware pots on the windowsill were missing. Everything, the accumulation of a lifetime of study, was gone. Sophie had never seen a more horrifying sight in her life. She thought she was going to be sick.

Her mother's steps sounded behind her. "You see?" she said at her shoulder. "We did what was necessary."

Sophie turned stricken eyes toward her mother. She

couldn't find any words, no way to express the rage, horror, betrayal, and misery she was feeling at that moment.

"Don't look at me like that," Caroline snapped unhappily. "When you've gotten over your fixation on botany and you're married with lots of babies with no dirt under your fingernails or stains on your gowns, you'll be grateful we did this. It was for your own happiness."

Sophie couldn't bear it. "It was for *your* happiness," she choked out. Pushing past her mother and away from the grisly image of her gutted study, Sophie ran upstairs and into her room. She slammed the door behind her—a ridiculous, childish gesture that was supposed to make her feel better but didn't.

In a frenzy, she paced her room like a caged animal, clenching and unclenching her fists. It was as though she had been eviscerated, the pain was so intense and deep. God. *God.* What was she going to do? How could she stand it? Everything was gone. Her love was gone.

Sophie, who hadn't cried when she fell off her pony and twisted her ankle at age six, who didn't weep when she accidentally burned herself reaching for the kettle at age ten, and had faced down England's most feared kidnapper without a shedding a single tear, now collapsed at the foot of the bed, sobbing brokenly.

Hours passed. Or maybe days; Sophie couldn't tell. She cried until there was nothing left in her and the tears gritted her eyes like sand. Empty, racking heaves shook her body. She tried to move but found she could only lay in a heap, as though she were a marionette with broken strings.

Someone entered her room, but Sophie couldn't speak or even raise her eyes to see who it was. A bowl of soup was left to turn cold. Eventually, she was left alone.

She was able to drag herself over to her couch and tumble across the stiff cushions. Through swollen eyes, she saw that night had fallen; the room was dark and silent except for the faint sounds of wind in the trees outside. Sophie had always liked her room because it faced the back garden and she could stare for long periods of time at the flower beds and grassy lawns, cataloguing the plants in her mind, extolling their virtues and smiling over their idiosyncrasies. She might have a look, but it seemed pointless knowing that her one dream had been stolen from her under the pretext of parental duty.

Everything seemed pointless now. She'd spent her life studying botany and she was supposed to instantly forget it, learn all the skills she found completely useless, turn herself into a pretty, empty ornament to decorate some man's home, or take delight in card parties and fashion journals, like her mother.

"I can't," she said aloud, tipping her head back against the sofa. "I just can't."

"Can't what?" a man's voice asked nearby.

Stifling a scream, Sophie attempted to jump up, but she was so weakened from crying she tumbled to the floor. A pair of hands immediately came at her and she tried to fight them off.

"Jesus, Sophie," the man said, grunting as her foot connected, "hold still."

She knew that voice. She hadn't thought to ever hear it again.

"Ian," she said softly.

"Let me help you up. What's wrong?" She felt herself gently being picked up and carried over to her bed. She did not argue as he draped her across the mattress, and she could barely manage a whimper of protest as he removed her shoes. Sophie closed her eyes when she heard the candle being lit, unable to look at its glare with her sensitive, tear-swollen gaze.

"God, Sophie," he breathed. She felt the mattress sag with his weight as he sat beside her. "What happened to you?" His hands brushed over her face, whisper-light, the roughness of his fingertips rasping against her tender skin. Even in the depths of her confusion and misery, she was surprised at his tenderness.

She opened her eyes and felt her heart shrivel. He was so perfectly handsome, and he was staring at her with such pity. She couldn't abide pity.

"Nothing . . ." she mumbled, turning her head away. "I . . . it's nothing."

His silence told her that he didn't believe her, but he did not press her further. The mattress shifted again as he rose, and she heard the sound of liquid being poured. Once more she felt the exquisite gentleness of his hands as he supported her head and brought a glass to her lips. "Drink this," he commanded. She took several swallows of water before he carefully lowered her head back to the pillow.

The water helped. She revived a little, and propped herself up on her elbows to look at him.

Ian had pulled up a chair to her bedside. The candlelight exaggerated the arch of his eyebrows as they folded down in a frown of concern. After her long and miserable day, he looked like a storybook prince come to rescue her. But Sophie knew he was no prince, and there would be no rescues.

"What are you doing here?" she asked. "How did you get in?"

"I'll answer your questions on one condition," he said, resting his forearms on his knees. "You must answer mine when I ask them. Agreed?"

Sophie managed a nod.

He leaned back in the chair and folded his arms across his chest. "I'd driven a few miles when it dawned on me that we each have something the other needs."

"We do?"

Ian nodded. "Your work and mine—they're very similar. You're trying to figure out how two plants manage to help the other thrive when they should kill each other, and I'm trying to understand what makes a person love. The more I got to thinking about it, the more I realized that we're after the same goal. What did you call it . . . symbiosis? Your definition of symbiosis sounded exactly like love."

He picked up the glass and made her drink a bit more. "It seemed ridiculous to me that we should be working on the same theory by ourselves, when we could combine our knowledge and talents and work together. We could find our answers that much faster, and with better results, by pooling our resources. 'Blackpool, you idiot,' I said to myself, 'you just left England's greatest botanical mind. If anybody knows anything about plants, it would be Sophie Andrews.'"

Sophie had to smile at that.

"But I knew your parents wouldn't exactly throw wide their doors and welcome me in like the prodigal son. So I left my wagon at the village, walked back, bribed the gardener—"

"You what?" Sophie gasped.

"There's no love lost between the staff and your

mother. He was glad to help out. He showed me
which was your room, I climbed the ivy, got in
through the window, and now here I am."

Sophie almost laughed, but it came out more like
broken coughing. Ian offered her the water, but she
waved it away. "I'm sorry to tell you this," she gasped,
collecting her breath, "but all your work was for nothing. You should go before someone finds you, someone
who won't be as easy to bribe as Wallace." She forced
herself to meet his eyes. "I want you to leave. Now."

He stood and walked to the open window, turning
his back to her. Bracing his hands on the casement, he
looked out into the garden. He was going to climb out
the window and out of her life for good. She wanted to
be glad—he was doing what she asked—but bitter disappointment threatened to choke her.

After a few moments, he turned around and leaned
against the casement. His face was hard and set, so
unlike the charming, lighthearted mountebank she
had known earlier.

"We had an agreement, and I'm not leaving until
you honor it," he said, grim.

"What agreement?" Her heart jumped a little.

"I'd answer your questions if you answered mine."
He walked over to the bed and stood, looming over
her, more menacing than she had ever seen him before. Sophie realized just how much bigger he was
than she, how much stronger. She gulped.

"Your time has come, Miss Andrews."

Chapter Seven

"What do you want to know?"

He sat back down in the chair, spreading the skirt of his coat behind him in a gesture so practiced, so fluid, Sophie could have sworn he'd been maneuvering through manor houses his whole life. Closer to eye level, he seemed less threatening, more familiar, but she could not shake the feeling that Ian Blackpool held back his strength considerably.

"What happened to you?" he asked without preamble. "When I left you this morning, you were as lively as an apple blossom, and now I find you unable to stand, barely able to speak, and your face streaked with old tears. No, don't hide behind your hands. Tell me what happened."

Sophie knew she was a terrible liar, so telling him anything less than the truth would register immediately on her face. Alforth always said she was much easier to read than her botanical books. Even so, she did not want to conceal herself from Ian Blackpool. She wanted to trust him.

In as few words as possible, she told Ian what had happened that afternoon: her parents decision to stop her work in botany, the blame they put on her shoulders for the kidnapping, and the complete and utter removal of her books, instruments, and collections.

"All of it?" Ian asked, frowning.

She nodded. "Not even a dried-up weed remained. I'm like Dante in the dark woods, without a path, without direction, and no Virgil to guide me."

Ian wasn't fully listening to her. She could see the anger on his face and took a strange measure of comfort that he was almost as outraged about her exile from botany as she. He understood the gravity of her loss. It was rare for anyone except Alforth to appreciate how much botany meant to her, how empty her life was without it. "Bastards," he muttered angrily to himself as he rested his chin in his hand. "They shouldn't have done that."

"According to them, it was exactly what they should have done. They would be remiss as parents otherwise." A mirthless smile touched her lips. "But you see, I'm no good to you anymore. You've gone to all this trouble for nothing."

He turned a sharp, hawklike gaze on her. "Why do you say that?"

"Didn't you hear me?" she cried, pounding her fist on the bed. "They took it all. *Everything*. I'm worthless now. To myself, and to you."

"My dear Sophie," he said, leaning forward, "there is more to life and learning than can be found in books. I'd wager you have more knowledge stored in that pretty head of yours than any library can hold."

"You're flattering me," she said, abashed and a little pleased despite herself.

He shook his head. "I'm not. I've traveled very far, Sophie, and met many men who claim to be learned, but none of them can hold a candle to you. You have a great mind. A Persian scholar once told me, 'It is only when the scrolls are lost can we truly learn.' It's the same with you. Don't be hindered by something as insignificant as paper and leather bindings. You're better than that."

Sophie didn't know what to say. No one had ever spoken such things to her before. Alforth tried to be encouraging, but she knew that most of her studies, and she herself, baffled him. He praised her the way people praised Brunelleschi's Dome: awestruck, but without an understanding of how she worked or why. This mountebank, Ian Blackpool, somehow possessed an understanding of her that no one else, not even her beloved uncle, had ever been able to grasp. She didn't know how it could happen, but it had. The fact that she was now barred from her work made this realization all the more bitter.

"It doesn't matter," she said at last. "My parents won't let me work anymore. And they certainly will not allow me to work with a mountebank."

Ian slowly shook his head. "Sophie," he said, reproachfully, "for someone with such a powerful mind, you're thinking too small. In the grand scheme of things, parents are but an obstacle to happiness."

Sophie stifled a laugh. "I can't imagine what kind of father you would be."

"I'm never going to be a father," he said flatly.

"Never?" Her eyes widened in surprise.

"Never."

"Can't you . . . ?" She trailed off in embarrassment. He caught her meaning and looked alarmed, and a bit insulted. "I can," he said hastily. "But I'm never getting married, so there will be no children for me."

The idea that someone as handsome, clever, and charming as Ian would spend his life alone—regardless of his profession—struck Sophie as rather tragic. He seemed made for the constant love of a wife, and she had a feeling he would be a wonderful husband. Attentive, whimsical, physical. Yet she couldn't say she was entirely disappointed with this news. The idea of him taking some strange woman to wife made her feel an odd stab of something she'd never felt before: jealousy.

"Never?" she asked again.

He seemed about to answer, but instead said sharply, "Don't change the subject. If you truly want to pursue botany, you won't let something as inconsequential as parents get in your way."

"Parents are hardly inconsequential," she muttered. More thoughtfully, she added, "Though mine never cared before yesterday *what* I did with myself." He looked at her with prompting, questioning eyes. "As long as I didn't make a nuisance of myself, no one seemed to mind my work. Well, my mother didn't mind. My father . . . was indifferent." Indignation began to surface again as she thought of it. "Only when I might attract attention to myself did they take botany away from me. I think my mother is more afraid for her own reputation than mine. 'Oh, there goes Caroline Andrews,'" Sophie mimicked. "'She's got a daughter who mucks about with plants and thinks she's as good as a man. What kind of woman would raise such a virago? Let's not have her over for tea.'" She gave a harsh laugh. "Yes, that's worth destroying your child's life—an untainted social calendar."

"Going against your parents isn't the end of the world, Sophie," Ian said thoughtfully.

"How would you know?"

He gave her a little smile, half contemplative and half ironic. "I'm the original prodigal son. When it came down to choosing between my father's wishes and my own, I chose my own."

Intrigued by this new information, Sophie began to speak, but just then there was a tap at the door. Both she and Ian froze, their eyes locked together, and understanding finally dawned on her that having a man in her bedroom alone at this hour was completely improper.

"Who is it?" she called, tearing her gaze from Ian's. She was afraid that if she waited too long to speak, whoever was on the other side of the door would simply let themselves in.

"It's Alforth. I've brought you something to eat." There was a little pause. "May I come in?"

"One moment," Sophie said, stalling. Dear God, what was she going to do? Even Alforth, as liberal in his opinions as he was, would do something terrible if he found Ian in his niece's bedchamber. He might make good on that threat delivered in Little Chipping; he might bring the whole house down around them, summoning the local law to throw Ian into gaol. Any number of horrible possibilities ran through Sophie's mind. She turned to Ian to urge him to hide, but he was gone. Sophie frowned. He seemed well-used to hiding himself in ladies' bedrooms.

"Sophie?" her uncle asked quietly, poking his head around the door.

"It's all right, Uncle A, come in."

He did so gingerly, shutting the door behind himself quietly. The genuine concern on his face made her feel like weeping all over again. She was going to have to lie to him, and lie well, in order to protect herself and Ian. She had no choice. Alforth carried a tray over to her bedside table, laden with tea and Sophie's favorite lemon tarts. Her uncle must have asked Cook to prepare them specially, which made her deception all the more painful.

He looked quizzically at the chair pulled up to Sophie's bedside but shrugged it off and sat down. Worry creased his face as he looked at her, taking hold of her hand. "You're not even dressed for bed," he said unhappily. "How are you, my dear? You look feverish and your pulse is racing. Shall I fetch a doctor?"

"I'll be fine," she said hastily.

"Will you?" Alforth scowled. "Damn it, Sophie—pardon my language—I told Caroline not to do it. Said it was a mistake, that you weren't to blame for any of what happened with McGannon. I said, 'If you take that girl's work away, you might as well tell her not to breathe,' but she was adamant. Nothing I said could convince her otherwise." He sighed, patting Sophie's hand. "Sometimes when Caro gets an idea in her head, not you, I, or the Great Lord Almighty can change her mind."

Saying nothing, Sophie tipped her head down. She could barely speak, overcome with a hurricane of emotions. Fury at her parents, contrition and gratitude for her uncle, a trembling, fearful excitement, knowing Ian was hiding in her room. This wasn't like her. She led a quiet, introspective life. Everything had changed since she met Ian Blackpool.

Alforth muttered an oath under his breath. "I haven't made you feel any better, have I? Curse me.

Perhaps I should leave and we can talk about it in the morning. Yes," he said, standing as he made up his mind, "I'll let you get some rest. We'll figure out something tomorrow, some way to fix this whole mess, though"—he pressed a kiss to her forehead—"I don't know how."

He was nearly to the door when Sophie said, quietly, "Uncle A . . ." He turned. "Thank you."

With a sad smile, he said, "Enjoy the lemon tarts, my dear. And sleep. I'll see you at breakfast."

A gust of breath burst from Sophie as the door to her room closed and Ian popped out of her wardrobe. What a clever devil. She stifled the urge to laugh as she saw one of her stockings clinging to his broad back.

"Is he gone?" he asked.

She nodded. "I've made up my mind."

Ian looked at her piercingly. She could tell that her answer meant a great deal to him, even if he did not want her to know it. More than that, her answer meant that everything in *her* life was going to change irrevocably, for good or ill. Everything rested on her decision.

Taking a deep breath, she said, "I'm going to do it. I'll work with you." She added, "I'm not sure how I'll manage it, but I will. If being a dutiful daughter means giving up my life, my happiness, then I don't want to be dutiful. I want to be me, Sophie, the botanist."

There was that smile of his, the one that made her insides collapse in upon themselves from the sheer gorgeousness of him. She was surprised he hadn't tried to charm her into helping him, but had actually appealed to her sense of self and reason. He respected her, in a way no one else did. It was a heady gift.

"This is good news," he said with a grin, coming to

stand beside her bed. "*Very* good news. We'll make terrific progress, you and I. You'll see. Are those lemon tarts? I love those." He had an infectious energy, picking up a tart and taking a bite of it, practically humming with excitement over this new development. Sophie had a sudden wish to be that tart as he ate it with so much relish. She blushed at the thought. He wiped crumbs from his wonderful mouth and began to pace, thinking aloud about how they would meet, where, and countless other details.

She was overwhelmed, unable to grasp much more beyond the sheer gravity of her decision. "Since you're so adept at sneaking onto my property," she said, interrupting his eager monologue, "I'll meet you by the orangerie tomorrow, around midmorning. It's far enough away from the house so no one will see us." The notion of a clandestine meeting with this handsome mountebank filled ever fiber of Sophie with an exquisite agony. She was going to do it. She was striking out on her own, defying her parents, defying everything, for her chance at happiness.

Ian finished the tart with an animal sound of pleasure. "Give my compliments to the cook. Better yet, don't. We're going to do some great work together, Sophie. I know it." He braced his hands on the headboard of her bed, smiling down at her, pleased with her, pleased with himself. And then something changed. The air grew heavy around them as he stilled. Sophie saw the flare of interest in his eyes, could almost feel the tenseness in the lean body arching over her. She lay still across her bed, staring up at him. For a brief, alarming, delightful moment, Sophie thought he might touch her, kiss her. How she wanted him to. How disastrous it would be if he did.

"Do you know," she blurted. "I've never had a man in my bedroom before that wasn't a relative or a servant."

Success—of a limited nature. He pulled back sharply with a small frown, a little aggravated, a bit confused. He laughed, but it was strained, and he walked toward the window.

"I'll see you tomorrow, then," he said, throwing his leg over the casement. "Thank you for the tart."

It was only after he left that Sophie realized she had forgotten to tell him about her stocking, still draped across his back, held against him like the silken remains of a promise she meant to keep.

As she made her way downstairs for breakfast, Sophie checked her reflection in a mirror. She looked for signs in her face, some kind of visible feature that revealed her new, secret life, the life that began today. Nothing. The same constellations of pale freckles, the same honey-colored hair pulled back into a chignon, and, sadly, the same cup-sized endowments that made only the gentlest of curves above the dip of her bodice.

She scolded herself as she turned away. Of course no heavy-lidded siren would be staring back at her from the glass with a knowing and artful smile. Everything was different, but outwardly she was the same, which would make the deception of her parents easier. They could never know. As for Alforth . . . Sophie had yet to resolve how to sort out the business with her uncle. Rebelling against her mother and father was one thing, but she could not deceive the one member of her family who loved and valued her as she was.

This troubled her a good deal, which ultimately worked to her advantage as she entered the dining room. She couldn't have her parents see her full of excitement and energy, particularly since the last time she and her mother had spoken, Sophie had been weeping hysterically over her broken dreams. Too much happiness would certainly raise suspicion. While she distractedly filled her plate at the sideboard, a meditative frown creased her brow. She would have to tell Alforth eventually about her arrangement with Ian Blackpool, but perhaps she would give it some time and let the situation with her parents cool down.

"You look quite well this morning, Sophie," her mother said loudly, interrupting her thoughts. "Much improved since yesterday."

Sophie looked up, startled. As was their custom, her mother sat at the farther end of the table while her father, at the opposite end, read his correspondence. Alforth generally took a cup of coffee in his room, disliking conversation before ten o'clock.

"Simon, doesn't Sophie look quite well this morning?" her mother asked without taking her eyes from her.

Her father came up from his poached eggs and news. He glanced at Sophie quickly. "Yes, quite well," he answered, and dove back down again.

"Thank you, Mother," Sophie answered. She took a sip of tea. "I had a revitalizing night."

Caroline nodded approvingly, smiling and holding her teacup delicately with her fingertips. She was clearly relieved that Sophie was not planning a repeat of the previous day's unpleasant scene and began to relax. Leisurely, she began to nibble on her scone and chat about some new doings in the neighborhood—

social functions and gossip that Sophie never cared about.

She didn't bother trying to insert herself into her mother's ongoing monologue, but sat back and observed her parents from a newfound perspective.

Even her parents had a symbiotic relationship, Sophie mused, but one that wasn't entirely beneficial. Some plants co-existed peacefully together for a time, but eventually one had greater needs—for sunlight, soil, water—and killed off, or damaged, the other. Her mother reminded Sophie of a giant, delicate hothouse rose, full of show but fragile when removed from its environment. And her father resembled unassuming roadside clover, taken for granted, utilitarian.

Sophie bent her head over her breakfast to hide her smile. She wouldn't be able to begin her work with Ian if she continued with such seditious thoughts. Her face would betray her.

After a while, Caroline's narrative trailed off. In the ensuing silence, Sophie noticed that her mother began to become increasingly agitated, glancing at the door every few moments and suppressing a look that could only be described as smug.

"Are *you* feeling all right, Mother?" she asked.

"Wonderful," Caroline chirped, smiling brightly, too brightly.

"I think I'll go take a turn in the garden." Sophie began to stand, but her mother's cry and outstretched hand stopped her.

"No! I mean," she said, collecting herself, "we've hardly spoken about your trip to London, my dear. How were the playhouses? And did you see the new fashions for the Season? Were they marvelous?"

"I wouldn't know," Sophie said flatly. "I spent my time at the Chelsea Physic Garden, working."

Her mother didn't know how to respond to this overt reference to Sophie's forbidden employment, so she smiled tightly instead. "Yes, all the same, I'm sure you saw *something* of London itself."

"A little. But, Mother, I'd really like to get some fresh air, so if you don't mind—"

Sophie had nearly made it out the door when the footman blocked her way. He held a calling card in his hand, which made her step back and frown in confusion.

"Bring that here, Linus," her mother said. Sophie watched as her mother read the card with a triumphant little smile.

"Who's calling at this hour?" Sophie asked.

Her mother began to rise from her chair, and Linus hurried over to assist her. "Sophie, dear, you are indeed a most fortunate young woman. Never forget that." She hooked her arm around Sophie's waist in a gesture that might have been interpreted as maternal if not for its singular abnormality. "You needn't worry any longer about how to look after yourself when your father and I pass on."

"I hadn't been," Sophie said with a frown.

"Linus, show him into the drawing room," said Caroline over her shoulder. The footman left the breakfast room at once.

"Show who? Mother, what is going on?"

Releasing her daughter's waist, Caroline took hold of Sophie's hands. She noted with approval that they were, at last, clean and free of all soil or lingering traces of botany. "Lord Charles Vickerton is waiting for you in the drawing room, Sophie," she said exultantly. "I sent word to him last night that your unhealthy and unfeminine obsession with botany had been thoroughly done away with, and he expressed renewed interest in pursuing your acquaintance."

Sophie gaped. She could not have been more surprised if her mother had suddenly begun quoting Linnaeus verbatim.

"You mean," she said, once she regained her ability to speak, "he'll take me off your hands now that I am no longer allowed to study botany?"

Caroline wrinkled her nose in distaste. "Don't be crude, Sophie. Lord Charles is a fine man, one of the most eligible bachelors in Gloucestershire. He's come all the way from Cheltenham to see you this morning."

"But I don't want to—" Sophie began to protest.

"Sophia Annabelle Francesca Andrews," her mother snapped, "what you *want* and what is best for you are two entirely different things." She placed her hands on her daughter's shoulders and turned her to face the door. The strength of her mother's grip surprised Sophie, and she was still sufficiently bewildered by Caroline's request that she dumbly obeyed. "Now, you and I are going into the drawing room together to greet Lord Charles. I expect you to be on your best behavior. No sulking. No talk of plants. Smile. Be charming."

"That's a lot to remember," Sophie muttered as another footman opened the door to the breakfast room.

Caroline fixed her daughter with a sharp glance. "None of that," she said pointedly. "If you do not amend your attitude immediately, I can easily arrange your removal to our estate in the Outer Hebrides. With only the sea and the sheep to keep you company, you'll have plenty of opportunity to reflect on your manners. So, will you behave?"

Sophie stared at her mother, incredulous, horrified. Her mother had never threatened her before, but now the menace of exile was being dangled before her. Sophie felt as if the world had been turned on its head. Nothing was as it seemed anymore. Her indifferent, coolly beautiful mother would make good on her threat if she didn't obey. She began to believe Ian's words—parents obstructed happiness, rather than provided or protected it. Seeing that she had little choice in the matter, she nodded stiffly.

"Excellent." Caroline beamed. She inclined her head toward the waiting footman, and the door to the drawing room was opened. As they entered, a young man with sandy blond hair sitting in a chair quickly got to his feet. "Ah, Lord Charles," Caroline exclaimed cheerfully, "what an unexpected delight!"

"The pleasure is mine, Mrs. Andrews," he said, bowing over her hand but staring at Sophie. "Entirely mine."

Ian was early. He didn't expect Sophie to be at the orangerie for another hour or two, but his restless energy had made him unable to bear the sight of his caravan for very long. He'd slept badly, too. Hundreds of thoughts and images had swirled around his head, disturbing his peace. One very compelling image had been Sophie Andrews lying on her bed, slim and lovely as a willow, her clothes mussed, her hair beginning to come out of its pins, a flush in her cheeks that revealed how aware she was of him. He'd been close, very close, to taking advantage of her. Thank God she had brought him back to his senses. One couldn't just sport with a woman like Sophie, and he had nothing to offer her but a dalliance.

He paced around the orangerie. It was an impressive building, built recently in the classical-revival mode. Orange trees and other warm-climate plants stood in rows, well-tended and warmed by the sun streaming in through the windows. The Andrewses weren't titled, but they had wealth and position just the same. A fine orangerie like this one required masses of money and ready labor. He'd seen some of that labor on his way over. Discreet inquiries told him that the Andrewses were the major landowners in the area, with hundreds of acres being farmed around Cabot Park. And they had a household full of servants with practically a wing to themselves. The building itself was old, warm brick, two stories shaped roughly like an *H*, with sloped rooves and ivy-covered walls. Cabot Park was a fine example of good, sober architecture from the last century, costly and dignified. Sophie might have been cavalier about her role in society, but it was clear she belonged to that society more fully than she realized. No young woman who came from all this could ever break away entirely.

Seeds of doubt were beginning to take root in his mind. Even as he smiled at the botanical metaphor—Sophie's doing, most likely—he wondered if he wasn't making a giant mistake by collaborating with her. It had seemed like a good idea last night, but now he wondered if his gains would outweigh her losses. He'd been given a convenient excuse to back out even before their partnership had begun. Her parents had banned her from her work.

The idea infuriated him.

Smothering the impulse to put his fist through one of the expensive windows, Ian reminded himself that his interest in Sophie was purely practical. The secret to love could be found in her botanical knowledge. It would be plain stupid of him to ignore such a rich resource just because he found her attractive, or because his chest constricted when he thought of the utter misery on her face last night. He'd never seen anyone so without hope, without purpose, and, he admitted, it frightened him a little—both her despair and his reaction to her. How could anyone claim to help her by taking away the thing she loved most? He had wanted to do something, anything, to make her smile again. But he wasn't being charitable with his suggestion that they work together. He was motivated by pure self-interest.

Voices, a man's and a woman's, interrupted his thoughts. Ian quickly dodged behind a column to hide himself. He would not be seen as a welcome presence at Cabot Park. He planned on waiting until whomever it was went away, but he could not resist poking his head around the column when he recognized one of the voices as Sophie's. He spotted her walking down a garden path, her hands folded carefully at her waist, her lively eyes downcast, every inch of her the composed young lady.

Who the hell was she talking to?

Some young buck, around Ian's age, walked beside her, dressed in the latest male fashion from Paris and thoroughly sure of his place in the world. The way he looked at Sophie was purely proprietary as he gamely chatted on about God knows what. Damn it, Ian could punch that smug bastard right in the face! Staring at Sophie as if she were a piece of meat in the butcher's window, and he a starving dog in the street. Yes, she looked unbelievably pretty in her violet gown, the sweet, pale, freckled expanse of her chest rising above the bodice of her dress, her dark golden hair framing her face, but that was no excuse for Lord Hound to leer at her.

Unless, Christ Almighty, she *wanted* that fool to leer at her.

Ian flattened himself against the column as Sophie and her beau—she'd never mentioned him before, damn it—came nearer.

". . . when I received your mother's letter with the highest of spirits," the blighter said. "How could I not? Yet before I set out this morning, I found myself quite nervous. I was half afraid you'd forgotten me." It was clear from the man's voice that he'd been afraid of no such thing, but rather trusted he would leave an indelible impression on the minds of young ladies everywhere.

"Of course I remember you, Lord Charles," Sophie said quietly.

Why *of course?*

Lord Charles laughed. "And I have never forgotten you, my dear Miss Andrews. May I call you Sophie?"

No, he may not.

"As you wish," Sophie murmured.

Was that acceptance or denial? Ian could not tell. He looked down and noticed that his hands had balled up into fists.

The footsteps stopped just on the other side of the column, and when Sophie and Lord Charles spoke next, their voices sounded right beside Ian.

"I look forward to seeing you on a more regular basis, Sophie," Lord Charles continued. "And I'm sure we'll find each other's company more than agreeable." God, Ian couldn't understand how Sophie could tolerate being spoken to in such a condescending way. "Your parents have given me permission, and I fully intend to make the most of that."

"Pompous ass," muttered Ian.

"What was that?" Lord Charles said.

Sophie began to cough. "Nothing."

"I could have sworn I heard someone speaking."

"Probably just the gardener," Sophie said quickly. "He's alone most of the time and talks to himself. Yes, I'm sure it was the gardener. He's always going on and on, saying things he shouldn't to the wrong people. He really should *keep quiet.*"

Point taken.

"You ought to dismiss such an insolent servant," sniffed Lord Charles.

"I'll just have a word with him right now," Sophie said. "This may be a while—he's hard of hearing—so you ought to take your leave."

"Are you sure I shouldn't stay? Just in case?"

Sophie attempted a laugh. "Oh, no. He's really quite tame. More bluster than bite. It honestly would be for the best if you left now, Lord Charles. I'll give your regards to my parents."

At least the fool had enough brains to recognize the fact that he was being dismissed. "Very well, Sophie. But I'll see you again. Soon."

There was a horrible moment when Ian could actually hear Lord Charles's lips on Sophie's hand. And then his solitary footsteps sounded on the gravel path back to the house.

Sophie materialized in front of Ian, a look of fury and amusement combining in her lovely face. "You dreadful, awful man!" she cried. "What in heaven's name do you think you are doing, eavesdropping on my private conversations?"

Love in a Bottle

"Who the hell was that?" Ian demanded right back.

Sophie looked surprised. "Lord Charles Vickerton. He came at my mother's request."

"You never mentioned him before." Ian pushed away from the column with his shoulder and began to pace through the rows of citrus trees.

"Why should I have?" Sophie jogged along beside him. "He's just some suitor my mother picked out for me."

"And how do you feel about him?"

Sophie blinked. "Feel?"

Ian stopped and turned abruptly. She nearly collided with his chest but managed to stop herself in time. "Are you going to marry him?"

For a moment she only stared up at him, and Ian realized he'd gone too far. He didn't even know why he was asking her, for pity's sake. Before he could turn tail and flee, or apologize, or even breathe, she began to laugh. "Marry? Lord Charles? Don't be ridiculous. As you said, the man's a pompous ass. Besides which, the only reason he's interested in me now is because my mother told him I had given up botany. But you and I both know," she added with a smile, "that it simply isn't true."

Right. Botany. It was the reason he was here, after all, skulking around like some lothario from a cheap novel. Ian reminded himself of this fact even as he felt a strange, unwelcome sense of relief at hearing Sophie's dismissal of her would-be beau.

"I half thought you wouldn't show up today," she admitted shyly. A sudden flush spread across her cheeks, and she turned away to examine the leaf of a lemon tree to hide her embarrassment. Ian loved the way she blushed, as though she'd been told the

135

lewdest, most risqué joke and found it both amusing and horrible.

"This project is very important to me," he said. "Obviously I'll show up."

A flash of disappointment crossed her face, but she quickly masked it. "I suppose we ought to make plans, and work out some kind of schedule. Research has to be done in an orderly fashion. Linnaeus is a great believer in order."

"First," Ian said, stepping closer, "I have something for you." He smiled, flicking his gaze to her mouth, then back to her eyes.

She gulped. "What?"

"A surprise. Close your eyes."

Sophie closed her eyes, and waited.

GET UP TO 4 FREE BOOKS!

You can have the best romance delivered to your door for less than what you'd pay in a bookstore or online. Sign up for one of our book clubs today, and we'll send you **FREE* BOOKS** just for trying it out...**with no obligation to buy, ever!**

HISTORICAL ROMANCE BOOK CLUB

Travel from the Scottish Highlands to the American West, the decadent ballrooms of Regency England to Viking ships. Your shipments will include authors such as CONNIE MASON, SANDRA HILL, CASSIE EDWARDS, JENNIFER ASHLEY, LEIGH GREENWOOD, and many, many more.

LOVE SPELL BOOK CLUB

Bring a little magic into your life with the romances of Love Spell—fun contemporaries, paranormals, time-travels, futuristics, and more. Your shipments will include authors such as LYNSAY SANDS, CJ BARRY, COLLEEN THOMPSON, NINA BANGS, MARJORIE LIU and more.

As a book club member you also receive the following special benefits:

- **30% OFF** all orders through our website & telecenter!
- **Exclusive access** to special discounts!
- **Convenient** home delivery and **10 day examination period** to return any books you don't want to keep.

There is no minimum number of books to buy, and you may cancel membership at any time. See back to sign up!

*Please include $2.00 for shipping and handling.

YES! ☐

Sign me up for the **Historical Romance Book Club** and send my TWO FREE BOOKS! If I choose to stay in the club, I will pay only $8.50* each month, a savings of $5.48!

YES! ☐

Sign me up for the **Love Spell Book Club** and send my TWO FREE BOOKS! If I choose to stay in the club, I will pay only $8.50* each month, a savings of $5.48!

NAME: _____

ADDRESS: _____

_____

TELEPHONE: _____

E-MAIL: _____

☐ **I WANT TO PAY BY CREDIT CARD.**

☐ VISA   ☐ MasterCard   ☐ DISCOVER

ACCOUNT #: _____

EXPIRATION DATE: _____

SIGNATURE: _____

Send this card along with $2.00 shipping & handling for each club you wish to join, to:

Romance Book Clubs
20 Academy Street
Norwalk, CT 06850-4032

Or fax (must include credit card information!) to: 610.995.9274. You can also sign up online at www.dorchesterpub.com.

*Plus $2.00 for shipping. Offer open to residents of the U.S. and Canada only. Canadian residents please call 1.800.481.9191 for pricing information.

If under 18, a parent or guardian must sign. Terms, prices and conditions subject to change. Subscription subject to acceptance. Dorchester Publishing reserves the right to reject any order or cancel any subscription.

JOIN NOW!

Chapter Eight

She had no idea what to expect. Ian Blackpool had the special gift to continually surprise her. She never would have anticipated his unexpected anger at seeing her with Lord Charles—Lord Charles *Vickerton*, for goodness' sake, the very *last* man she'd ever consider as a beau, or anything else. She could never keep up with his twists and turns.

That didn't stop her from closing her eyes.

"Hold out your hands."

She did so.

The orangerie was warm, far warmer than it was outside. She felt the tropical humidity press down across her chest, along her neck. In this heated climate, she felt overly aware of him, his body, the very real male presence of Ian standing close to her. He shifted and she heard a rustling noise, as though he drew something out of a sack. She hadn't seen him carrying anything, but he had a gift for trickery, and she easily believed he could pull flowers from the air. He *had* played the escape artist with her, after all, helping her to extricate herself from the confines of her parents' will.

He put something solid and rectangular in her hands. She ran her fingers over it. A bound spine, the pleasant ruffle of paper. A book. No, something even more familiar.

"My sketchbook," she cried, opening her eyes. And there it was, the by-product of her long years of hard work. She opened the book and saw all her drawings and notations, the plants looking back at her from the pages like old friends returning from a long journey. She couldn't believe it, and passed her hand back and forth over the pages to prove that they were real. She gazed up at Ian. "I thought they'd taken this, too," she said, her eyes growing damp. "I thought I'd lost everything."

"You left it in my caravan." He seemed almost shy under the power of her unfiltered emotion. He, who was always supremely confident, didn't quite know where to look or put his hands. "I thought you would want it back."

God, she might cry again. Somehow, her solid existence on dry land had turned into a tossing sea, swelling and dipping at a moment's notice. Through her tear-spiked lashes, she saw Ian, hawk-handsome, struggling and failing to keep from looking pleased with himself. He liked giving her back the book more than he wanted to admit.

"Of all the books I've ever received," she said, impulsively throwing one arm around him while the other cradled the sketchbook, "this one has been the greatest gift."

He nodded, his own arms wrapping around her waist. "My pleasure."

Simultaneous awareness dawned on them both—the closeness of their bodies, muscle pressed against muscle through layers of fabric, the humid air of the orangerie increasing the heat and moisture of their breath. She saw the responsiveness flare in his eyes as he gazed down at her, just as she noticed the trickle of perspiration running down the square line of his jaw and felt his quick inhalation expand his chest against her own.

Ian's mouth came down on hers. It was sudden but inevitable. Sophie tipped her head back to meet him. She knew the difference between this kiss and the one they had shared on stage. This time he wasn't surprised by his desire to kiss her; in fact, he was strong, sure of himself and what he wanted. His lips moved against hers with a hot purpose, tracing the shape of her mouth, learning her textures. He tasted of chamomile and tobacco. Her mouth opened for him and his tongue dipped in to stroke hers. She heard his growl of satisfaction as she blossomed for him, soaking up his possession of her.

He pulled her harder against him, and her palm came up to press against his chest. With a soft slide and *thump*, the released sketchbook moved down the front of her dress and came to rest on the floor between them. It was so warm; he felt alive and physical against her, his mouth shaping and exploring her own, his fingers in her hair and rubbing against the tingling flesh of her scalp . . . kissing never felt like this before. She knew that if Ian had asked anything of her at that moment, Sophie would have agreed to it without thought, would have thrown away everything and spent her life like this, always like this, wrapped up in his arms and his mouth and his warm, slick caresses.

And then there was only still air against her body where Ian had been. In a fog, she opened her eyes and saw him staring over her shoulder, his own gaze sharp and alert. She started to reach for him, but he took her hands in one of his own.

"What—?" she asked, but he pressed a finger to his lips.

"Sophie?" her uncle called. "Lord Charles said I'd find you back here. Hello?"

His familiar tread sounded on the path toward the orangerie. Two steps, the click of his cane. Alforth was coming nearer. And the orangerie had few solid walls that two people could hide behind.

Ian's hands came up and she frantically tried to bat them away, then realized he was trying to fix her hair. She couldn't imagine what she might look like, having experienced few things in her life equal to his kiss. It seemed as though her blood had thickened and filled every part of her. Her cheeks flamed. She was panting, and saw that his own chest rose and fell at an alarming rate, as though they had both been running full speed around the garden. Their hands collided as she tried to replace the pins that had come loose from her chignon, but she soon realized he was doing a much better job than she, and left him to his work.

The door to the orangerie opened. "Sophie?" Alforth said. She bent down and quickly snatched up her sketchbook, clutching it against her chest to hide her telltale breathlessness. Ian had stepped back, took off his hat, and held it in front of himself. He'd been able to compose himself more quickly, but she could see the muscles in his throat working reflexively.

Alforth appeared, holding a piece of paper in one hand. He started at the sight of Ian, then frowned in puzzlement. "What are you doing here? I thought we'd agreed—"

"Mr. Blackpool and I are going to work together," Sophie interjected brightly, too brightly. "He's got a lovely botanical project, and we're going to collaborate on it." The back of her neck went cold as she realized she had no idea how Alforth would react to this news. He could turn around right now and tell her parents everything, and life as she knew it would cease altogether. She thought of the lonely estate on the Hebrides and shivered.

Taking hold of Alforth's hand, she said, "I was going to tell you earlier, but there wasn't any time. You know that my life without botany is completely empty." He didn't answer, so she continued. "I have to do this, Uncle A. What are my options? Life as Lady Vickerton?" She grimaced.

Sophie shot a look over at Ian, but he seemed unable or unwilling to speak. Glancing back at her uncle, she saw him shaking his head. Oh, Lord. He was going to forbid it. The floor of the orangerie pitched under her feet.

"Sophie, Sophie," Alforth said with a sigh. "Sneaking around with a mountebank on your own family's property? Pursuing work that has been expressly forbidden by your parents? It won't do. It won't do at all."

Even more painful than giving up botany all over again was Alforth's disappointment in her. He'd always been her champion, and she'd thrown that away through her dissembling. Sophie bit her lip to keep from crying.

"No," Alforth went on, "if you two are going to do this, you'll have to do it right."

Both Ian and Sophie looked quickly at Alforth. Sophie grew light-headed. Did she hear him correctly?

"You'll have to be more discreet. Meeting at Cabot Park is simply out of the question. Anyone could find you here."

Sophie dropped Alforth's hand and embraced him tightly. She smelled his familiar cologne as she squeezed her eyes shut. He patted her on the back. "Thank you, Uncle A," she whispered.

"I know what it's like to want something very badly and not be able to have it," he said tenderly. "I loved Violet and you love botany. She was kept from me, but I won't let anything keep you from what you desire." He held her back at arm's distance. "But you need to be careful."

She nodded. "I know."

Alforth turned to Ian, his expression much less pleasant. "And you, *Mister* Blackpool," he said sharply.

Ian held up his hands, an appeasing smile on his face. "I will protect her at all costs, Mr. Morley."

"Have a care for her reputation," Alforth insisted.

"Uncle A!"

He ignored her protests and fixed solely on Ian. "I am relying on you to be a gentleman at all times. Otherwise, my boy, I will happily kill you."

Sophie wanted to sink into the ground in mortification. She wondered what Alforth would make of the scene he had interrupted moments earlier. Surely, for such a kiss as that, he would have tried to skewer Ian from roots to petals.

But with perfect composure, Ian answered, "You have my word, sir. I have always treated Miss Andrews with the utmost respect." Sophie realized then that one of Ian's remarkable skills was his ability to lie. He did it very well. The thought disturbed her.

Alforth, fortunately, did not look to Sophie for confirmation of Ian's promise. He would have seen her guilt plainly inscribed on her face.

"Very good," her uncle said with a firm nod. "We'll have to come up with a plan so you can meet and work without being found out."

"*We?*" Sophie repeated. "I don't want you to get into trouble on my account, Uncle A. If blame is to be assigned, I want to be the only one accountable."

"My dear, your heart is in the right place, but unfortunately you aren't in any kind of position to fully protect yourself." He ambled over to a bench and slowly sat down, waving off Sophie's gesture of help. "A young lady of quality is at the mercy of her parents until she marries. And after that she must obey her husband."

Sophie made a strangled sound of displeasure, causing both Ian and Alforth to laugh.

"Your uncle is right," Ian said, surprising Sophie. "You're too vulnerable to go into this on your own. I should have realized." He frowned as he picked up the discarded cloth sack.

A sharp flash of disappointment shot through Sophie. Too many obstacles were being thrown in her path, and she feared her return to botany would be over before it began. But she wouldn't let it die without a fight.

"I see your determination, child," Alforth said, clasping the top of his cane with both hands. "And that is why I must help you. I fully accept the risks. Besides," he added with a shrug, "the only real threat is Caroline's anger, which I have dealt with many times before. She is my sister, after all."

•

"I can't imagine what it must have been like to grow up with her," Sophie said with a shudder. "It must have been dreadful."

Alforth looked at her sharply. "Caroline suffered a great deal as a girl. We had a drunken father and an inconstant mother who let the household run over with filth. You may have observed her horror of dirt of any kind." When Sophie nodded, he explained, "Even the poorest cottager in the village kept a cleaner house than our mother. Everything was made worse by our father, who was so inebriated he even kenneled his dogs in the dining room, not to mention the mess created by his drinking companions. When Caroline was old enough, she took over the task of cleaning, but our home was large and it always over-whelmed her. As a male, I could take refuge away from home, but Caroline had no such recourse. She's endured much. And she wants to ensure that her daughters never suffer as she did."

"I . . . had no idea," Sophie whispered, horrified and stunned by this new information. She'd always thought that her mother had sprung from the earth fully formed in her adult perfection. Sophie's grand-parents were long dead by the time she had been born, and much of their family history had died with them.

Alforth said with a shake of his head, "It's not something she willingly discusses. She's a good woman with a good heart, even if she is often blinded by her own desires."

Sophie glanced over at Ian, realizing too late that she was discussing private family business in front of him without any consideration for his awkward posi-tion as an outsider. But he had gracefully absented himself from the conversation with Alforth, feigning rapt interest in the new pineapple plant. For a mountebank, he possessed a great deal of tact, and she felt a swell of gratitude toward him.

Turning the topic back to more urgent issues, she said, "Mr. Blackpool and I were just discussing how to go about meeting when you arrived." Goodness, dishonesty came a bit too easily to her all of a sudden. It must have been Ian's influence.

"Miss Andrews needs to be able to stay away from home for long periods of time," Ian said, returning from his inspection of the plant.

"How long?" asked Alforth with a raised eyebrow.

"Just during the day, Uncle," reassured Sophie. She sat down beside him. Maybe she and Ian were not as successful in concealing their kiss as she originally thought. Alforth was taking a lot of interest in her physical well-being all of a sudden. "I promise to come home every evening. But I can't get any work done if I have to keep popping back to check in with Mother."

Alforth chewed meditatively on his lower lip as Sophie rubbed her nose in thought. Niece and uncle pondered this question together, while Ian tapped his hat against his thigh. His voice interrupted everyone's thoughts.

"On my way here I noticed a new house being built," he said. "The grounds weren't even laid out yet. I heard one of the workmen mention your name."

"Yes, they're building my new country estate," Alforth confirmed. "Whenever I come out from London, I stay with Caroline and Simon. I'd been planning on keeping a permanent residence in Sevendowne for some time but never got around to it. The house is mostly finished, but, as you said, the grounds haven't been planned yet. I was thinking of hiring one of those new improvers from London to come out."

"Why do you mention it?" asked Sophie. She noticed that the quickness of Ian's intellect registered in the features of his handsome face, so that the activity of his mind made him even more attractive—if such a thing was possible. And only a few minutes earlier, that man had given her such a kiss. . . . Sophie forced herself to pay attention and not become diverted by Ian's masculine beauty.

"Sophie's parents have forbidden her from continuing her botanical work, but perhaps they wouldn't object to her interest in gardening," Ian suggested.

"I'm not a gardener," Sophie immediately objected, but as the words left her mouth, she began to see the sense of Ian's words. "Yet gardening is such a ladylike pastime," she amended, "so very delicate and respectable."

"It's an innocuous way for a young woman of quality to spend her time," Ian said with a smile.

Alforth looked from Sophie to Ian and back again, his confusion evident. "What are you two getting at?" he demanded, thumping his cane on the ground. "Sophie hates gardens. Don't you, Sophie?"

"Unless the garden in question happens to be *your* garden, Uncle A."

"But I don't have a garden!"

"Not yet," Ian said. "But you will. And Sophie is going to plan it for you."

Alforth still looked incredibly confused.

"Think of it, Uncle A," Sophie said excitedly, placing a hand on his arm. "If we tell Mother that I will be over at your new house planning your garden, I will have enough freedom to work on my botany. Mother will think I'm at your house, but instead I'll be with Mr. Blackpool."

"I see," Alforth said with dawning comprehension. "Yes—I think I understand you. So every day, you can walk over to my new house and meet Blackpool on the way. Then you'll both be at liberty to continue your botanical work."

"Exactly." Sophie beamed. She darted a triumphant look at Ian, thrilled at the prospect of carrying on her botany studies, and also extracting sparks of pleasure from having their minds work in concert. She hadn't had a partner before, and never one as handsome as Ian. Sharing his thoughts was almost a physical sensation. She liked it. Quite a bit.

"Would you agree to that plan?" Ian asked. "We'll be using you as our alibi, you understand."

"Yes, yes, the old man has finally put it all together," Alforth huffed, more exasperated at his own sluggishness than anything else. Sophie understood that he wasn't particularly enjoying the process of becoming an old man, an annoyance of which she could not blame him. She also realized that she was going to share his fate: growing old with no one beside you. It was a sobering thought.

Of their own volition, her eyes strayed to Ian, but she quickly snapped them back to her uncle. Entertaining notions of marriage was a ridiculous waste of time. But still, she couldn't help but wonder . . .

"Seems sound enough," Alforth determined. "We can talk to Caroline this afternoon."

Grateful, Sophie squeezed her uncle's arm. She stood up as Ian shook Alforth's hand. "Much appreciated, sir," he said.

"Don't make me regret my decision, Blackpool," Alforth said sternly, holding Ian's hand in his grip.

"I won't."

Alforth pulled his hand away, then noticed, as if for the first time, the piece of paper that now lay crumpled within his palm. "Dear Lord, I almost forgot to tell you," he said, blinking in surprise.

"Tell us what?" asked Sophie. Her brow creased with concern.

"It's a good thing I found you out here, too, Blackpool," Alforth continued. He held out the paper. "I received word this morning from Constable Euwer—the man who went to arrest McGannon."

An involuntary shiver ran along Sophie's back as she remembered the hardened criminal and the threats he had uttered before succumbing to Ian's drugs.

"When the constable and his men got to McGannon's hideout, the blackguard was gone," Alforth explained. "His men, too. Cleared out, leaving only some trinkets behind."

Ian looked grim. "Damn. The dhatura was old. It probably only knocked out McGannon and his gang for an hour or two."

Sophie swallowed hard. "What does that mean?"

"It means, my dear," Alforth said, lines of concern etched into his face, "when you and Blackpool are out in the field, you have to stay together. McGannon is on the loose."

"No, it's a ridiculous idea," Caroline snapped, setting down her teacup with a decisive click. "How can you even suggest it, Alforth?" She gave her brother a sharp, disapproving look as he sat across from her at the little table in her private parlor. Sophie, too, sitting alert and edgy on the chaise longue, was given a censorious glance.

"Be reasonable, Caro," Alforth tried to persuade her. "You can't just take away the girl's life's work and expect her to carry on as if nothing happened."

"I can and I will, particularly if I am acting in her best interests. Sophie's botany," she said with a delicate shudder of distaste, "cost her all her opportunities of finding a husband. The moment I let Lord Charles know that she had given up the horrible habit, he came over immediately to renew his courtship. That is proof enough that I acted in the right." Caroline toyed with a biscuit on the painted china plate, crumbling it apart and then dusting the remains from her fingertips in one elegant gesture.

"Planning a garden is not the same thing as botany, Mother," Sophie said. She gripped her elbows with her hands, but forced herself to sit tall before her mother's critical scrutiny.

Caroline thinned her lips. "Semantics," she insisted. "It's all the same mucking about with plants, and I won't have it. Not when Lord Charles has revived his interest in you."

"But think . . ." Sophie continued, rising up and coming to stand beside her mother. She saw the flare of displeasure in Caroline's gaze as she stood taller than her and immediately dropped to the floor to kneel beside her. The theatricality of the gesture both appalled and gratified Caroline, and she tipped her chin away from her daughter in an artfully choreographed movement not unlike something one would see on the London stage.

Sophie knew her mother well enough to understand

she had a part to play in her drama, so she continued. "Everyone says that gardening is one of the most refined pastimes for a lady of quality. And it *is* different from botany. I'll only concern myself with what looks pretty and pleasing to the eye—none of that mannish book reading and," she added pointedly, "*no dirt.*"

That got Caroline's attention. "Really? You won't be up to your elbows in mud?"

Sophie shook her head, and Alforth chimed in, "Not a bit. I'll make sure that Sophie merely plans the garden and supervises the work. I won't let her so much as touch a granule of soil."

This bit of hyperbole might have gone too far, but Sophie could tell her mother was actually giving the idea some thought. A flash of hope bloomed in her chest, and she knew she had to push on while her mother's resolve wavered. "Won't Lord Charles be pleased when he finds out that I've turned my attentions to proper, genteel pastimes? He'll see that my abilities are not solely limited to objectionable scientific dabbling. Rather, I will become that much more attractive in his eyes. He will know that I can run a household and have refined aesthetic sensibilities, and I will make him proud before the eyes of his peers." The words Sophie spoke tasted like the bitterest dandelion greens, filling her with repugnance. She knew, however, that it was precisely what her mother wanted to hear.

Caroline tapped her slender fingers on the edge of her plate. "Lord knows you cannot sing or play the pianoforte," she mused. "And your embroidery is barely adequate. But gardening . . . yes . . . you could arrange flowers cut from your own garden in vases.

Lord Charles would like that very much. He appreciates feminine qualities."

Sophie exchanged cautiously hopeful glances with her uncle, careful that her mother did not see.

"I've made a decision," Caroline said at last. "I want you to go to Alforth's every day to design his garden. We must make sure Lord Charles keeps his interest in you. But if I see so much as a spot of dirt on your apron when you come home, the whole scheme is off. Do you understand?"

Sophie nodded readily, not bothering to correct her mother's sudden belief that the planning of Alforth's garden had been her own idea.

"Very good. Give me a kiss, child, then take yourself off. Close the door behind you."

Dutifully, Sophie gave her mother's dry, smooth cheek a peck, then stood to leave the room. Behind her mother's back, she gave Alforth a wide, celebratory smile and a wave, then did as her mother ordered. The door clicked shut behind her and she headed outside, into the sunshine.

Alforth remained in his sister's parlor, however. He watched as she rose from her seat like a swan taking flight and glided to the window to look out into the side gardens. A rare look of wistful uncertainty crossed Caroline's face.

"I *do* want what's best for her," she said, "despite what you may think."

Carefully, Alforth got to his feet and ambled to his sister's side. He covered her hand with his own and was surprised when she didn't pull away. "I know," he said.

"I had no one to help me through my coming out," she said without resentment. "Everything I did myself. Hired the companion to take me to London, let the town house in the city, bought my gowns, everything. It was a wonder I managed to catch Simon."

Alforth chewed on his lower lip. "I'm so sorry, Caro, that I wasn't there for you when you needed me."

She gave him a small, bittersweet smile. "You were off being a brave soldier. I would have followed if I could, but I never blamed you for leaving."

Sophie appeared below in the garden, her hat dangling down her back as she bent to inspect some hollyhocks. Whatever hesitation Caroline's daughter felt inside the house at Cabot Park was now gone entirely. She moved with unaffected security and ease through the garden, a young woman confident in her ability with plants, who nevertheless found everything that grew to be delightful. "Of all my girls, she is the only one I was never able to fathom. Whenever I looked at her, I could see how different she was. Not just from her sisters, but from everyone around her. And that difference frightened me. It still does. She's smarter than Henry, you know. By miles." Caroline sighed. "Brains never helped a woman, though. And Sophie knows so little of the world," she said as she gazed down at her daughter.

"Perhaps it is time to let her see it, then," Alforth suggested gently.

"Perhaps," Caroline agreed, but as an agreement, it was tentative. With a sudden exhalation, she visibly and deliberately shook off her pensive mood, pushing away from the window. Alforth dropped his hand. She made herself appear composed as she folded her hands at her waist. It was her great skill, the one thing that had managed to ensure her social success when her parents were well known to be wild and unreliable. "I shall send word to Lord Charles today. He will dine with us tomorrow night. If I have my way, Sophie will be engaged to him within the month. And," she added, drawing herself up, every inch a gentleman's wife, "I *always* have my way."

Chapter Nine

Ian raced up the hill, his long legs easily making the climb as his mind marveled at what he was doing.

If he had anticipated that working with Sophie was going to involve sedentary pondering of imponderables, his expectations were shattered by the sight of her darting through woodlands and meadows, her sketchbook tucked under one arm, her hat hanging down her back, and her face smiling. Over her shoulder, she called, "You simply *have* to see this. Just over this ridge. Come *on*."

Ian followed, feeling not unlike a satyr chasing after a nymph. He wasn't so sure of his reward once he caught her, though. It probably did not involve the acts he saw painted on the sides of Greek urns, more's the pity.

Watching her retreating back as he ran behind her—she moved remarkably well for a woman burdened down with panniers, stays, skirts, and other feminine ridiculousness—Ian knew himself well enough to acknowledge that he was deep in lust with

Sophie Andrews. It was the only way he could explain the fact that he had kissed her yesterday in the orangerie after he had expressly forbidden himself from any kind of extensive physical contact with her. Damn him, she'd looked so incredibly lovely, the heat from the orangerie causing her skin to flush and dew, her green-brown eyes full of gratitude and pleasure, with the lingering traces of relief Ian felt that she didn't want to marry the fool courting her. She'd presented him with an irresistible concoction, and desire—chemical, of course—had made him act.

Those same chemicals told him now that he'd like nothing more than a few hours—hell, make it a few days—alone with Sophie in bed.

Ian smiled wryly to himself as he watched her disappear into the shrubbery. Chemicals didn't care about class or responsibility or honor or duty, or any of the social barriers and customs that prevented Ian from following Sophie and gently but firmly removing her pink dress and hanging it on the branches of a tree. Yet whatever chemicals were ricocheting through his body right now, he knew they were not the same as the chemicals he sought to isolate, the ones that held the key to love.

That was the reason he followed when Sophie's voice called out from the shrubbery, "Just a little farther. I promise."

"I haven't done this much running and crawling," he said, pushing his way through the dense undergrowth, "since I got trapped inside the Sultan of Ahmadabad's harem."

"How did that happen?" she asked. She waited for him, crouched down in a clearing, her face alight with excitement and energy.

"I was with a Muslim doctor, acting as his assistant

while he consulted on a mysterious illness that had befallen one of the sultan's wives." Ian managed to break free from the clinging thicket and now found himself in the clearing, a small enclosed space bordered by trees and lush with plant life.

"Did the sultan have many wives?"

Ian shrugged as he dusted off his knees. "Four or so."

Sophie laughed, rising. "Yes, how prosaic. Only four."

"It wasn't uncommon."

"And how many children as a result! Imagine trying to remember all those birthdays. No," she said with a smiling shake of her head as she looked at him. "One husband with one wife is enough for me."

The conversation was taking a turn toward the uncomfortable. "But *this* sultan's wife," he persisted, "had been complaining of an unexplained sickness for some time. The doctor and I were ushered into a private room and had to examine the wife behind a screen. Muslims do not allow people outside of a woman's family to see her," he explained. "The wife ordered everyone but myself out of the room, popped out from behind the screen, and said that she wasn't sick at all, she just wanted to meet the white Christian man who was assisting the doctor."

Sophie gasped and laughed. "I don't need to guess how you got locked inside the harem after that."

Ian realized too late that this wasn't the kind of story one should tell a young lady of good breeding. At least she wasn't ignorant in the ways between women and men. No, Ian had empirical proof that Sophie had a strong foundation of knowledge in that area—and whatever she didn't know, she learned at an accelerated pace.

He caught sight of her pale, freckled skin above her bodice and made himself look away. She was a ripe peach waiting to be plucked, but damn, he wasn't the man who was going to do it.

"We ought to get to work before we lose too much light," he said.

She frowned a little at his abrupt change of subject but recovered herself quickly. "This clearing has a number of plants that should interest you," she explained. She walked over to a knee-high plant and held its trefoil of leaves between her thumb and forefinger. "*Trigonella foenum-graecum*, also known as fenugreek." She plucked a few seeds from its white flowers. "These are chemically very potent. I've heard that some nursing mothers take it to help produce milk and overall, it, ah, aids lubriciousness."

Ian watched, charmed, as the imperturbable scientist blushed. He pocketed the seeds.

"I'll add them to the mix," he said with a laugh.

She tried to smother her embarrassment by returning her focus to the plants. "Did you know," she said enthusiastically, walking to a group of blue flowers growing in profusion, "that Linnaeus's classification system is sexually based?"

"I wasn't aware of that."

"It's true." She waved him over to stand beside her, a full, artless smile curving her mouth. A loud alarm went off inside his head, but he decided to ignore it, remembering the adventures he had lived by disregarding his inner judgment. As he stood next to her, she pointed to the tall threads standing in the middle of the flower, each tipped with fuzzy black motes. "Linnaeus organizes plants based on the number of stamens, their lengths, and whether they're distinct or fused. This

Geranium pratense—meadow cransebill—has ten stamens. It consists of an anther and a filament. Do you see them?"

Ian nodded as she gently ran the tip of her finger up and down the long, thready strand. "The stamen are the male sex glands of the plant," she continued, her voice instructional. Ian's throat went dry as he watched, hypnotized, her finger go slowly up and down the filament. She had no idea what she was doing. "The female sex glands are in the pistil, which is right here in the middle."

"Interesting." Her wrist was narrow, but the pulse that leapt beneath the skin was vital, animal, carrying her blood deep within her body. Sophie's hands showed that she used them: her fingers were tapered but capable, with short, rounded fingernails like pale peach-blue petals. She had strength in her hands, an able grip, and the potential to connect solidly with the physical world. His world.

"Everyone thinks flowers are so dainty, so genteel and suitable for ladies," she said with a chuckle. "But they don't know the truth." She bent closer to speak softly in his ear, her breath warm and sweet against him. She was being conspiratorial with him, but Ian became unbearably aware of her slim body next to his, her active energy that needed only the most gentle encouragement toward sensuality. "Flowers are just sex organs, the generative act of plants. If we could take sex and make it into an object, a *thing*, it would look like this." She nodded toward the blossom still held between the tips of her fingers. She ruffled its silky petals. "Strange, isn't it?"

Ian nodded, his gaze shooting back and forth between the sight of her fingers caressing the flower and the amused smile that quirked her full lips. She had an unbelievable mouth.

"I wonder if that means," she continued musing blithely, "that roses are more passionate at lovemaking than daisies?"

"What?"

Her eyes fluttered shut, and he could see Sophie conjuring up an image in her mind. Her lovely, nimble mind. "Roses can be so rich in color, so intense," she reflected, "but the petals are deep and soft to the touch. Also," she added, opening her eyes and blushing again, "they have such an intoxicating scent."

He watched the color come into her cheeks, delighted by the carnality she couldn't seem to suppress. "The daisy, while pretty in its way, is hardly so complex. Plain and sensible are hardly the qualities one seeks in a lover."

"And what would you know of such things?" Ian asked, his own smile dark and aware. He drew himself up to his full height, nearly a foot taller than Sophie, even as he arched slightly over her. His hand could almost completely enfold her upper arm and he flexed it to reinforce the idea. It was a subtle menace, calculated to remind her of the differences between them.

"Nothing," she said, her voice small. She raised her chin, trying to face him down, yet they both knew he had the greater strength. "Except books and what the kitchen maids will tell me."

"And what do they tell you?"

"Mostly daisies."

He had to laugh at that. Drawing himself up closer to her, he said, "But there's a world of roses out there, Sophie. Lush, full roses thick with perfume so that you can grow dizzy and nearly swoon."

"There are?" She turned wide, dilated eyes to his.

Again he nodded. "Not just cottage roses but giant roses I can span with my hand, lasting for days and days. A person could get lost in such roses and never return. You wouldn't want to."

"Days?" Her pulse began to flutter in her throat.

"Roses are only one kind, though." He stood directly behind her, not touching her with his hands, but fully against her so that he only needed to tip his head down to follow the curve of her neck, down to the creamy flesh of her décolletage, and further along the colorful cotton expanse of her skirt. It was almost as though he had *become* Sophie, looking down and seeing not himself but her, as though they had fused to become a new hybrid. "Exotic orchids bursting with color and shape, clusters of bluebells, charming yet abundant, sweet little buds of violets and, of course, *honeysuckle.*"

This last flower caused her to tremble. Ian felt it through his own muscles, his body a willing receptor to the signs of her own. He thought she was going to fall back against him in full surrender. His hands were already coming up to catch her. He knew what she would feel like—wonderful.

"So it's quite logical, really," Sophie said cheerfully, straightening and brushing pollen from her hands as she stepped to the side, "that you should look to plants for the answer to your questions about love. Flowering plants *are* love incarnate."

His laugh was self-deprecating. "That's damned fortunate."

Sophie tried to laugh, too. She seemed nervous, overly bright, as though she had negotiated a narrow escape. He wanted her to trust him. No; he wanted her to fear him. She ought to.

"Yes, we've got a lot to work with, but not much time," she said, rubbing her nose. "I'm expected back at Cabot Park by four. Lord Charles is dining with us tonight." She made a face. "It doesn't seem fair that someone as unpleasant and obsequious as Lord Charles can sit at our table as much as he pleases just because he has a title and a fine town house in Cheltenham. But you," she continued, turning to Ian, "are perfectly amenable—"

Ian scoffed at this description of himself, but she persisted.

"It's true," she sniffed. "Don't pretend you aren't. You're ten times more interesting than Lord Charles, but the only way my parents would admit you to Cabot Park is through the servants' entrance. And all because you don't have a title."

"That's not the only reason," Ian pointed out. "If I were an industrious tradesperson who'd made good through the 'Change, or maybe the vicar"—Sophie laughed at this—"they might be more sanguine about my prospects."

She sobered. "Why did you become a mountebank? Surely there had to have been better ways to make money. And," she added, her forehead creasing, "you could be respectable."

"We've different ideas about what's respectable."

"I'm serious."

"I am, too," he countered. "Miring myself in social expectations, pretending to be something I'm not—that's not living."

"Think of everything you've missed!"

"I have my freedom."

"Freedom to cozen farmers and villagers out of their money," she returned hotly. "Freedom to live out of a wagon. Yes," she said, fuming, "I can see you've made an even trade."

The depth of her anger surprised him, but it wasn't entirely unexpected. She was butting up against a decision she knew nothing about and could never understand. "One of the reasons I chose my profession," he said, fighting to keep his voice even, "is because I would never have to explain myself to anyone. No one has any expectations of a mountebank, and I like to keep it that way." The implication in his words was obvious.

She looked stung but did not back down. "Your life is your own, of course. You can live it as you choose. Yet I think it's a waste. You're an intelligent man who could do anything if you set your mind to it. You could be a great scientist or a professor at a university, but instead you squander your talents." Sophie did look away then, staring hot and hard at the tree branches overhead with shining eyes. "I'll never have your choices."

"I'm not nearly the man you think I am," he said quietly after a moment. "But you're right; it isn't fair that I have choices you don't. I wish to God I could give you even a fraction of the independence I have now. I know you'd make better use of it."

Sophie gave him a small, sad smile. Ian knew he wasn't making things easier, yet there was little he could do for her in his current position. Maybe he was helping, though. The sooner she realized the inequality of the world, the better off she would be. Illusions and hopes only made a person vulnerable.

She had been walking around the clearing as they spoke, but now she exclaimed and plucked some green stalks growing nearby. "*Avena sativa*," she explained, coming to stand next to Ian. "Wild oat.

You've heard that expression, 'sowing your wild oats'? It's because of this plant. Green wild oats are fed to stallions to make them more spirited and increase their libido. It's definitely something that should be investigated."

"I'll make a distillation tonight," he promised, adding the stalks to his growing store.

"What's in the elixir you sell now?" She sat down on a carpet of soft grasses and propped open her sketchbook in her lap. She fished around in the pocket of her apron, then looked up blankly. "I haven't anything to draw with," she said. "They took all my pencils and pens." She appeared completely lost, stymied by the will of her parents.

Cursing softly to himself, Ian dug a piece of chalk out of his own pocket. He couldn't comprehend the actions of her family—they seemed deliberately cruel when she deserved much better.

"Oh, how wonderful." She beamed up at him. "Thank you." Her face glowed with gratitude and joy.

He took entirely too much pleasure out of her happiness, and he could practically see her unprotected heart offered to him in her upturned hands. He reminded himself, even as new desire curled in his belly, that she wasn't far out of girlhood. A clandestine collaboration with a man on the fringes of society—it was a breeding ground for romance or, at least, what she would perceive as romance. But nothing could be less possible. He would have to tell her.

Yet looking down at her natural, fresh beauty, pure admiration for him in her hazel eyes, Ian told himself he would make everything clear to her—later.

"The elixir is made of roots and plants I discovered abroad," he said instead, sitting across from her and stretching out his long legs. "Star anise, some Chinese herbs called *fo-ti* and *ginseng*, the root of the Indian *ashwaganda* plant, and a few others for flavor and color."

"Like roses," she said with a sly smile.

He nodded, enjoying their private joke. "Yes, roses, too." *You're a fool, soaking up this girl's attention like some damned withered plant because she makes you feel more noble than you really are.*

"I tasted them when I tried the elixir in Little Chipping," she said. The chalk in her hand flew across the page as she spoke. "I think that might actually work . . . a little," she added quickly.

"Oh?" He raised his eyebrow a fraction as he leaned back on his elbows.

"I felt a bit . . . odd, after I drank it," she confessed. "Kind of flushed and confused. I couldn't be still. And I could *feel* things, like the air on my skin and the breath in my lungs. I felt as though I wanted something, but I didn't know what." She looked up at him through the light brown fringe of her lashes. "What does all that mean?"

"It means," he said with something halfway between a laugh and a groan, "that I've managed to make a fairly decent aphrodisiac."

"Ah." The scratch of the chalk on the paper combined with the intermittent bird song. "But that's not love, is it?" she asked after a pause, still bent over her work.

"No," he agreed. "It isn't love." He gazed at her, the filtered sunlight turning her hair into a whiskey-colored nimbus, freckles dotting her face like amorous punctuation, her teeth catching her lush bottom lip in concentration. "It's just sex."

A few more strokes of the chalk and she straightened, holding open her sketchbook for his inspection. It was a drawing of him—his profile, as he looked off into the distance. She'd managed to capture something in his expression, a warring impulse, caught between ambiguities, both calculating and hopeful. It was unnerving to see himself so accurately rendered, not just his exterior self but the interior as well.

She looked at him expectantly. He made himself laugh.

"What an ugly specimen," he said, using the tip of his boot to shut the sketchbook. "Not for lack of talent on your part," he added, seeing her dissatisfaction. "Plants make a far more attractive subject than mountebanks."

She wasn't happy with his dismissal but accepted it. She opened her sketchbook and took another quick look at her drawing, shrugged, then shut the book again firmly.

Ian stood, helping her up, too. He felt the burning afterimage of her hand in his own and realized he was becoming seriously fixated on Sophie Andrews's hands. He wanted to know what they would feel like against his bare skin, what they could do to him with only a few caresses.

"Let's get moving," he said. He held several branches aside so Sophie could move ahead of him into the woods. "We've spent far too long wasting time."

Chapter Ten

Sophie and her mother sat silently bent over their needlework. Dinner with Lord Charles was over and they had retired to the drawing room, waiting for the men to finish their port and Alforth's cigars.

This was always the most uncomfortable part of the evening for Sophie. She and her mother had so little to discuss. It was no wonder that of all the feminine arts, Sophie had learned needlecraft. It was the only acceptable pastime her mother allowed after dinner, and it prevented strained conversation.

Now male voices sounded near the door, causing her mother to set aside her embroidery hoop and direct a charming smile toward whomever approached. Catching a warning look from her mother, Sophie reluctantly followed her example and made herself smile when Lord Charles, her father, and Uncle Alforth came into the drawing room.

"At last, the revivifing company of our beautiful ladies!" Lord Charles cried, still carrying his glass of port. He made an elaborate bow, spilling a bit of the drink onto the floor. A footman hurried to clean it up as Lord Charles ambled toward Sophie.

She rose from her chair to give him a polite curtsy, then resumed her sewing.

Her parents and Alforth conversed in quiet tones at the other end of the drawing room, trying, without being too obvious, to listen in on Sophie and Lord Charles.

The man in question paced around her, one hand still holding his glass and the other resting on his hip in a flamboyantly self-satisfied gesture. As he walked, Sophie studied him out of the corner of her eye. His evening clothes were exceptionally fine, blue satin covered in golden floral embroidery, lace frothing across his neck and at his wrists, golden buckles at his knees and matching silk high-heeled shoes. He had powdered his sandy hair. Lord Charles had fine features, the by-product of good breeding, and was neither too tall nor too short. She'd heard at various balls that he was, indeed, one of the area's most eligible bachelors, quite rich and refined and considered handsome by most. But even before Sophie had met Ian Lord Charles had never appealed to her. And now that Sophie *did* know Ian Blackpool, poor Vickerton really had no chance.

"I hear that you are planning your uncle's garden," Lord Charles said with a smile.

"I am."

"I'm pleased," he said. He put one hand on the back of Sophie's chair, and she leaned forward slightly to avoid touching him. "At first, I was a trifle concerned. Your parents had assured me that you had discarded your botanical mania—something wholly inappropriate for a woman, and certainly one of your station—so I thought perhaps you had returned to your old ways."

"But that is not the case," Sophie said, trying to sound as mild as possible when, in fact, she wanted to stab her needle into his hand and dash from the room.

He laughed and drained his glass. The footman hurried forward to refill it. "No, indeed. I feel it is most important that a woman not be idle, for idleness breeds a disregard for the person. And it is critical that a woman be at all times fair and pleasing to those around her. That is what a woman does best. She is," he continued, leaning down to speak softly in her ear, "her husband's greatest possession, his finest ornament."

Sophie didn't answer, could barely even breathe, she was so enraged.

"And you, my dear Sophie," Lord Charles went on, flicking his eyes down the front of her gown, "are indeed a fine ornament. You would make your husband proud. You would make *me* proud."

"How gratifying," she murmured. Fortunately, Lord Charles chose to see this comment as a bit of playful banter, so he moved back with a laugh.

"Yes, gardening is an admirable pastime for a woman, and I endorse it heartily." He came around to sit at the far end of the chaise, propping his elegant shoe on his knee. "As is sewing," he remarked, noting her diligence at her work. "What is it that you labor at?" He craned his neck to observe the patches of fabric in her lap.

"Some scraps of cloth I am piecing together for a quilt," she improvised. "Mother encourages me to make things for our tenants." Ordinarily, Sophie helped the farmers on her family land by determining which seeds would yield better crops and sometimes assisting in their own kitchen gardens, but she didn't think Lord Charles would appreciate or understand these acts.

Lord Charles nodded his approval, much as her mother had done earlier. "Very good. I keep my main residence in town and have my steward tend to my land, but it is an excellent idea to make sure the farmers know where their income comes from, remind them of who keeps them fed and clothed. Acts of charity reinforce this marvelously well."

Sophie nearly pointed out that it was, in fact, the tenant farmers who kept Lord Charles fed with rich meats and clothed in Parisian silks, but, glancing up and catching her mother's hawkish gaze, she merely nodded serenely and continued her sewing.

And so, for the rest of the long night, until Lord Charles finally made his bows and left, she took secret gratification in knowing that her mundane, feminine task of sewing was going to provide her with the most extraordinary day of her life.

Ian stepped out of his caravan, clad only in his breeches, boots, and a thrown-on shirt he didn't bother to button. He was alone at the back of Edward Chesterton's farm, having paid the yeoman farmer in advance for the privilege of boarding his wagon and horse for the duration of his time in the area, however long that might be. Chesterton had given him the use of a sheltered acre, partially wooded and largely uncultivated, so Ian need not observe the rules of polite society when it came to his dress early in the morning. He gathered his hair back into a queue and tied it with a strip of leather.

Idly, he wondered what people would think if he stopped cutting his hair and wore it in a turban, like the Sikhs. Either it would be very bad for business or very good.

He set his shaving kit on the top step of the wagon and hung a small mirror on a hook from the back wall of the wooden caravan. As he meditatively whipped up foam in his shaving cup, he understood that eventually he would have to take several days off his work with Sophie in order to pursue his true vocation. He had bottles and bottles of Blackpool's Elixir that needed to be sold, and he no longer had automatically regenerating coffers. Though he didn't want to be away from Sophie for very long, it would be impossible for a young lady of breeding to accompany him as he hawked his goods in public markets.

He frowned at his image in the mirror as he shaved with a pearl-handled straight-razor. Their time together could not last forever, but he wanted to sustain it for as long as possible. It had been a long time since he'd enjoyed another person's company as much as he did Sophie's. She was serious and playful at the same time, with a deep wellspring of intelligence that sometimes awed him. He liked her idealism tempered with a more sanguine view of the world, and her insistence that things could always be better.

She was, he realized as he rinsed off the last vestiges of the shaving foam, the kind of woman who made a man want to improve himself.

Damn it, he didn't *want* to improve himself. He was happy the way he was.

He blotted his face with the towel. As he did so, one eye glanced into the mirror and saw Sophie standing ten feet behind him, holding a basket and staring.

Fortunately, he had strong nerves. Otherwise he would have jumped a good yard into the air. Instead, he deliberately set down the towel and turned to face her. He watched as her eyes traveled down to his chest, widening slightly at the sight of the dark hair that curled there, and moved even further down his abdomen. A deep blush filled her cheeks as she realized that the hair on his chest trailed down into a thin line, disappearing under the waistband of his trousers.

As if she were touching him, he felt the muscles in his belly leap. She licked her lips. Ian bit back a groan.

Forcing his fingers to be steady, he slowly buttoned his shirt. He would not let her see how much her gaze affected him.

"I didn't expect to see you until later," he said, his voice deliberately casual.

"No, I, ah . . ." He didn't know if it was better or worse that she was as flustered as he. He tried to recall some meditation techniques a guru had shown him, slowing his mind and removing himself from his body even as he went about getting dressed. He ducked inside the caravan and put on his waistcoat, draping his coat and cravat over his arm as he came back out again. She was still standing there, lips parted and eyes glazed.

"How was your dinner with Vickerton?" he asked, turning back to the mirror to tie the plain stock of his neckcloth. He cursed himself. What difference was it to him how her dinner with the embroidered fool went?

She recovered herself, like a sleeper awakening, as Ian shrugged into his coat. "Tedious," she said with a wry smile. "At least he approves of my 'gardening project,' or so he told me. In fact," she added with a laugh, "he is most pleased because it will keep me from becoming a slattern. Lord Charles is very concerned with my appearance."

"I don't doubt it," Ian muttered, giving his coat a sharp tug to align the fit. He could just picture that jackass drooling more over Sophie than his five-course meal. She probably looked lovely, clad in some evening finery, with maybe a ring or two ornamenting her slim hands and pearls draped around her elegant neck. Ian would never see Sophie dressed for dinner, a fact that filled him with an inexplicable sadness. He could well imagine her in the glow of candlelight, smiling at him over the soup, running the smooth instep of her foot over his calf while the fish was being served, letting her graceful and capable hand climb up his thigh as the roast was being carved. And then, for dessert . . . He almost shivered.

"At any rate, I won't have to endure him again until Sunday," Sophie continued, unaware of the direction Ian's thoughts had taken, "when he's accompanying us to church."

Another privilege denied Ian. Well, he told himself, he'd made his bed. Too bad it was solitary.

"How did you know I was here?" he asked as he cleaned up the camp. She stepped back and watched him.

"Alforth told me you were ensconced at Edward Chesterton's. They're good friends."

"He's a man of the people, your uncle."

"Alforth doesn't care for society." Sophie shrugged. "I suppose I take after him in that respect."

"You'd rather toil in the dirt," Ian said with a smile. "Which explains your early appearance."

Sophie shook her head. "No, actually. I remember hearing some of the servants talking when some traveling actors came to town, and they said that if a mountebank wanted to do business in this area, he had to have a zany. What do you plan on doing about that?"

Ian sat down in the open doorway of the caravan so that his legs stretched out in front of him. He balanced one heel on top of the toe of his boot. In answer to her question, he shrugged. "I'll manage. I always do."

She shook her head. "You ought to do better than just *manage*. You should be the best mountebank Gloucestershire has ever seen. They ought to talk about you years after you've gone, and say to their grandchildren, 'Ian Blackpool sold the entire town of Moreton bottles of his elixir and the next spring, the population tripled!'"

He folded his arms across his chest and laughed. "I appreciate the sentiment, Sophie, but I don't feel the need to excel as you do. If I can unload a dozen bottles or so, I'll be happy."

"Well, *I* won't," she insisted. "Which is why I've come up with a plan."

Oh, God, another plan. Ian slowly stood, regarding her suspiciously. "What kind of plan?" he demanded.

With an angelic smile, Sophie reached into her basket. She pulled out a jacket, a bit crudely made but able to stay together. It was a patchwork coat, consisting of diamonds of multicolored fabric sewn together like a harlequin's jacket. Just what a zany traveling with a mountebank might wear. In Sophie's size.

"No," Ian said. He stepped forward. "No, I won't let you. A genteel young lady knows nothing of the life of a performer," he said. "Before our meeting in Little Chipping, I doubt you'd ever even *been* on a stage before. You wouldn't know what to do."

He watched her blush at the memory, just as his

own body stirred to life recalling the kiss they had shared, but he tried to force his response away. He was making a point, damn and hell, and a fine example of rectitude he would be if he pointed more than his finger at her.

"It is true that I never did step onto a stage before then," Sophie conceded, pushing through her embarrassment. "But I'll have you know that when I was eleven, I saw a troupe of performers come through Sevendowne and was simply mad after that to become one of their members. It baffled my father and horrified my mother when I taught myself all manner of tricks and japes. I even learned how to juggle. Observe." She pulled three apples from her basket and, true to her word, began to juggle them deftly, only a slight bobble at the beginning indicating that she was not a strolling player. With a small flourish, she caught each apple in turn in the basket, then bowed.

He clapped his hands and shook his head at the continuing unfolding enigma of Sophie Andrews. "Simply because you have a talent for comic business does not mean that I will allow you to serve at my zany."

She didn't back down. With careful patience, she explained, "But the servants were sure. Only those with Merry Andrews have any success around here. As long as we're collaborating together, you won't be able to travel very far to places that are more open-minded about mountebanks. As a consequence," she continued judiciously, "your income will suffer, and all in direct correlation to me. So you see," Sophie concluded, looking quite sure of herself, "in good conscience, I cannot let you work alone. It will reflect quite poorly on me. You don't want that, do you?"

Ian knew she was trying to talk him in circles and applauded her audacity. Her request to join him wasn't only about his finances and her sense of obligation. As Sophie began to taste freedom, she needed more ways to stretch herself, learn her own power. What could be more forbidden, more daring, than doing something everyone in her family and her class would disapprove of? He didn't want to deny her this. With an exaggerated sigh, he said, "Far be it from me to let your self-esteem suffer."

Her bravado slipped as the reality of his acceptance sank in. "So you'll let me be your zany?" she asked.

"Only if you want to," he said quickly, giving her a way out.

She swallowed and nodded. "I do," she answered, tipping up her chin to give herself confidence. He felt his chest constrict with admiration. Whatever Sophie was afraid of, she made herself face that fear, just as she sought new experiences with the enthusiasm of a seasoned adventurer. "Today would be an excellent day to go to Cheltenham; they're having a fair that draws people from all over the area. I already told my mother that I would be doing some further canvassing of gardens and won't be at Alforth's, so she shan't go looking for me."

Ian smiled in appreciation. "You have thought of everything."

"Yes." She agreed with her own smile as she lifted up the lid of her basket. Inside were two rolls, split and filled with meat and cheese as she had done on the road to Sevendowne days before. "More of Sophie's Special, in case we get hungry. But we should go soon. By the time we get to Cheltenham, the fair will be in full swing and," she added with a waggle of her eyebrows, "we don't want to miss the best customers."

"Then you should change." He nodded toward his caravan. "Go ahead. I promise not to spy."

She blushed again but nodded and quickly went into the wagon, shutting the door behind her. He realized that she had come prepared for their change in plans, since she had been dressed in a plain quilted skirt and coat instead of a gown. Then his mouth dried and his palms grew damp. He could hear her moving around inside the caravan. She was taking off her clothes, removing her jacket, clad only in her stays and chemise. She was right by his bed. The door to the caravan wasn't locked.

He took a step toward the wagon, but stopped as she opened the door. She was wearing the harlequin jacket and grinning. He quickly smothered his incipient lust. She hopped down to the ground and held something up in front of his face.

"I'd *wondered* where this had gone," she exclaimed.

Filmy fabric brushed against him and he reached out to capture it in his hand. It was her stocking, which he'd found draped across his coat several nights before as he was getting ready for bed. Knitted of fine silk, it held the echo of the shape of her leg, with delicate floral clocks embroidered at the ankle. She had found it, which meant she knew that he had kept it enshrined next to the Buddha statue on his little table. She didn't know, however, that he touched the stocking ritualistically throughout the day. He would be sorry to see it go.

Before he could mumble an excuse, she tucked it daintily in his pocket. He looked up at her in surprise. "You keep it," she said with a curve of her mouth. "I've got too many of the blasted things. Now," she went on briskly, "let's get your horse and get on the road. We've got quite a day ahead of us."

She had no idea.

Cheltenham was the most fashionable city in Gloucestershire, attracting numerous visitors to its healing mineral waters. Some said it rivaled even Bath as a spa town, but Sophie had never been to Bath and could make no comparisons. She rode beside Ian through the bustling streets made more crowded by the fair, watching the throngs of people and taking in the noise and happy confusion. She visited Cheltenham several times a year; it had lost its savor of novelty a long time ago, but this was the first time she had ever come to town as a mountebank's zany. Thus the city was reborn in her eyes and she observed everything around her with a rapidly beating heart.

It was very likely that people she knew or who were acquainted with her family might be in the crowds, so Ian had provided her with a demi-mask he'd purchased in Venice several carnivals ago, and an old floppy hat to cover her distinctive honey-colored hair. Female harlequins, called columbines, weren't entirely unknown, but one who spoke with a cultured accent was much more singular. And as much as Sophie wanted Blackpool's Amorous Elixir to make an impression in the minds of the populace, she did not want to attract the wrong kind of attention. So she and Ian had agreed she would perform in pantomime—mute—which would present its own set of challenges.

As Ian maneuvered the caravan through the streets, her mind kept running down two very different routes. One, going over her routine, which would draw and sustain a crowd long enough to buy the elixir. And two, returning over and over again to the spectacular image of Ian Blackpool *en dishabille*. Sophie had seen farmers working on hot days without their shirts and had found the sight mildly interesting, but she'd never before considered a man's body to be truly beautiful. Ian's was exquisite. His skin was lightly golden, the muscles beneath lean and sculpted fine as a Grecian statue, with delicious ripples of taut flesh all down his flat abdomen. The dark hair had surprised her a bit, and she couldn't help but follow it down until it vanished from sight into his breeches. His hips were narrow and chiseled, and even now she had to suppress the desire to flatten the palms of her hands against his belly.

"Whoa!"

Sophie looked up sharply, brought out of her heated thoughts by Ian's command. At first she thought he was speaking to her, attempting to curb her overheated imagination, but then chuckled at herself as she saw him pull the mare's reins up to wheel the caravan into position.

Ian settled them between a woman offering ready-made clothing and a man selling honey. He had explained to Sophie on the ride over how to get ready for a show and, recalling his instructions, she got to work. There were other performers walking the streets— some with trained animals, jugglers, musicians—but Ian's exceptionally decorated caravan was already beginning to draw a crowd.

"I'll finish setting up the stage," Ian told her. "Go and mingle with the crowd."

With her pulse hammering in her throat, Sophie began her career as a zany. At first, her actions were tentative, mostly dancing and a bit of comic stumbling. But as passersby began to pay her more attention, she became more bold, interacting with those around her. She drew on her limited experience playing charades and began to ape the actions of the people in the crowd. A man with an ample belly attempted to walk past, and Sophie walked behind him, exaggerating his gait into a waddle. The crowd pointed and chortled. She pulled faces at children, who shrieked with laughter and hid behind their mothers' skirts. As a larger crowd began to gather, she found more and more people to toy with, her confidence growing. One couple consisted of an exceptionally tall man and a diminutive woman, and another couple was a squat dumpling of a man with a lanky, coltish woman. With great gestures, Sophie let everyone know that these pairings were ridiculous and, breaking the couples apart, she rearranged them so the two tall people and the two little people were matched. Dusting her hands together in a pantomime of satisfaction, the assembled group applauded and cheered.

She felt giddy with possibility, thrilled with the freedom afforded by her disguise. She wasn't accustomed to being so physical, shutting down the intellectual part of her personality and simply letting herself *be*. Certainly, she'd never interacted with so many strangers before, people who did not know her and would never know her, and the effect was liberating. It was wonderful, almost as wonderful as discovering a new flowering plant. She couldn't help the smile that spread across her face and wound its way into her soul.

Glancing up, she saw Ian standing on the stage,

smiling his gorgeous smile at her, delighted and surprised and proud of her performance. The crowd was quite large, drawing people away from other stalls to observe her antics. Between her clowning and Ian's able skills as a mountebank, they would sell every last bottle of elixir he had prepared. Sophie moved around the jostling crowd, preparing to join Ian on stage, when she turned and ran right into a man pushing his way through.

"Get out of my way," snapped the man. "Boorish hussy!"

Sophie could not move, though. She found herself staring right into the annoyed blue eyes of Lord Charles Vickerton.

Chapter Eleven

She was frozen, utterly paralyzed by shock and horror as she stared at him and he stared back at her down the length of his aristocratic nose. Of all the people she wanted to avoid while serving as Ian's zany, Lord Charles ranked at the top of her list. Oh, God! What if he recognized her? Would he rip off her mask and demand that she come home right away? Would he tell her parents? And what would he do to Ian, a mountebank corrupting one of England's well-bred daughters?

Sophie shot a quick glance at Ian, who stood ready and alert at the edge of the stage. He would help if she asked him to. But she didn't want his help. She wanted to manage Lord Charles on her own.

"Remove yourself at once, trollop!" Lord Charles spat, waving his lace handkerchief in the air.

She realized with a giddy lurch that Vickerton didn't recognize her beneath her demi-mask and hat. Why should he? Lord Charles only saw the Sophie he wanted to see, refined and demure in her expensive clothing, eyes downcast, agreeable and nonthreatening. Relief expanded through her—replaced almost at once by anger and the desire for revenge. She'd had to endure his loathsome comments throughout his visits, his pompous declarations about women as pretty ornaments, and his leering, sticky gaze.

Instead of stepping aside to let him pass, Sophie puffed out her chest, parodying Vickerton's haughty posture. She gazed at Lord Charles with an exaggerated sneer of disdain, waving a hand in front of her nose as though she smelled something quite foul. The crowd of farmers and shopkeepers had now turned its attention to this newest antic and began to howl with laughter as Sophie continued to satirize Lord Charles, the nobleman, much to his exasperation.

"Stop that at once!" Lord Charles took his gold-tipped walking stick and rapped it angrily on the ground. Sophie mimicked him, using her own imaginary walking stick. The crowd hooted.

With a disgusted sneer, Lord Charles turned on his heel and jostled his way out of the crowd.

A blossom of triumph opened in her chest. Perhaps her revenge had been childish—but it felt amazingly good.

She scampered back to the stage. Everyone was now fully prepared to give Ian their complete attention after the ridiculous scene.

He stood next to her and gave her hand a squeeze, which caused her heart to contract with happiness. "Beautiful work, Sophie," he murmured into her ear, and gave her a conspiratorial wink.

Then Ian launched into his routine. It was much the same as it had been in Little Chipping, except for the fact that Sophie stood to the side of the stage, pantomiming along with Ian's quest for the true essence of love. She was the regal sultan withholding the secret to everlasting passion, the fierce tigers guarding the formula, the lonely bachelor and the bored wife. Ian spoke; she acted. They moved in perfect harmony, each playing off the other like musicians taking a simple tune and making it more complex, more delightful, by turns. If her earlier actions with the crowd had given her a sense of freedom, working with Ian felt unbelievably freeing, their two minds operating as one, a symbiosis that grew and became its own living entity.

She marveled at her ability to perform, and even managed to convince the crowd that she couldn't bear the thought of kissing Ian. That took more skill than she thought she possessed.

"Now observe," Ian directed, "as Daisy drinks Blackpool's Amorous Elixir, and marvel at the change." He uncorked the bottle and, after chasing her around the stage and catching her, affected to force Sophie to drink it. This bottle contained nothing more than distilled water, but the crowd didn't need to know that.

Everyone waited as Sophie pretended to feel the potion coursing through her body. Slowly, she turned to Ian. The crowd made a sound of expectation. Ian also waited. They had rehearsed that Sophie would put her arms around his neck and give him a simple, close-mouthed kiss. But Sophie had something else in mind.

The fires built in her, so that everything she had experienced that day blazed: convincing Ian to let her join him, her triumph with the crowd, humiliating Lord Charles, and her desire for Ian. It all combined into one scorching ball inside her.

She walked deliberately toward him, female power surging through her veins. She felt as though she could do anything. The world was hers. And he would be, too. At first, Ian did not understand her intent, but his eyes widened with surprise as she reached up and pulled his head down for a kiss.

This, Ian realized, was not what they had rehearsed. Sophie's lips against his were hungry, demanding. She opened her mouth, drawing him in, her tongue stroking his own with deliberate, fiery seduction. He didn't try to resist her, didn't want to, as he wrapped his arms around her, one hand cupping her bottom through her simple skirt and the other resting near the side of her breast. She pressed herself into him, soft yet fierce, and everything but the feel of Sophie retreated. Her fingers wove into the hair at the nape of his neck while she gripped his biceps with her free hand. How could anyone mistake Sophie for a dry intellectual? She was flesh and fire in his arms. The only cogent thought Ian could form was to wonder why he'd waited so long for this.

"What an endorsement!" someone in the crowd shouted, and approving claps and cheers followed.

As they had before in Little Chipping, Ian and Sophie broke apart, dazed and disoriented. He recovered a little faster, giving silent thanks for the full skirt of his coat, and launched back into his patter. His mind was far away as words continued to form and move out of his mouth of their own volition. He guessed that he was making sense, since the audience nodded and clapped when appropriate. Ian risked a look over at Sophie. She was also managing to continue her work as a zany, but she, too, wore a confounded expression.

Then it was over. People queued up to buy love in a bottle, as both Ian and Sophie doled out the elixir and collected money.

"This has been one of my best days yet," Ian remarked once the crowd had dispersed. "We took in three times as much as normal."

She stuffed bills and coins into a small wooden box. "You ought to live in style for a goodly bit of time. What's this?" Sophie looked up, puzzled, as he pressed some money into her hand.

"Your cut," he explained. "I'd never have done so well without you."

"I can't take it," she insisted. "The money is yours."

"It's *ours*. Besides," he continued with a grin, "think of this as the first money you've ever actually earned for your hard work, instead of someone providing you with pin money."

She seemed to like that idea quite a bit, and cheerfully stowed her earnings in her pocket. Even beneath her mask, she looked undeniably pretty, and delightfully pleased with herself.

He was going to have to do it. He couldn't simply let her kiss him like that, and kiss her in return, and not lay down some ground rules. Otherwise, sooner rather than later, he was going to have her. And that was something that could never happen.

"Listen, Sophie—" he began.

"Blackpool, old friend!" a voice cried out behind him.

Cursing whomever had interrupted him, Ian turned to face the intruder, fully prepared to tell him to piss off. Instead, he was shocked and pleased to see a familiar, smiling face.

"Radé!"

The other man jumped up onto the stage and enveloped Ian in an effusive bear hug, then leaned back and grasped his forearms with his sinewy hands.

"I didn't expect to see you in these parts," Radé Valariu said jovially.

"The same goes for you, you goat!"

"I am glad to have met up with you today," the gypsy said. "I have heard some distressing news through the Rom and wanted to get the word to you as soon as possible."

"What news?" asked Sophie, alarmed.

Radé looked around furtively, then lowered his voice. "Men like you, mountebanks, have been found badly beaten over the past few days. They say they were set upon by the highwayman Dan McGannon."

Sophie gasped, one hand flying to her mouth. Ian pressed her more tightly against him even as he absorbed what his friend was telling him.

"It seems as though he is looking for someone, some mountebank who has done him a great injury," Radé continued. He shook his head. "I pity whatever poor soul offended him, for it is certain that this McGannon will kill him, and make him suffer in the process."

Ian did not speak, only nodded. He didn't want to tell his friend that *he* was the man McGannon was looking for, since that kind of knowledge, even in the most well-meaning hands, could turn deadly. Sophie had begun to tremble. Ian held her tighter.

"For your safety," Radé went on, "it would be best for you to disappear for a little while, at least until this madman finds his prey and ends his short, miserable life."

"Thank you for your news," Ian said, shaking his friend's hand by clasping his wrist, the gypsy way. "Will I see you again?"

Radé waved his hands. "Perhaps. We shall be encamped outside Cheltenham for the next month or so. Let us hope our paths cross. Until then." He took Sophie's hand and pressed a gallant kiss there—a gesture that many women would have swooned over, but Sophie merely smiled politely. With another wave, Radé disappeared into the crowd.

Sophie looked up at Ian, fear whitening her eyes beneath the mask. "What now?" she asked, chewing her bottom lip.

"Now I go into a brief retirement from the mountebank business," Ian said cavalierly, trying to lighten the mood. "I'm all yours, Sophie."

They took a longer, more out-of-the-way route home, trying to avoid traffic and eyes that might spot Ian's distinctive painted caravan and pass the information along. McGannon could be anywhere, or have informants. Recalling Radé Valariu's news about the brutalized mountebanks made Sophie shudder.

For her protection, Ian made her ride inside the wagon, but she had opened the hatch between the inside of the caravan and the driver's seat so she could talk with him.

"Do you think he knows your name?" she asked.

He knew who she was referring to. "I doubt it. He wouldn't leave a trail of beaten mountebanks behind him if he did. Otherwise, it would have been easy for him to track me down and finish his business."

"You sound so casual about it," she said, almost reproachful.

"What do you want me to do, Sophie?" Ian shifted in the seat so he could look at her over his shoulder. "Cower in terror? Run screaming into the hills?" He turned back to the road. "As you said once before, there's no point in histrionics."

"Don't be ridiculous," she snapped, irritated by his indifferent attitude. "You ought to seek out some kind of law enforcement—perhaps they can help, give you some protection."

Ian snorted. "The law generally isn't fond of people like me. I'm sure they'd see my situation as a problem taking care of itself."

"But we could—"

"Damn it, Sophie," Ian growled, "enough. I don't need you smothering me."

Sophie started, completely shocked. He'd never spoken to her like that before, or anybody else, for that matter, as far as she knew. At first she could only blink in hurt confusion, but anger quickly replaced that hurt.

"You're right," she said, in a cool and unyielding voice she had heard her mother use repeatedly. "I won't make the mistake of being concerned for your welfare again."

With that, she shut the hatch. The inside of the caravan was dark, but she didn't notice, she was too busy fuming. Her fear for Ian's safety had fast transformed into outrage. Perhaps she was overreacting, but she never once thought that Ian, who had always been a good friend and ally in the time she knew him, would reprimand her for something she didn't feel was an offense. Yes, she cared about him, which was *not* the same as smothering. It wasn't. How on earth could he think that?

Several minutes passed. She sat on Ian's bed in the darkness, the caravan swaying slightly from side to side as it moved down the road, the horse's hooves making a steady rhythm on the earth. There were still many miles to Sevendowne, made longer by her self-imposed isolation. Sophie realized that without fresh air and light, she would probably get sick inside the wagon. All over Ian's bed and his possessions. The thought almost made her smile. It would serve him right.

A tap sounded on the hatch. Sophie ignored it.

The tap sounded again.

"Go away," she called.

"Open up, Sophie," Ian said.

"No. Leave me alone."

There was another moment of silence. And then the little door opened, spilling sunshine inside the caravan. She squinted, holding her hand in front of her eyes.

"It opens both ways," Ian explained dryly. She could just see part of his shoulder and a sliver of jaw and ear. Sophie cursed to herself, and pointedly turned away from him so that she faced the rear of the wagon. Her eyes roved, catching sight of his traveling chest, a stack of books tied down, crates holding bottles. Yes, the caravan was filled with him, with Ian, and she hated him right now. She contemplated jumping out the back and walking the rest of the way home.

"I wouldn't."

She looked sharply over her shoulder, but Ian was still facing the road, not even sparing her a glance. Somehow, he'd read her thoughts.

"It's a long way back to Cabot Park," he continued conversationally. "You wouldn't make it home until long after dark, and your parents would wonder where you'd been. I don't think they'd appreciate your explanation."

Curse him, he was right. Sophie continued to sit in incensed silence, not giving him the privilege of a response.

"Look, Sophie," Ian said, "there's something you should know about me."

"I don't wish to know a single thing about you," she countered, but she wasn't speaking the truth. She burned with questions about him, but whenever she had tried to pose them in the past, he evaded answering by regaling her with stories of his travels. How ironic that he was granting her wish at a time when she wanted to keep him at a distance.

He ignored her comment. "Do you know why I'm looking for the secret to love?" She didn't answer, so he continued. "It's because I can't."

"Of course you can," she said automatically, turning back to face him. The idea was so absurd, she didn't bother to check her response. "Everyone can love."

He shook his head. "Not me. I may esteem and value certain people, but I can't love."

"What about your parents?"

"Do you love yours?" he countered immediately.

"I respected them once," she answered cautiously.

"But you don't love them."

"I . . . don't know," she finally said. "But I know I love my uncle. We are discussing you, however."

"Like you, I respected my father, but love . . . that's something else. He probably feels the same way."

"What about your mother?"

"She died giving birth to me."

"I am sorry."

Ian nodded. "It's a shame I never knew her. I cannot love her absence."

"Being unable to love one's parents doesn't mean one cannot love at all."

He exhaled, and flicked the reins. "Don't think I haven't considered that. But I know from thirty-one years of experience that love just isn't possible for me. Somehow, I was born without the chemicals that cause a person to experience love. Passion, attraction, admiration, yes. Love, no."

Sophie edged nearer the hatch so that only the wooden wall separated her from touching Ian's back. "I don't fathom you at all."

"Seven years ago, I was going to be married."

Again, she started. The idea that he had once planned on taking a wife stunned her, and provoked a churning unhappiness inside. Rationally, she always knew there had to have been other women in Ian's life, and though that thought didn't please her, she had taken comfort in the hope that he hadn't considered actually marrying them.

"From your silence, I can tell you're taken aback."

Sophie didn't know how to explain her feelings to him, didn't know if she wanted to. "I thought you were never going to marry," she said at last, her throat dry.

"That revelation came later," he said, a wry smile quirking his lips. "But at that point in my life, I was twenty-four and, I thought, ready to take a wife."

"Yet you didn't."

"No, I didn't." He pulled on the reins. The horse slowed, then stopped, and he turned around fully to face her through the small hatch. His handsome face was tight and tense as he regarded her pointedly. Sophie felt as though she were hearing his confession. "I couldn't. I realized I didn't love her, and never could."

Her shoulders sagged with relief. "That does not mean—"

"Why didn't I love her, Sophie?" he demanded. His eyebrows had drawn together, arching down fiercely. She realized that the question troubled him strongly, more strongly than she had originally suspected. Sophie understood at that moment that there was a great deal more to Ian Blackpool than she was aware of, as though what she knew of him was a tiny cluster of flowers and the rest of him lay buried beneath the earth in a giant knotwork of roots.

"She was beautiful, charming," he continued hotly, "laughed often and easily. Everyone who knew her said she was one of the finest women they had ever met. She would have made an excellent wife. And she liked me, loved me possibly. But I couldn't do the same. No matter how much I tried. I liked her well enough, yet I just couldn't make myself love her." He looked off to the side, scanning the tree-lined horizon for something nameless and formless. "I vowed I would never marry without love. And so I left her, left England. Tried to find the answer to a riddle I couldn't solve."

"Simply because people tell you that you ought to love someone doesn't mean that you should or can," Sophie pointed out. "Love isn't a candle that can be lit and extinguished whenever you want. Either the flame exists between two people or it doesn't. You needed to find a better match."

Ian smiled grimly at her pun, but he shook his head. "I thought so, too. But everywhere I've gone, every woman I've met, I thought to myself, 'Is she the one? Can I love her?' The answer was always the same: no."

Sophie wondered where she fit into the long catalog of women Ian had known over the course of his life. Most likely she was an amusing footnote, the lady botanist who panted for his kisses. While her pride and heart stung from this notion, she made herself focus on his perceived dilemma.

"Don't you see," she said gently, "by promising to withhold yourself from marriage without love, it proves that you *are* capable of feeling it, that you know it can exist for you if you only gave it a chance. If," she added, her voice barely a whisper, "you found the right woman to share it with you."

"Someone like you, Sophie?" he asked without rancor. His eyes scanned her face, his expression kind but not exactly adoring.

She gulped, the blood draining from her face. She hadn't expected him to ask her so directly. "Why not?" she managed to counter.

Ian dropped the reins in one hand, reached through the hatch, and cupped her face tenderly. She found herself leaning into his rough, strong palm, grasping it with her own hand and closing her eyes to simply feel his skin against hers.

"Aside from the fact that I am a mountebank and you are a lady," he said quietly, "I can't. You're a wonderful woman and I'll make no secret about my desire for you, but I cannot love you, Sophie. I cannot love anyone."

Tears began to sting her eyes, and she blinked furiously to keep them back. She pulled away from his hand, straightening her back and forcing her voice to stay level. "I see."

Ian took hold of her chin and gently made her look directly at him. She compressed her lips together, willing herself not to let him see how fragile she was at that moment, how his rejection had cut her more deeply than she could fully understand.

"I don't want to hurt you," he said. "And that's why I don't want you to care too much about me. Sooner or later, we'll have to say good-bye, and when that time comes, I don't want you to feel any regrets. I don't want to break your heart."

"That's very . . ." Her voice faltered a little, and she paused to collect herself. "That's very thoughtful. But you needn't worry yourself about me, Ian." Sophie managed to fix a bright, false smile on her face. "I'm quite sure that I haven't any heart left to break."

Chapter Twelve

At last, they had found it.

Weeks of ever-widening searches had turned up no evidence of the peach-leafed bellflower growing symbiotically with the sessile oak. Sophie had begun to think that it was impossible, that these two plants could never co-exist without one destroying the other.

Yet here they were, growing together in a densely wooded forest. Sophie wasn't sure where *here* was exactly, but she felt as though she had been in these woods a thousand times without ever truly looking around her.

"Let us get to work right away!" Sophie said to Ian happily, but she could not help the sharp pierce of melancholy that came with her discovery. Once she made her observations and was able to isolate the property that allowed this strong, masculine tree and this trim flower—so delicate in comparison—to live together, their collaboration would be at an end.

Perhaps Ian was aware of how bittersweet this occasion was. As she gently prodded in the soil around the bellflower, she noticed he had suddenly disappeared from her side.

She tried to shrug. It was bound to happen eventually, his disappearance. She ought to accept it now with good grace. Sophie spread the bellflower's protective sepals to uncover the blossom and turned its pistils toward the sessile oak, yet she knew cross-pollination was futile. They were two different species. She couldn't stop herself from wishing, though.

"I'm not leaving yet," Ian murmured, suddenly pressing her against the oak with the length of his body. "I may not leave at all."

Joy assailed her. She swelled, bloomed, opening her lips as his came down on hers. They kissed and kissed for what seemed like days and days, until she grew dizzy. She could feel her wetness, her own petals unfurling completely. She was exposed and ready.

And then—oh, Lord—he was inside her, permeating every part of her. She knew, *knew* intuitively, that she'd found what she had been looking for. She wanted to weep, to cry out blessings. Surely something was going to explode, she wanted him, she wanted, she wanted—

Her own moans woke her.

Sophie opened her eyes and found herself staring at the canopy of her bed. She ran shaking hands over her face as she tried to sit up. Realizing that her strength had vanished, she leaned back against the headboard and stared with unfamiliar eyes around her bedroom in the bright light of morning. Everything seemed strange and hurtful, jagged with sharp edges and painfully distinct, after the liquid unity of her dream.

God, that *dream.*

Carefully, Sophie swung her legs around and lowered her feet to the floor. After testing her legs and finding that they wouldn't collapse out from under her, she padded over to her washstand and poured some water from the china pitcher into a bowl. She splashed her face, trying to erase the memory of her dream-mating with Ian from her sleepy mind, but her body betrayed her.

She was still hot and panting for him, right this moment, and she could tell that her body was prepared for a joining that would never take place. When was the last time a dream had affected her this way?

Looking at the image that stared back at her in the glass, pupils dilated, cheeks hectic and pink, Sophie knew that only Ian could wreak such havoc on her perfectly ordered existence.

Ever since their outing to Cheltenham, they'd both been careful to keep their distance. It seemed no good would come of an attachment. A fortnight had passed since that day when they had decided to try to avoid the threat of McGannon. It had been a solid two weeks of scientific study, during which Sophie had set up a small laboratory in a corner of the caravan to help organize Ian's botanical extracts. They had been traveling extensively throughout Gloucestershire in search of the sessile oak and peach-leafed bellflower, with Ian searching for the secret of love in the plants Sophie studied. No success yet in either department, but she had become ambivalent at best with regard to their quest.

Working closely with Ian all this time had been an exercise in pleasurable torture. And she could tell that he felt the same way about her. Well, she thought, turning away from the glass, at least they shared desire. He wanted her. She might be sheltered, but Sophie could tell when a man desired a woman. Yet whatever she felt for Ian, it went beyond a physical need.

How far beyond she didn't know, and wasn't sure she wanted to know. It didn't matter anyway, since he'd been very explicit in telling her that any feelings she had for him could not be reciprocated.

Or would not—if there was a difference.

She sat down in front of her vanity and undid her braid. As she ran a brush through her long, wavy mass of hair, she tried to laugh at herself. What a goose, entertaining sentiments for a roguish mountebank, like a character from one of George Lillo's melodramatic plays. But it didn't seem so funny and ridiculous when it was her own heart withering on the vine.

A tap sounded at the door, and Sophie's maid appeared with some tea.

"Do you have a sweetheart, Meredith?" Sophie asked as she was laced into her stays.

Her maid's eyes met hers in the glass, then looked down, a blush spreading over the girl's face. "I've been keeping company with someone, miss," Meredith answered shyly.

"Someone from the village?" Sophie's panniers were tied on next, followed by her petticoat.

"Eh, no, miss. What gown shall I fetch you?"

"The blue-checked cotton, I think. Who, then?"

Meredith returned from Sophie's closet with her gown draped across her arms. She looked a bit uncomfortable, ducking her head to avoid Sophie's probing gaze.

"I promise I won't tell anyone," Sophie said as she

settled into the dress. "I'm quite good at keeping secrets."

"You mean like that you've been seeing some mountebank during the day, miss?"

Sophie whirled around, gown undone. "How do you know about that?" Panic clutched at her.

The maid shrugged genially. "We all do, miss. All the servants. One of the men working at Mr. Morley's new place told us." She smiled, a bit apologetic. "Cabot Park is small, miss. Everyone knows everyone's business."

Sophie felt the room tilt. She'd been so smug about her clandestine meetings with Ian, thinking that she had fooled her parents for a fortnight. But she had overlooked a whole army of people in her haste. She should have been more careful. She should have considered. Grabbing Meredith's hand, Sophie implored, "Please, Meredith, *please* don't tell anyone else about Mr. Blackpool. Especially not my mother."

In a surprising show of comfort, Meredith patted Sophie's hand with her free one. She seemed to realize the familiarity of the gesture and stopped in mid-pat. "Don't worry yourself, miss," she said, gently removing her hand from Sophie's. "Nobody will tell tales about *you*, and especially not to your mother. You're a good mistress and," she added with another blush, "we all felt sorry for you when they took your books away."

"Ah," Sophie said, at a loss. The servants pitied her. How strange. "Well . . . thank you."

Meredith turned her around to get at the fastenings at the back of her gown. Slightly stunned, Sophie did her maid's bidding. "Everyone thinks that he's a hundred times better-looking than Lord Charles, miss,"

Meredith confided. "With such a smile on him that could charm even the coldest heart. And he's a thousand times more friendly than Lord Charles, too. Just the other night he gave William the footman a wonderful salve to help his swollen joints. And he didn't charge him anything. William said he felt like a young stripling again. He even did some high jumping to prove it."

Sophie almost laughed to think of the sober-faced footman leaping up and down, but she was more interested in all the new information her maid was giving her. Ian had been making his services available to the servants without her knowledge, interacting with them, socializing with them while she had to endure the upstairs unpleasantness of her parents and Lord Charles. She felt unease stirring within her. She did not mind him spending time with servants so much as the fact that he'd never mentioned anything to her about it; had, in fact, been leading something of a secret life after they parted company at the end of the day. She wondered if he didn't trust her. It seemed a ridiculous idea, especially after everything she had done with him and for him, but there didn't seem to be any other explanation.

"Sit down, miss, so I can finish dressing your hair." Meredith's instructions punctured Sophie's pensive silence.

As she watched her hair being coiled up into a neat bun and pinned into place, Sophie managed to rouse herself enough to ask, "You never answered my question, Meredith."

Placidly, the maid asked, "And what question was that, miss?"

"Who's your sweetheart?"

She must have seen that Sophie would not be dissuaded or distracted, so Meredith confessed bashfully, "John Driscoll, miss."

"Uncle Alforth's coachman?"

Meredith nodded. "Yes, miss. We started taking walks together a few months ago, and going to church together. I believe he is going to ask me to marry him."

"Do you want to marry him?" Sophie asked. "It's all right if you don't."

A shocked look spread across Meredith's open, artless face. "Of course I want to marry him! He's gentle and kind, and I think he's handsome, though some say he looks like a colt. He's the most wonderful man in the world." She seemed to glow with happiness and love with her description, and Sophie realized that she was actually jealous of her maid.

"When that day comes," Sophie said, attempting a smile, "you will have my most hearty felicitations."

Her hair done and her clothes in place, Meredith stepped back to let Sophie rise. She bobbed a curtsy. "Thank you, miss. Perhaps someday I can say the same to you."

The strained smile still on her face, Sophie answered, "Perhaps. Now I had better get downstairs. My parents do enjoy quizzing me at breakfast." She opened the door.

"Oh, but your father's in his study with Lord Charles," Meredith said. When Sophie could only stare in astonishment, her maid continued, "They've been in there since eight this morning. Nobody had any idea Lord Charles was such an early riser, but your father seemed to expect him."

Sophie managed to mumble out a thanks and hurried downstairs. A firm believer in reason and the scientific method, she usually scoffed at the idea of intuition. Cool logic had always been her friend in the face of emotional upheaval. Yet Sophie could not comfort herself with the practices of Galileo and Isaac Newton. As she made her way to her father's study, she had a very bad feeling about all of this.

He never enjoyed mornings. Ever since his collaboration with Sophie had begun, however, Ian had found himself getting up earlier and earlier to be ready to meet her. Rising from bed had become almost exhilarating, as though he were looking forward to greeting the challenges of the day. No, he amended as he pulled on his boots, he didn't look forward to the challenges so much as he anticipated seeing Sophie's sunny, pretty face and teasing her, or telling her stories until she laughed and called him ridiculous. He couldn't think of a better way to start the day.

Except waking up next to Sophie. That would be a piece of nirvana he would gladly welcome.

Ian shook his head, smiling wryly to himself as he finished dressing inside his caravan. He would never wake up next to Sophie. He wouldn't do anything with her beside collecting plant specimens and recounting tales. He knew the words to this song by heart, having memorized it weeks earlier. Hell, he'd even sung it to Sophie on their return from Cheltenham and, like a good scholar, she had also committed it to memory. She hadn't tried to kiss him since then, though Buddha and Krishna and every other deity knew well that Ian was being eaten alive by his craving for her. Damn it all, his education had been too good, so even now when he burned for this woman and he knew she wanted him, too, he was possessed by cursed honor and principle and had not touched her except in the most fraternal way he could muster.

Maybe he ought to lend her his copy of the *Kama Sutra*, let her explore possibilities outside the rigid English code of conduct. Ian laughed aloud, imagining Sophie applying the principles of her adored scientific method to sex, testing a position and carefully taking notes at the same time.

A picture of Sophie arched in one of the *Kama Sutra*'s more exotic congresses caused Ian's head to grow light and his groin heavy. Perhaps he ought to contemplate something else as he waited for her arrival this morning. It wouldn't do to have him greet her with a smile and a rampant erection. Then again, presented with such a spectacle, she could apply some of her scientific thoroughness to study *him* in depth instead of flowers.

All right, idiot, enough. You just want a woman, any woman. It's been over a month and that's a damned long time. He wouldn't be so obsessed with the delicious Miss Andrews if only he could muster some other female company.

Ian opened the door to his caravan and smiled in surprise at the young woman standing there. "And now I can grant my own wishes," he said with a laugh, stepping down.

She frowned, not understanding him, of course. Then she recollected herself and smiled in return. It was Mary, the daughter of yeoman farmer Chesterton, a girl Ian had seen many times in passing and spoken to once or twice without truly registering her presence. Yet here she was now, big as life, lush and cheeky at twenty years old and very glad to see him. She was holding a gigantic orange-striped cat, one of the rulers of the barn, who looked perfectly bored by everything around him.

"Morning, Mr. Blackpool," Mary said with a bouncy, breathy laugh. She set down the cat and tugged at her braided copper hair. "I thought maybe you'd left by now with Miss Andrews. I was planning on tidying up around here a bit while you were away. Bachelors," she added with a sly grin, "are always so messy."

Ian raised an eyebrow. "Do I look like I need cleaning?"

A smile curved her lips as she pressed herself against him. "Mr. Blackpool," she murmured, threading her arms up to wrap them around his neck, "you are very, very dirty."

She kissed him, her overripe body leaning into his, her mouth open and bold. Mary was a girl who'd done a lot of kissing in her day, and she did it well, with a sense of practice and assurance Ian recognized from some of the finer courtesans he'd met in his travels. He kissed her back, though he kept his hands lightly at her waist. Her lips promised him healthy, vigorous sex with no complications and no need for attachment. Maybe wishes did come true after all.

As he kissed her, though, he found himself distant and unmoved. Everything about young Mary Chesterton should have aroused him, but the only feeling he could muster was impatience. He wanted this kissing to be over and done with. Mary's hot, eager mouth simply aggravated him with its demands. Demands he didn't want to meet. All he wanted to do was finish getting ready to meet Sophie.

Mary suddenly stopped, pulling back. "I'm of the mind that I like my men to be thinking of *me* when we kiss," she said dryly, meeting his eyes.

Rather than deny it, Ian simply unlaced her fingers from around his neck. He felt cross, disconcerted—angry at himself, Mary, Sophie, the damned orange cat slinking away to the woods, anyone who could be blamed. He wasn't sure what the hell was going on, but he didn't like it.

Mary, however, was more sanguine. With a cheerful shrug, she stepped away from him and adjusted her bodice. "If you change your mind, you know where to find me." She gave him a wink and began to make her way back toward the house, all pretense of "tidying up" forgotten.

Moodily, Ian kicked around his encampment. Never, not once in his whole life, had he been unable to summon desire for a pretty, willing woman. He'd always taken advantage of opportunity, and in his line of work he had quite a bit of opportunity. But after a month of testing aphrodisiacs and self-enforced celibacy, the best he could manage with Mary Chesterton were some halfhearted pecks. He hadn't even made a move toward her ample breasts. Damn it all, he didn't know what was wrong with him. Perhaps he needed some of his own elixir. His body was failing him for the first time.

"Was that Mary Chesterton I passed?" Sophie's voice asked.

Ian looked up to see the woman herself walking toward him, looking bright and luscious in a pale blue cotton gown and freshly starched apron. She smiled, and all the parts of his body that Ian had begun to question suddenly sprang to life, leaping to greet her as eagerly as one did a long-awaited spring. Even his heart had begun to increase its rhythm at Sophie's approach. Ian groaned silently, cursing himself.

"Yes, she offered to clean up," he said, passing his hand over his face, "but we decided everything was neat enough, and she left."

"Are you well? You look a bit . . . colicky."

Ian snorted a laugh. "Yes, colic is definitely what I am feeling right now." He leaned back against the caravan, crossing his arms across his chest, feeling indeed like a thwarted, unwell baby. "What remedy can you give me for it?"

His ill temper seemed to catch her off-guard, since he had been so careful to remain jovial and playful whenever they were together since their argument in the caravan. But right now he didn't feel much like shielding himself or her with a lighthearted facade.

"I'm not an herbalist, so I cannot say for certain," she answered cautiously. "If I had a copy of Blackwell's *Herbarium*—"

"You and your damned books," he spat out.

Her eyes widened in shock and indignation. Gathering her skirts around her, she said, her voice precise, "I came to give you my regrets that we won't be able to work together today. But since you've decided to be an ass, I don't regret it at all."

Remorse was both immediate and unwelcome. He hated himself for lashing out at her like a callow boy denied his sweets, yet he was shaken deeply by his overwhelming desire for Sophie when he had felt nothing for Mary. As Sophie turned to go, Ian heard his own voice calling out to her. "Wait, Sophie. I'm sorry; I didn't mean it."

She regarded him over her shoulder, narrowing her

eyes. "If you are angry with me in some way, I wish you would simply come out and say so instead of playing games," she said. Her tone was cool, with an edge of hurt beneath.

It was unavoidable, Ian thought. No matter his warnings to her, and himself, sooner or later he was going to hurt her.

He exhaled deeply, stepping nearer so she was within arm's distance. "I'm not angry with you, Sophie. I'm just . . ." He searched for the right words.

He knew he couldn't tell her the truth—that he was obsessed with her, with her shrewd, nimble mind, her dexterous hands, the tender skin revealed at the nape of her neck, the inner recesses of her, both mental and physical, that he could never quite possess. He was so obsessed with her that he no longer knew himself anymore or, at least, he had lost track of the identity he had forged for himself seven years before.

Very slightly, she had moved to face him, peering at him closely as he struggled for some kind of answer.

"I'm a bit cagey this morning," he managed at last. "Not quite used to staying in one place for so long." He tried to shrug casually, but it didn't feel appropriate or even accurate, so he let the gesture die in an awkward raising and lowering of his shoulders.

"You needn't stay on my account," she said, holding his gaze steadily. A golden corona ringed her pupils, and today her eyes were more brown than green. Those eyes were like the shift from summer to autumn and back again. He could study them for hours. "If I do locate the sessile oak and the bell-flower, I can write to you and describe my findings."

"How would you find me? My home is my caravan—I have no location to receive your letters."

She did look away then, just a tiny flick of her gaze to the side, fixing on the brightly painted wagon in question. "I would think of something," she answered softly.

"And then let you take all the credit for my scientific discovery?" he asked. "No, I think I'll stay just the same."

"*Your* discovery?" she repeated, facing him fully, disbelieving.

He grinned at her, at himself. "Yes, my discovery. Haven't I been trekking across half of Gloucestershire and Warwickshire looking for these plants? Madam, you sorely underestimate me if you think I will quietly roll over and give you all the glory."

Sophie laughed, a small sign of forgiveness. And Ian eliminated an easy way of disentangling himself from their collaboration. He honestly had no idea anymore what he wanted for himself. He wanted the secret to love, he knew that much. But the world kept changing, the poles reversing, and here he was, grinning at Sophie Andrews like a happy fool, when what he felt like was a *mystified* fool.

"But did you say that we aren't meeting today?" he asked casually. He put his hands in his pockets because he was fighting the temptation to reach out and pull her into his arms. And then . . . he had a good idea what would come next, a wonderful idea . . . but the end result would not be so wonderful. Sophie would be hurt, and badly, with himself the culprit.

She nodded, her laughter quickly fading into a little frown of concern. As if sensing his prickliness, she avoided him and walked over to the open door of the caravan. She peeked inside at the tiny laboratory she had set up. A look of pure longing crossed her face as she contemplated the rows of bottles, each with a distillation of plant extracts, and the notebook in which she kept her precise notes in careful, slanted handwriting. Sophie didn't know it, but after she used her laboratory, the inside of the caravan smelled of her, the warm, grassy, sunny scent of her flesh permeating the wood and the fabric covering Ian's narrow bed. When he fell asleep now, he was surrounded by her. It was no wonder his dreams were full of Sophie. And her dreams, no doubt, were full of plants.

"Yes," she answered, distracted. "Lord Charles is having an assembly tonight in Cheltenham and we must attend."

"*We* meaning your family?"

"Mmm." Sophie turned and leaned against the top step of the caravan. "Lord Charles came to Cabot Park this morning and spent almost an hour with my father in his study."

Ian tensed. He did not like the sound of that at all.

"I asked what it was about, but no one would say," she continued. "All my mother told me is that Lord Charles is hosting a large formal ball, and as much as I tried to get out of going, I have to attend. Mother wants me to spend the day getting ready—but why I have to waste a whole day I cannot fathom." She picked at the flowers woven into the fabric of her gown, dissatisfaction plainly written in her sweetly beautiful face. "I hate assemblies," she said grumpily.

"I thought all young women loved parties." He ambled over to her, touching the toes of his boots to the tips of her little shoes peeking out from under the hem of her skirt. "Dancing, cards, music . . . flirting," he added with a gentle nudge of her shoe.

"I *do* like to dance," she admitted, a wry smile tugging at the corner of her mouth. She gave him a playful kick in response. "But there's altogether too much scrutiny at these kinds of events. I can never really enjoy myself because I'm afraid that I'll spill champagne on the host, or talk too loudly about fructification, or any number of social debacles."

"You'll be fine," he assured her. He wasn't so sure about himself, though. Ian thought of Sophie bejeweled and bedecked in her finest gown, parading before a host of undeserving eyes that included Vickerton but not himself. And what would he do with himself all night? True, he and Sophie parted company each day at sundown, but the thought of trading stories at the tavern, or sitting around inside his caravan and catching up on his reading of the *Mahabarata,* while lovely Sophie danced with unworthy boors made him want to throttle someone. Preferably Vickerton.

"I wish you could come, too," she said suddenly, then blushed at her own forwardness. "I mean," she amended, "at least I would have someone to talk to about things that really matter."

"Like fructification," he offered helpfully. "Which is what, exactly?"

She laughed in exasperation. "Have I taught you nothing? Fructification is the reproductive organs of a plant." As she realized the implications of what she was saying, she grew flustered all over again, Sophie tried but could not meet his eyes, as though swamped by an uncomfortable memory. At last she pushed herself to her feet, and Ian had to step back awkwardly to avoid colliding with her. Things grew rather strained between them for a few moments as they negotiated what had been a large field but was now a very small space.

"I have to go back," she said with a sigh, once she had established some distance between them. "I had to sneak out of the house and I'm sure Mother will be looking for me."

Ian found himself strangely at a loss for words. He honestly didn't want her to go to Vickerton's damned ball, mingling with people of her own class, leaving him alone to contemplate his choices. As he mulled over this prospect, he saw Sophie looking at him expectantly. He wasn't sure what to say. He knew she wanted him to ask her to find some way to avoid the ball, to stay with him instead. The fact that they shared the same desire sparked a flare of alarm in Ian. He had to disappoint them both.

"Be sure to dance the Siege of Limerick tonight," he managed finally, attempting a smile. "And don't mention reproductive organs of any kind, botanical or otherwise."

Clearly this was not what Sophie had hoped he would say. Unsure what to make of his strange farewell, Sophie merely raised her hand in parting and left for home by way of the forest, saying nothing.

Well, this is a fine state of affairs, Ian said to himself, watching her until she disappeared from view. The whole day free. He could do whatever he pleased until tomorrow.

It was going to be a long twenty-four hours. Staring at the space where Sophie had been, Ian could feel something building inside him, an inevitable slide into recklessness that he had managed to tamp down during the course of the past few weeks. His control began to slip—it was a physical sensation as palpable as an exhalation. The floodgates opened. And he welcomed wherever the deluge would take him with the dark pleasure a man afraid of heights might feel balancing on the edge of a deep chasm.

Chapter Thirteen

Sophie sipped at the glass of negus in her hand, watching the crowd and telling herself she ought to be having a good time—if not for her own enjoyment, then at least to spite Ian Blackpool.

Everyone was dancing the Siege of Limerick, and she had deliberately rebuffed a request to dance this particular set. That will show him, she thought heatedly. Sophie fanned herself, both to cool her temper and to stir a bit of air in the crowded, overheated assembly room. She knew she was being childish and irrational. Ian wasn't here, so what difference did it make which sets she danced and which she didn't, or if she was having a pleasant time? But, blast him, it wouldn't have hurt him to tell her that he would miss her, even a bit, the way she would miss him. She felt that her suspicions were now confirmed, and his interest in her hardly matched the way in which he had pervaded every aspect of her life, both waking and sleeping.

That was not entirely fair. He would never feel

what she felt, not because he did not want to, but because he *could not*. She was given little comfort from this, though.

Images from her dream flitted back into her mind, intertwined bodies and spreading petals, and she fanned herself harder to keep the telltale flush from her cheeks.

"Sophie, you will ruin your hair!" her mother scolded at her elbow. "Your fan must not be abused so."

An automatic apology sprung to Sophie's lips as she turned to Caroline. "It's very hot in here," she said by way of explanation.

"Yes, your father has gone to seek the relative cool of the gaming room," Caroline answered. "Alforth refused to come. Impossible man. He hates such events. And it is quite a crush Lord Charles has provided this evening." She and her daughter looked around the assembly hall, one approving and the other barely tolerant. Sophie glanced at her mother surreptitiously, admiring even as she was intimidated. Her mother had powdered her hair so she looked like a queen, with a rope of pearls threaded through her silver curls. She wore an elegant ice-blue satin gown with an abundance of Flemish lace and carried an ivory fan. Caroline looked the epitome of cool sophistication.

Sophie, against her mother's wishes, had picked her favorite gown—an almost severely simple cherry taffeta of Spitalfields silk, the lustrous fabric embroidered only slightly with tiny flowers at the low neckline and elbow-length sleeves, with the barest froth of lace peeking out. The sack gown was fitted and fell down her back in two heavy pleats from her shoulders to the floor. Her petticoat was two shades darker than the gown itself, more embroidered than the rest. Also to her mother's dismay, Sophie had rejected jewels, powder, and cosmetics, wearing only a nosegay of violet pinned to her stomacher and violet flowers tucked into her simple hairstyle. Her one consolation to Caroline's desire for show were creamy pearl earrings.

"I do wish you had powdered those freckles of yours," Caroline whispered behind her fan. "You look as though you've spent the entire summer in the garden."

"I suppose that I have," Sophie murmured back. She, too, had noticed earlier in the day that the many hours outdoors with Ian had turned her into a wild-looking creature with brown skin, golden freckles, and pale honey-colored hair. She shrugged now as she had shrugged then. If she was destined to look common, so be it. Her freedom was worth more than her vanity.

And though she had received many approving glances from gentlemen this evening, her vanity still stung at Ian's dismissal of her earlier that day.

Blast it, why did he have to keep reappearing in her thoughts like an unbidden spirit?

"Stop frowning so," her mother chided, breaking into her thoughts. "You look cross, and if you look cross, Lord Charles will think you didn't enjoy your dance."

She hadn't, actually, between Lord Charles's leering at her, Caroline's pointed glances, and the speculative looks of the guests. Sophie felt as though she were on display, ogled and assessed like a broodmare. "Mother," Sophie said tightly, her patience at an end, "I am twenty-three years old and if I choose to frown, then, by God, I will do so. Kindly keep your criticisms of me to a dull roar so I may enjoy the music."

Caroline gaped at her, startled by her daughter's unusual outburst.

"If I may offer a word of advice," Sophie said, setting down her glass, "you may want to close your mouth. People will stare. Now, excuse me, I think I'll get some air. It's much too stuffy in here."

Before her mother could respond, Sophie sailed through the crowd. She did not try to suppress her feeling of triumph, minimal and petty as it was. She seldom had any opportunity to stand up to her mother. The one aspect that dampened her spirits was the fact that it had been her irritation with Ian that had fueled her sudden fortitude against Caroline. She wanted to owe her courage to herself and no one else.

She really did need a bit of air. Lord Charles had filled the ball with everyone from the local gentry and people coming from as far away as Oxford and Somerset. The Vickerton town house was too small to accommodate such a crowd, so the Cheltenham assembly room had been let instead. As she made her way through the crowd, Sophie murmured greetings and nodded to the faces she had known almost her whole life, though there were individuals here and there she was unfamiliar with. Life outside London ensured a close network of genteel families, with a self-contained system of marriages that kept the stock pure and the company always the same.

Her parents wanted so badly to absorb Sophie into this world, where life consisted of a string of card parties, shooting parties, bridal parties, and any other number of parties that were designed to fill up leisure time but contribute nothing to humanity outside of their own sense of privilege.

She could not do it. If Ian felt that he was born

without the ability to love, then Sophie had been born without the aptitude for indolence. She had to make something of herself, be worthwhile, not decorative.

Almost reaching the doors that opened on to the balcony, Sophie was stopped by Lord Charles's greeting. She saw him maneuvering through the crowd to reach her, a smile of triumph on his face. And why should he not feel triumphant? The ball was a success.

She thought about pretending not to hear him, but she had looked up when he called and knew it would be impossible to avoid him. So she waited.

As he came closer, she took stock. He wore a fashionable bag wig and had lightly dusted his face with powder, though sweat had caused some of it to run. His suit was of emerald green satin, covered with heavy golden embroidery along the cuffs, pockets, and lapels. His yellow waistcoat shone like an egg yolk in the glow of hundreds of candles. He truly was a good-looking man, the height of fashion and refinement, and Sophie could not have been less happy to see him.

"Lord Charles," she said, dropping into a curtsy as he neared. She watched his eyes dart to the front of her dress as he bowed in return. "You have proven yourself an accomplished host this evening."

He pressed another glass of wine into her hand, which she didn't want, and drank from his own. "Indeed, Sophie, I look forward to the time when I may share my hospitality with a wife by my side."

"I assume you mean your *own* wife, sir, and not someone else's," she said dryly.

Lord Charles laughed, not an unpleasant sound, but certainly not nearly as affecting as Ian's laugh. *Stop it, Sophie.*

"Oh, my dear lady," Vickerton drawled, "you are wit personified."

"Alexander Pope may claim that title rather than myself," she replied. "I am only a humble botanist."

Sophie realized her mistake the moment the words left her mouth. Lord Charles had lost all pretense of humor and looked piercingly at her.

"Your parents had assured me you were finished with that claptrap," he said, his voice cold.

Sophie was suddenly tired of pretense. The novelty had worn off and now she wanted to come forward, make herself known as she really was. She realized that being with Ian had spoiled her, made her accustomed to being honest and unguarded. She did not want to lead two lives anymore. She wanted one life, whole and unbroken. "What if I were not finished?" she suddenly demanded. "What if a botanist is all I shall ever be? If the study of plants is my life, Lord Charles, will you keep spending every night at Cabot Park eating our food and playing piquet? Will you accept me as I am? Or will you flee for the safety of comfortable society?"

Her immediate reversal of the situation caught Vickerton off-guard. He looked around nervously, uncomfortable under Sophie's direct, sharp gaze and interrogation. "Please, Sophie," he muttered. "My guests are staring."

"A man of your standing should not concern himself with the censure of small-minded individuals," she answered. "I know that I would wish my husband to be as accepting of me as I was of him." She stared down into the dark wine in her glass and saw her reflection, tiny and dim, staring back at her. She felt as small as that reflection, adrift in the crowded assembly hall and lost under the deluge of music, noise, and expectation.

"Miss Andrews . . . Sophie, your father and I—" Lord Charles managed, but was cut off by the excited rumblings of the crowd.

Both Sophie and Vickerton turned their attention to the open door where new guests made their entrance. A country gathering such as this one employed no master of ceremonies to announce new arrivals, but the other guests were doing a fine enough job as they remarked on the latest to join the assembly. Someone new had appeared.

"Who the devil?" Lord Charles exclaimed, unconcerned about cursing in front of Sophie. "I don't know that fellow."

Sophie did.

Dressed in a suit of embroidered midnight-blue velvet, including the waistcoat, neckcloth snowy white against dark skin, legs lean and muscular encased in fine white stockings, hair pulled back and held in place by a large black bow, Ian Blackpool stood at the entrance of the ball, gazing around him with the surest sense of noblesse oblige Sophie had ever seen. He looked completely in command, totally at ease, ferociously masculine, and devastatingly handsome. If Sophie did not know that he made his living standing on High Street selling bottles of love potions, she would have bet her entire herbarium that he was of the gentry. More so than anyone in the room.

She was dumbfounded. Absolutely and utterly. And enthralled. Without exaggeration, he was the most beautiful man she had ever seen.

And he was looking right at her.

Her insides leapt, both with fear and excitement.

Sophie took a gulp of her wine and began to fan herself. She needed to hide the fact that she knew him, but more than that, she had to disguise her immediate reaction to him. Should anyone glance her way, they would see a woman who had entertained the most carnal fantasies imaginable about this newcomer, was entertaining them even now. Much as Sophie wanted honesty in her life, this was not the time to pursue it.

As if sensing his natural nobility, the crowd parted to admit him into the room. Slowly, confidently, Ian made his way toward Sophie and Lord Charles. She felt her heart slam inside her chest, unable to move, breathe, or do anything else but watch him come closer.

Oh, God, he wouldn't. He absolutely would not unmask her here, in front of Gloucestershire's finest families and biggest gossips. If he had decided to end their partnership, this would be the most spectacular way of all to do so.

Perceiving his guests' partiality for this newcomer, Lord Charles tried to straighten to his full height, but even so, Ian had almost half a head on him. Comparing the two men, one a refined dandy, the other a lethally magnetic male, Sophie could only muster pity for Vickerton. Standing in close proximity to Ian only brought out the lord's deficiencies and highlighted the mountebank's advantages.

Ian stopped before them and gave a bow that was both polished and slightly scornful. She did not know if his mocking was meant for her, Lord Charles, or the whole party, but she tried mightily to keep her features as impassive as possible. One thought did escape her in the midst of her turmoil: How on earth did a traveling charlatan learn to make a leg like a member of the House of Lords?

Instead of speaking to Sophie, as she had been bracing for, Ian turned his attention to the man standing beside her. She blanched. Ian had not been wearing a mask on the day of the fair at Cheltenham, and Lord Charles could have seen him plainly. She prayed that Vickerton had a faulty memory.

"Lord Charles," Ian said, addressing Vickerton like an old friend and smiling as he pressed a hand to his chest, "forgive my intrusion, but I was in town and heard that you were hosting an assembly tonight. I thought to myself, 'Why not look up the old fellow and talk about old times together? It will be an excellent surprise.'"

Vickerton blinked. "Do I know you?"

Ian chuckled as though Lord Charles had made a terrific joke and then sobered a bit when he realized that no joke had been intended. "You don't remember?"

Please, please, don't say anything about the fair, Sophie silently begged Ian.

"Ian Nichols, from university. I was a friend of Jack's."

"Jack? Jack Pringle?"

"Yes, Pringle, of course. You remember him, don't you?"

"Always getting into trouble with the bulldogs at Balliol." Lord Charles chortled, Ian joining him and looking decidedly more comfortable. "Yes, now it comes back to me. Ian Nichols, eh? I thought you looked familiar, but I just couldn't place the face."

Ian waved graciously. "After a few pints at the King's Arms, everyone's face gets a bit blurry around the edges."

"A few pints? In my day, it was a whole hogshead!"

The two of them laughed as though it were old times again, and Sophie thought she might actually faint with released apprehension. Ian's charm worked on men as well as women—that's what made him a successful mountebank. Lord Charles truly *wanted* to believe he and Ian were old friends, and so he accepted the first thread of possibility thrown his way. They continued to chat, Ian's answers vague enough, with a hint of specificity to reinforce their likelihood, and Lord Charles was happy to claim this handsome and smart newcomer as an old Oxford comrade.

Sophie watched and marveled. She thought she would have grown used to Ian's ability to reshape himself to suit his needs, but she was still astonished by how completely he could transform himself. If Alforth were nearby, they would be the only two in the room who did not fully believe Ian was an old schoolmate of Lord Charles. She felt profoundly uneasy in the midst of her relief. Not for the first time she wondered how well she really knew this man and who he truly was, underneath the complex layers of his identity. Though he'd satisfied her curiosity about his life abroad, never had he spoken in detail about his family, his origins, or anything of substance outside of his aborted plans for marriage.

Surely he had to be hiding something. Yet she didn't know what.

"And who is your charming companion, Vickerton?" Ian asked, interrupting her rumination. So it was Vickerton now, and not Lord Charles. *My, how fast you work, Ian.*

All smiles and puffed pride, Lord Charles said, "Sophie Andrews, may I introduce you to Mr. Ian Nichols? Ian, Miss Andrews."

Sophie had no choice but to curtsy and let Ian take her hand. "Mr. Nichols," she managed. They had both been scrupulous to avoid touching each other since the day of the fair, and now the sensation of his warm skin against her own, his fingers brushing the sensitive flesh of her hand, sent hundreds of tiny hot filaments through her. She was starved for his touch, even as its familiarity assailed her. Ian bent over her hand, a model of courtesy, but his eyes fixed hers with a look full of awareness, as though everything that surrounded her had suddenly fallen away and she was as bare as a young stripling buffeted by the storm of his gaze.

"A pleasure, Miss Andrews," he murmured, and then pressed his lips not on top of her hand, but on the tender flesh between her fingers. Sophie barely managed to stay standing. Damn it, what kind of game was he playing?

The musicians struck up a new tune, and Ian said, grinning, "Vickerton, you won't call me out if I ask your lovely Miss Andrews to dance." It wasn't a question, Sophie realized, but a subtle command. He still had not let go of her hand.

Lord Charles was easily manipulated. He smiled indulgently, with Sophie his prized possession being admired by his friends, just as he'd hoped. Except Ian wasn't his friend.

"Not a bit," Vickerton said magnanimously. "I insist. Sophie can be far too serious for her own good. Help her lighten her mood, Nichols."

With that benediction, Ian led Sophie toward the dancers taking their places. She wanted to pull her hand away and run from the room, take shelter in some far-off and forgotten corner, but Ian was touching her and, curse it, she didn't want him to stop. A fine scientist she was, letting pure emotion rule her judgment instead of reason. She knew she should disengage herself from his grip, excuse herself, and seek the safety of the ladies' retiring room. But she did not, of course. She sent him a mutinous glare as he stood opposite her on the dance floor. When the dance began in earnest, she saw that he knew the steps perfectly. Perhaps he had been a dancing master to noblemen. Sophie was growing weary of guessing.

"You don't look happy to see me," Ian said softly as they came together for the set.

"What are you doing here?" she hissed back.

He smiled wryly, acknowledging the fact of his transgression. "Can't a mountebank have any fun?"

She looked around with disbelieving eyes. The elegant room was full of brittle, polished people, laughing, fanning themselves, assessing those around them with calculating stares. A girl was introduced to a wealthy, older bachelor by her acquisitive parents. Roars of anger and triumph issued from the gaming room, where fortunes were won and lost over a single hand of cards. Even now, a red-faced man stalked from the room, pure rage in his face. The plant kingdom was much more civilized. "You call this fun?"

Ian shrugged as Sophie walked the steps of the dance around him. "Perhaps not."

"Then why risk exposure and possible scandal by coming here tonight?"

He seemed ready to toss a glib reply but paused and became more thoughtful. Sophie guessed he was marshaling his thoughts, preparing a response that was amusing and untrue. They went through a whole other figure before he said, almost too low for her to hear, "I missed you."

Any answer she had prepared died immediately as she absorbed this information. She had readied herself for whatever he might say to her, a fanciful tale, a boastful remark, but not this simple statement that seemed, she hoped, genuine.

"I—" she began. She tried to answer in proportion to his manner, but his expression was unreadable, opaque. Sophie wanted to cry out in frustration. Ian's structure was more complicated than any organism she knew, botanical, animal, or otherwise. He never did what she thought he would, and this tormented her as she was drawn in closer to him.

She would not play his game. She did not want to play any games at all. Finally, in challenge to his hooded glance, she told him the truth. "I am glad you came. I missed you, too."

That caught him by surprise, she noted, as his perfect footing caught very slightly. He righted himself before anyone else noticed, coming across the floor to take her hand in the final pattern of the dance. With an inward smile, Sophie realized that they were literally embodying the metaphor of their relationship, gingerly dancing around each other in the space of convention and expectation.

Ian had the body of an athlete and looks that could charm any woman of virtue into surrendering that commodity, but Sophie had the distinct impression that, for the first time, Ian was uncertain. Not very uncertain, but just a little, just enough to give her confidence. She smiled genuinely, her first of the evening.

The dance ended, the partners bowed to each other, and an emboldened Sophie bent down and whispered in Ian's ear, "Meet me by the ladies' retiring room. I want to talk to you."

Without letting him speak, she glided past him, not even looking over her shoulder. Sophie was not a believer in certainties—recent events had obliterated any sense of security she might have once possessed—but she knew with absolute faith that Ian would follow her. He had to. They still had the rest of their dance set to finish.

It had been a mistake to come. A mistake to tell her why. He was deliriously glad he had done so. Ian watched Sophie sway from the room with a command of herself she had never shown before. Perhaps that was the reason he had infiltrated Vickerton's damned ball—to see her thus, magisterial, sensual, evolving yet further into an exotic hybrid. She was delicious in her dark red dress—he would pop her whole into his mouth if he could.

He moved from the dance floor to grab a glass of wine, knowing he could not immediately quit the room right after Sophie. For all his audacity, some part of him had to keep functioning logically, and so he took a few swallows of wine—it wasn't very good, and a poor substitute for the taste of Sophie—and noticed an exceptionally striking middle-aged woman frowning at him from across the assembly hall. Ian placed her as Sophie's mother almost at once. It was encouraging to see how well Sophie would age, since Caroline Andrews was one of the most attractive women in attendance. And she was using her beauty like a weapon now, showing Ian with all the imperiousness she could muster that she was very, very angry with him. Something about Ian's dance with

Sophie had shown Caroline that there was more going on than a simple set. No, she didn't like him, a stranger, muddying up the waters.

Alarm ricocheted through him. God, there could only be one reason for a ball like this. He had to get to Sophie.

Ian took a step to follow her, but Lord Charles appeared in front of him. "Did you say you were a fellow of Balliol, or was it Trinity?" he asked.

Thrusting the glass of wine into Vickerton's hand, Ian answered, "Yes," and left immediately.

He heard Lord Charles stammering behind him, but his thoughts were elsewhere. As he maneuvered through the crowd, he saw several women smile invitingly at him behind their fans, a few gentlemen scowling, and Caroline Andrews trying to approach him. He was trapped in a genteel maze. But he'd learned well in his time abroad and in the lower echelons of society. In a moment, he had slipped from the room.

The laughter of women told him where to go to find the retiring room. Fewer candles cast the corridor in a soft, dim light, and his shoes clicked on the wooden floor. He bowed to some young wives returning to the ball, who promptly burst into giggles, but saw no sign of Sophie. Had she somehow eluded him, left the assembly altogether in some misguided need for revenge? Revenge for what, he wasn't certain. Ian was on the verge of returning to the ball when a door opened beside him and Sophie's arm reached out from the shadows to grab him.

"In here," she whispered.

He did not need further urging. He stepped into the darkness and heard the door close behind him. It had to be a small room, for it was full of the sounds of her gown, silk rustling against itself as she moved. The sound enveloped him as she came closer, with the dull noise of conversation, music, and dancing floating in. The thick, undulating scent of violet filled his lungs. She wore it in her hair and pinned to her bodice. He wanted to crush the purple, scented flowers with his hands, his mouth, as she stood near him. In this darkened little room, he was disoriented, and he used her as his guide.

"This is an extra gaming room," she explained. He felt the warm air of her breath near his collarbone and his body turned immediately to hers.

His eyes were growing accustomed to the dark, and he was able to make out a few details. Windows lined the wall, ambient light filtering in, pale edges appearing on the surfaces of some empty card tables, a lone chair, gilt on the plaster wall decorations, and Sophie. He remembered the night they drove from McGannon's hideout to Cabot Park together, the way the moon had turned her ethereal, too lovely to be touched.

Much had changed since then, mostly his need to feel her, know her. Diffused light gilded the curve of her neck into her shoulder, turned her hair into a halo, and shadowed her expression. He reached out for her, but she moved away, so his fingertips brushed against silk taffeta.

"How do you know that friend of Vickerton's?" she asked. "Jack Pringle?"

"I don't."

"But how—?"

"Everyone knows someone named Jack. I let Vickerton fill in the details, and just agreed with him."

Her laughter, low and whiskey-colored, washed

over him. He watched her move near a card table, run her fingers over its inlaid surface. "And what about all that information about Oxford? Surely a mountebank never attended university."

"I've been to Oxford Town," he said, which was true. "It didn't take long to figure a few things out."

"And how did you know the dance steps? Where did you get your clothing?"

"Is this why you've brought me here? To ask all sorts of questions?"

She turned to face him, bracing her hands on the back of the table and leaning back. Her breasts were pushed forward, the light forming gold half-moons on her skin, and he knew they would be fragrant with violet. He realized then that there wasn't a damn thing he could do to stop himself; desire was there beside him, whispering such honeyed words into his ear, pushing him nearer and nearer to Sophie. He wasn't strong enough to resist. He did not want to be strong, not anymore.

"No, I—I want to know why you came here tonight."

He took steps toward her. "You know why."

Sophie shook her head. He could sense a hundred different emotions in her: bravado, excitement, hope, some fear. And here she was, alone with him in a darkened room. He would explode in a minute. Then, as he drew even closer, so the fabric of her skirt enveloped his legs and all he had to do was bend forward a little and their torsos would touch, she nodded slowly. "Yes," she said at last, "I think I do know."

He placed his hands atop hers as they gripped the edge of the table. He wanted to press himself down onto her, but his arms bore his weight and he moved so that the full lengths of their bodies were in contact. She gasped, tipping her chin up to look at him, but, he hoped, not to protest. Her mouth was inches from his own.

But he wanted more than that. He wanted . . . oh, merely everything, and more. He thought of her family so close by, the ninny Vickerton presiding over his country ball like a tiny potentate, and, even more dimly, his own father far away. Mainly, he thought of Sophie, soft and tight against him, eyes shining in the shadows as she regarded him. And he bent his head to kiss her neck.

Ian felt rather than heard her intake of breath against his lips as he tasted her skin, tiny spasms of sensate pleasure as he drew his tongue down her throat to rest in the hollow at the base. She was satiny, floral, corporeal. He'd never tasted her skin before and grew intoxicated from it, from her. His hands still held hers down, though she tried briefly to tug free, and he moved lower to lavish kisses on her breasts.

"Ian—" she cried softly, and then moaned with her head thrown back as his mouth trailed along the delicate flesh. *Ripe*. The word flitted into his mind as he caressed her with his mouth. He released her hands so he could touch her with his own, though the stiff fabric of her stays frustrated his attempts. He cursed dressmakers as he struggled to learn her body, his hands cupping her breasts from the sides. Her fingers wove into his hair, pressing him closer as they both leaned onto the table.

"Damn," he cursed, and thrust his hands under her skirts to touch her more fully. Through the oceans of silk and petticoats, he found her legs. She wore fine

stockings, gartered at the knee, and beyond that—
"God, Sophie"—the bare skin of her thighs. He
kissed her fully on the mouth and she licked his lips,
urging their mouths apart, mewling, while his hands
moved upward, over the incredible geography of her
legs. Shapely and lean from hours walking through
fields and forests, unbearably sleek beneath his
rougher hands. When he lifted her up so she sat on
top of the card table, her legs wrapped around him.
One of her dainty shoes clattered to the floor. Neither
of them noticed.

Ian's finger brushed the hem of her drawers. She
shuddered but did not pull away. Delirious with the
feel of her, he moved higher, edging past the lacy hem
to the juncture of her thighs, where he found damp,
soft curls. She cried out again and slowly, very slowly,
he began to trace intimate patterns against her folds,
and he wanted so badly to claim her then, he used
every drop of control he had available to hold himself
in check. As he touched her with growing boldness,
he began to move his hips against hers. He couldn't
stop himself. God, touching her most private place
like this beneath yards of silk, hearing her softly
keening out his name again and again as she surren-
dered to him, he thought he would weep with erotic
longing. He'd been right: She possessed an innate sensuality that humbled him even as he ached with sexual need.

Then he slipped one finger inside her and had to
swallow her cry with his mouth. No assembly would
be large enough to drown out her sounds of pleasure.
She gripped his arms with surprising strength, nearly
lifting herself off the card table. He was momentarily
surprised to find no maidenhead because he knew

without a doubt she was a virgin. He'd heard of girls born without them, or losing that intimate barrier through riding or being active. Lord knew that Sophie was an active woman. He had proof enough before him, around his fingers. Then he stopped caring about her maidenhead because she was moaning and gripping his shoulders, her head back, her eyes half-closed. With deft fingers, he caressed her. God, she was tight and hot and liquid, moving faster, until her cries came closer and closer together and, at last, she bit into his shoulder to stifle her scream as her body tensed, arching up. Then she fell back, lying across the table fully, panting.

"Ian, Ian, what was that?" she murmured, trying to pull him down with her.

"The beginning," he growled. "But I don't think this table will hold us both. Come here."

Bonelessly, she slid into his arms as he tried to gather her up. He had to move her; maybe they could lie on the floor. He didn't really care about that or the assembly hall full of revelers separated by a mere wall, or anything else. He had to have her. Right now.

A profusion of silk skirts and pliant limbs. She could not seem to gain control of her body, but she weighed little and he began to ease her slowly to the ground. At least there was a rug to cushion them. He knelt between her legs as she stared up at him through heavy lids, her hands coming up to run over his face, his shoulders, down his arms. He caught one of her hands and pressed it to his mouth.

"I've wanted you for a long time," he breathed against the heel of her palm.

"I've wanted you my whole life," she whispered back.

That should have made him stop. She tried so hard to be fearless, but he could damage her in ways she had no way of imagining. He hesitated for only a second, gazing down at her, her eyes sleepy with need, her body ready for him. He could not stop. Lowering himself on top of her, Ian pushed her skirts back up. Then his hands went to the buttons at the front of his breeches. The only thing he needed now was her.

"Sophie? Sophie?" A voice that could only be Caroline Andrews's sounded in the hallway. Ian stilled immediately. "Have you seen my daughter?" she asked someone. There was a mumbled reply.

For a few seconds, Ian thought he might actually go mad. He looked down at Sophie, her eyes squeezed tightly shut and her throat working reflexively.

"Maybe she'll go away," she whispered.

"I already looked in the retiring room," Caroline said, her tone edgy. "I thought I saw her leave with . . . never mind . . . I'm sure she's around somewhere. Perhaps in one of these rooms."

Ian was on his feet in an instant, lunging for the door. There was no lock. The door swung open at the same moment he stepped behind it, hiding himself from view. Light poured into the room, hard and glaring, and Ian saw that Sophie had sat up, blinking, and was trying to straighten her dress.

"What are you doing in here?" her mother demanded. "Lord Charles wants you in the ballroom."

"I was feeling faint," Sophie said, sounding hazy, "and needed somewhere quiet and dark to lie down."

"For goodness' sake, Sophie! What will people think?" Caroline stepped into the room to help her daughter reassemble herself. Ian took advantage of

Mrs. Andrews's distraction and noiselessly left the room.

He was shaking. He had acted like a green boy. One minute more and Caroline Andrews would have discovered her youngest daughter being thoroughly ravished on the floor of a gaming room in a public assembly hall. He felt as tense as a drawn bow, ready to snap at the slightest movement. He was unbearably hard, almost throbbing. Resting his head against the wall in the hallway, he forced himself to take several deep breaths. All he needed to do was get out of this place without anyone noticing him. Not Vickerton, not Sophie's family. No one.

And then? He had no idea.

He did know that if he endured any more disruptions when he was with Sophie, both his patience and his sanity would shatter. The last time he had suffered such a case of sexual frustration, he'd been fourteen and groping in a hayloft with a dairy maid. In that instance, his gratification had been postponed by a few hours, and the dairy maid had been a willing but undistinguished partner in what was to become his deflowering. Everything he'd experienced that day was but a tiny dot in comparison to the monstrous, savage hunger he felt for Sophie.

He put his finger in his mouth—the same finger he'd had inside her. It tasted of violet's and Sophie. But his reverie ended when he heard Caroline Andrews say, "I don't understand how you lost one of your shoes!" He made himself shove away from the wall and mechanically walk into the assembly hall.

The crowd retreated from his vision as he moved toward the exit. He felt drugged, yet keenly alert at the same time. Ian did not want to risk looking back at Sophie as he fled. He didn't think even his skills at dissembling could disguise the fact that he'd been deep in the throes of lovemaking with her when they had been ruthlessly interrupted. Yet as he neared the door, he sensed that Sophie had come into the room. He wanted to turn, to see her again, but felt that somehow everything would fall apart if he did.

This must be what Orpheus felt like, he thought, with Euridice trailing behind him out of Hades. One look would damn them both.

Suddenly, the music stopped. The crowd quieted. Behind him, Vickerton's voice rang out in the silent room. "My friends, may I have your attention?"

Now. Go now, when no one will notice your departure. But he couldn't leave. He still faced the door, bracing one hand on the jamb in preparation for flight, letting Lord Charles's words contend with his back. If anybody noticed the insult, they made no comment.

"Though I am glad to bring you all here tonight," Vickerton continued, "to dance, to drink, to make merry—" Someone in the crowd seconded that notion raucously. Lord Charles laughed with the rest of his guests and went on. "I own that I have an ulterior motive in calling everyone together. Much to the despair of my parents, I have been a bachelor for far too long, but I intend to remedy that situation this evening.

"Many of you have met my bride-to-be, and there are those who have known her all her life. It is my fervent wish to join our lives together, and I can think of no more deserving woman. Tonight, with the hearty approbation of her family, I make our engagement official." Vickerton paused, and Ian froze with dread. "Ladies, gentlemen, may I present to you my future wife, Miss Sophie Andrews!"

The assembly hall filled with the discordant sound of clapping and shouts of congratulations. Ian gripped the door frame until his hand ached and slowly turned around. He picked Sophie out of the crowd immediately. She stood, wedged between an exultant Vickerton and her parents, ashen-faced and stunned, as she accepted the felicitations of a hundred well-wishers. She looked as if she might be sick.

The desire to shove his way through the crowd, scoop her up in his arms, and carry her out of the damned Cheltenham Assembly Hall was overwhelming.

Instead, he forced his hand to let go of the door frame and propelled himself into the night.

Chapter Fourteen

Sophie ran.

She ran as hard as her heart and legs would allow. Through the warm night, lit by a full, pitiless moon. Down the road, across fields, through woods, anywhere she could go. She barely felt the sting of branches against her face or the sharp press of rocks through her thin slippers. No cognizant thought entered her mind—all she wanted was to lose herself in the pure physical mechanics of running.

She was wearing only her nightgown and rail, having changed out of her dress, stays, panniers, and petticoats. Her hair was unbound, streaming behind her. Violets were knotted in the loose tresses. If she looked like a madwoman escaping from Bedlam or some kind of female Lear, she didn't care. She was past caring about anything but the burning air in her lungs and throat, the span of her legs pushing and moving against the ground at her feet.

After Lord Charles's announcement, Sophie had

been too shocked to speak, to do much of anything but feel the force of a hundred guests converging upon her to wish her well in her new marriage. She had gone from the greatest pleasure she had ever experienced to one of the most awkward and appalling scenes she could remember. Sophie had been unable to correct the well-wishers. Squeezed as she was between her parents and Lord Charles, she could not move. She tried to find Ian. He was gone. Even this barely punctured the dismal bubble that engulfed her. Finally, she managed to turn to her parents and demanded to be taken home. She used no excuses, pleaded no headaches; she simply had to get out of there. Her mother looked as though she might argue, but one glance at her daughter's face made her reconsider.

Still too furious to speak, Sophie had been silent for most of the ride home. Her father stared at his buckled shoes and her mother tried to keep her chin high, but embarrassment kept overtaking her.

She heard her mother calling for her as she ran up the stairs into the house. She could not even wish her uncle a good night, rushing past him to get inside. It was late, most of the servants already gone to bed. After helping her undo the fastenings in her gown, Sophie dismissed Meredith immediately. She dressed for bed but found the prospect of sleep utterly impossible. Like a trapped beast, she whirled around her room, her mind churning with rage and sorrow.

She had to get out. She remembered that Ian had once climbed the ivy outside her window. In a short while, Sophie found herself tearing across the countryside of Sevendowne clad only in her white nightgown and robe—an angry ghost haunting the peaceful hills, searching for release and finding none.

It wasn't until she was standing in front of Ian's caravan that Sophie had any idea where she was going.

Her hand was upon the door pull before she'd given it any further consideration. Sophie would let herself be ruled purely by instinct tonight. Her fine machinations and careful deliberation had gotten her nowhere. Worse than nowhere—she was being forced into a marriage she didn't want by parents who viewed her with less consideration than one of her father's prize horses. *I am my own woman,* she thought to herself as she pushed open the door. *I can do what I please with myself.*

She found herself staring down the barrel of a pistol.

"Ian!"

"Jesus, Sophie," Ian muttered, lowering his weapon. "Give a man some warning." He was sprawled across his narrow bed, still dressed in his finery from earlier in the evening, though his coat had been discarded and lay in a heap on the floor, his cravat undone. In one hand he held a bottle, and the other grasped the pistol, which he was shoving underneath his pillow. He did not invite her in, apologize, or even sit up. Instead, he put the bottle to his lips and drank deeply, his expression opaque, his eyes never leaving hers.

Her gaze darted to the candle blazing next to her little laboratory. Its light was harsh compared to the moon's glow outside. "You shouldn't lie in bed and drink with a candle burning," she said, stepping in. "If you fell asleep, you could go up in flames."

He shrugged and wiped his mouth with the back of his hand. "It doesn't make any difference," he drawled. "I burn either way."

She leaned against the wall, unwilling to sit, and folded her arms across her chest. "Are you drunk?"

Ian contemplated the bottle, which was nearly empty. "Maybe." He looked over at her, gazing up and down with unconcealed interest in her barely clad figure. A steady intensity smoldered in his eyes. "Not drunk enough." He lay back fully, staring up at the low ceiling. "Shouldn't you be home, readying yourself for your new husband?"

Sophie almost thought he was jealous. The idea confused and gratified her even in the midst of her tumult. "I am not marrying Lord Charles."

He turned his head to stare at her, his eyes as hot as the candle flame. "That's not what he seems to think. Or your parents."

"They're wrong. Everyone is wrong. Do we have to stay in here?" she asked suddenly. "I need to keep moving. Come outside with me." Without waiting for an answer, she went out into the field.

Sophie heard Ian's footsteps behind her and began to walk into the forest, more sedate than she had been earlier, but still compelled to be in motion. She heard Ian curse behind her and take a few quick paces to catch up. His long stride easily matched her own. For some time they walked in silence, moving between the trees and picking their way through the grassy fields and glades she knew and loved. She wasn't sure what to make of Ian's mood, blacker than she had ever seen it, but at least he didn't try to jolly her up, tell her that everything was going to be all right, just wait until the morning. Only a few hours earlier, they had been entwined together, his hands exploring her most secret and hidden places until that wonderful paroxysm of ecstasy had overtaken her body.

She swallowed hard. She had been expelled from paradise without ever tasting the fruit of knowledge.

She glanced over at him. Was he thinking about their interrupted lovemaking? If he was, he gave no sign, resolutely striding beside her, deeply mired in his own thoughts.

Her legs finally grew tired, and she stopped in a small, grassy glade. The midsummer grass grew high and full, rustling and brushing against her legs. Ian drew himself up, his eyes watchful, gleaming in the moonlight. She was acutely aware of him, the muscular breadth of his shoulders, his height, his *prana*—a Hindu concept he'd taught her, which meant vital energy and life force. Sophie had scoffed at the idea when Ian had told her about it, finding it ridiculously unscientific, but now it made perfect sense. He was filled with this energy, this *prana*, as were the woods that surrounded them and the whole night.

She ran her hands over the bark of an elm. A good tree. Solid. Dependable. It asked nothing.

"Some people say that science teaches us to shun God," she said, touching the furrowed bark, "that it strips away the mystery of creation and turns the world into one vast laboratory." She turned and leaned against the tree, her wrists crossed behind her. "But they are wrong."

Ian did not speak, but steadily regarded her.

Sophie closed her eyes, listening to the soughing of the saw-toothed leaves, pushing aside all thoughts of genus and order and even, yes, Linnaeus. She could be at the bottom of the ocean. Waves cresting over her. Then borne aloft on tides and carried far out to sea, where she would dissolve into salt and minerals.

"The more I learn about botany," she said, opening her eyes and returning her gaze to Ian—still watching her, hawklike—"the more I believe what a great miracle God has worked." She smiled faintly; then the smile died. She looked at Ian, her own gaze level while her heart rioted within her chest.

He stared at her for a long time. She thought, feared, he would turn away, tell her to run home, back to her family and fiancé. But he didn't. Instead, Ian strode across the glade and kissed her, cupping her head with both hands. She opened her mouth to his immediately, keeping her wrists crossed behind her as she leaned hard against the elm's trunk. She wanted to open herself up to him fully, give him access to every part of her so he could know her as completely as one human could know another.

She tasted warm wine on his lips, his heated breath filling her up like the finest vintage. Her head began to spin as he pressed the lean length of his body wholly against hers, the fine fabric of her nightclothes giving her unmitigated access to his incredibly muscled physique. The kiss was deep, aggressive, fluid— he wanted everything and she wanted to give everything to him—and she felt the sinews of his firm thighs, the plane of his taut stomach, press against her own. There could be no mistaking his arousal. She shocked herself by pushing her hips into his. They gasped together at the contact.

God, she could kiss him like this forever, a spreading warmth curling out from between her legs. Her breasts brushed against the velvet of his waistcoat, nipples growing tight and hard from the sensation of soft, plush material with intractable muscle beneath. He tore his mouth away from hers. Before she could protest, he dragged hot, wet kisses down her neck, across her collarbone, lower, until his hands cupped her breasts and his tongue licked through the cotton nightgown and circled the stiffened buds, one then the other. A sharp cry erupted from her. His palms covered her, pushing her breasts together to bring them closer to his mouth. His thumbs ran back and forth over the peaked nipples as he gently tugged on them, then suckled, creating ripples of fiery sensation that spread throughout her body.

She brought her hands out from behind her, careless of the elm's bark that rasped against her skin, and pushed Ian back slightly. In answer to his questioning look, she began unbuttoning his waistcoat. She had to feel his skin, had to see him fully. Though she suffered the loss of his hands on her breasts, she endured it gladly as he began to help her with his buttons. Soon the waistcoat had been discarded and the full-sleeved white shirt followed shortly after.

He bent to return to his ministrations, but she stopped him.

"I need to touch you," she murmured.

Obliging, he let her fingers rove over him, closing his eyes and growling as she explored territory she'd longed to see. Her knowledge of anatomy was limited. Once her mother had found her reading Vesalius and immediately confiscated the book, horrified by the illustrations. Sophie mourned the loss then, but tonight she was glad, for as she tried to catalog the smooth muscles that bunched and flexed under her hands, reacting to her touch, no Latinate names or words came to her other than *beautiful*.

She reveled in the contrast between corded sinews and the patterns of crisp dark hair that swirled over his chest and edged lower, down his stomach. His body was almost spare, ascetic in its lean strength, but she could witness plainly the way her touch affected him. Each muscle in turn contracted slightly as he sucked in his breath. She let her hands move down the breadth of his arms as she leaned in and kissed where his heart thundered in his ribs.

Again she surprised herself with her boldness. She took one hand and slid it along his quivering stomach, past the waistband of his breeches, and let it rest along the hard flesh straining there, the root of him. She almost snatched her hand away. God, he was so big, thick as a sapling, there could be no possible way . . .

"Sophie," he groaned, pressing her hand firmly to his body.

No, they would find a way. She let him guide her, caressing the length of him, delighting in the immediate response as Ian sucked in air and said her name again and again. Through velvet, she felt the long, rigid shaft, the full head, rubbed her thumb against the ridge delineating the two. Feeling this part of him, he became both more human to her and more mysterious, separate. Here was the final proof that he was unlike anything she had ever known. She had lied to him—she was afraid. Afraid, but fearless, if that was possible. At that moment, touching him, learning her own power, Sophie felt anything was possible. With her free hand, she tried to undo the buttons of his breeches, but he stopped her.

"This will be over in less than a minute if you keep going," he said somewhere between a laugh and a growl. "I want to take my time with you."

Before she could speak, he'd pulled her slippers and robe off and, in one motion, gathered her nightgown and pulled it over her head. She wilted a little, suddenly shy under his gaze, but he held her hands to

keep her from covering herself. She felt as exposed as
a green shoot emerging in the early, cold spring, but
his eyes warmed her as he took her in.

"You're so lovely, Sophie," he said. "It breaks my
heart how lovely you are."

She didn't know how to answer this but was saved
from making any response by his own hands sculpt-
ing her body. He palmed her breasts, stroked the
slight roundness of her belly, gently brushed the
golden curls between her legs, pressed his hands
against the curvature of her thighs. Everywhere he
touched seemed to burst into awareness. She dimly remembered drinking his elixir in Little Chipping, and
the restless night she had spent in oversensitized,
waiting skin. She'd never experienced sensations like
that before, but they faded into tiny ripples compared
to the tidal wave rushing over her, in her, now.

And then he was lifting her up. He laid her down in
the grass and hastily pulled off the remainder of his
clothing. His buckled shoes clattered against each
other, his stockings fluttered to the ground like exor-
cised ghosts, followed immediately by his breeches.

There he was, absolutely naked. Sophie tried not
to gulp, but she couldn't help herself. It was one
thing to look at statues or paintings of nude men and
something else entirely to have a very handsome,
very aroused, unclothed man standing over her.

He did not give her long to ponder this new development, quickly coming to lie down beside her, covering half her body with his own and taking her mouth
with his.

"This is just how I pictured you," he said between
kisses, "since the day we met."

"The day we met!" she exclaimed, a bit shocked

but more flattered. Her arms wrapped around his shoulders.

"Yes," he answered, and as he continued to kiss her, his hands roved over her pliant body, stroking her stomach and legs. "Like a goddess in Botticelli's *Primavera*." He began to tease the juncture of her thighs. Unafraid of his touch, she parted for him, and they both moaned together as his clever fingers delved into her. She could feel how slick she was, as though her body was full of milky nectar and had only been waiting for him to tap it.

"I'm . . . no goddess," she managed as she arched up.

"You're better," he answered. He moved, arranging himself so that he was fully atop her now, between her legs and supported by his forearms. "You're earthbound. Full of life. Luscious. Sophie."

She felt him position himself so that he was poised at her entrance. She could actually feel herself blossoming for him, an unfolding of petals and a rush of heated blood. She recalled her riding accident when she was a child that resulted in the loss of her maidenhead, and was fervently glad there would be no pain. She only wanted him.

He rubbed the head of his penis against her cleft, testing, seeking, covering himself in her liquidity. She tried to keep her eyes open but his were shut, and she could see the incredible tension in his shoulders and neck, his jaw tight. He was restraining himself, for her. Sophie pressed the soles of her feet deep into the lush grass. She wished to welcome him inside her.

With an oath, he thrust fully within her. A small cry burst from her mouth—it wasn't pain exactly, but she felt herself being stretched, filled so completely she didn't think there would be room inside for anything but him. Strange. And wonderful, to have Ian as deep within her as humanly possible.

"Ah, Sophie," he breathed, resting his head in the curve of her neck, "you're so tight."

"I'm sorry," she said, and felt the warmth of his exhaled laughter on her throat.

"No, no. It's a good thing. Very good." He kissed the side of her neck, and she brought her legs up, hooking her ankles around his calves. An interior contraction told her she was going someplace new, but she wanted to be there, wherever it was. She raised her hips to see if he could be brought even farther inside. Ian groaned at her movement. "God, Sophie, I'm trying to go slow. But you're making it," he gritted his teeth as she shifted, "very difficult."

Sophie grasped the back of his neck and brought his lips down onto hers. Delirious, flushed, drunk on him and new discoveries, she kissed Ian with all the desire that had been building within her throughout the summer. "Don't go slow," she said into his mouth. "I need you too much."

He cursed and drew himself almost fully out. She began to complain at the loss, but before she could, he plunged forward again. An unearthly mewl jumped from her mouth as he set up an unhurried rhythm, in and out, again and again, the wet friction of skin sliding into skin that was almost too good, too exquisite to be borne. She gripped his shoulders hard as she tried to match his movements. His pace increased, and she could hear him calling upon Hindu gods in an animal growl. Every part of her felt him—her body, the hidden recesses within and the responsive flesh without, her thoughts, her soul, and she strained toward him, reaching, racing after the gleam of a promise fulfilled. She felt herself growing closer, nearing her goal, oh, if she could only get there. Faintly, she recalled her dream—it had only been that morning, a lifetime ago. Reality far outweighed the dream. No one ever told her it would feel so *good*.

"That's it, Sophie," he panted, low and heaving, "come with me."

She bucked and felt hundreds of muscles tightening and releasing in a cascade of pure rapture. Sophie flung herself into it. She was swallowed whole in the bliss they had created together. It was like the contractions of pleasure he had given her earlier at the ball, but this was a thousand times better because she could feel him inside her and could tell that he felt the same peaking sensations. Just as the edges of her euphoria began to fade into a more gentle gold, he stiffened, convulsing in short, hard strokes, invoking any deity that would hear him.

He collapsed, crumpling against her. His skin was damp with sweat and early-morning dew. She ran her tongue along his shoulder, tasting the musky salt of his flesh. His queue had come undone, and she ran her fingers through the thick, dark mass of hair that fell to his shoulders. His weight pinned her into the grass, but she didn't mind.

"That definitely wasn't daisies," she said when she could speak.

She felt his rumbled laughter against her still-quivering belly. Raising his head and smiling, he said, "Roses, I think."

"A whole bouquet of roses," she agreed. "Can we try lilies next? Maybe," she giggled, "tulips?"

Ian rolled onto his back, clasping one arm around her waist so she rolled with him. He slid out of her, and she frowned to lose him. "Next?" He raised one eyebrow. "Don't tell me you want another stroll in the garden already?"

She sprawled on top of him, feeling completely wanton and loving every moment of it. Laying naked in the grass with Ian—one of the great new pleasures in life. "I can't help it," she said, sobering as she trailed her fingers through the hair on his chest. "Now that I know what it's like, I never want to stop making love with you."

He tried to stay light. "Never? That could be tricky, especially when the winter comes. We might get snowed on, and think of the frostbite."

"We'll find a way to keep warm," she said. She couldn't begrudge him his levity. She felt awed by what they had just done, even as she longed to do it all over again.

A faint frown appeared between his brows as he raised his head and looked around. "Sophie," he said with an amazed whisper, "you are miraculous."

"Miraculous?" she repeated, astonished. "I . . . Thank you."

"We're actually *glowing*," he breathed. "I thought it was only a metaphor, but look."

Sure enough, she saw that both their bodies were glowing faintly in a way that had nothing to do with the light from the moon. A pale green illumination haloed their skin, turning intertwined limbs from corporeal to ethereal. It was mystical, beautiful, and, unfortunately, easily explained.

"Bio-luminescence," she said with a laugh, letting her head fall back.

"Bio-what?"

"That's the name I've given it. Light from living organisms."

"I didn't realize there was such a thing."

"Mostly I'd heard about it in the ocean, but it can occur in plants. Like this one." Sophie reached beside her and plucked a little weed, similar to a dandelion green, and held it up for his inspection. "It's a very rare plant, barely documented in Britain, whose juice actually glows when exposed to air. It's so uncommon, it does not have a name other than what local people might dub it. Some call it fairy grass, others St. Elmo's wort. Look." She snapped it in two and rubbed the sap onto her fingers. Sure enough, a gentle glow appeared on her fingertips.

Ian touched his fingers to hers, drawing some of the glow onto his skin. "Can it harm us?"

She shook her head. "It fades within an hour." He continued to rub his fingers against hers in a lazy caress, drawing them down the palm of her hand and over the sensitive flesh of her wrist. Patterns of light appeared where he touched, and though Sophie knew there was a scientific explanation for it, she half-believed that he *could* make her shine just from his touch.

She turned and pressed hot kisses on his chest and, out of curiosity, licked his small, brown nipple. She was rewarded by a sharp intake of breath and him pulling her up until she straddled him.

"I'm thirty-one, for God's sake," he growled. "I shouldn't be doing this so soon." But she could feel that he was already completely engorged, full against her stomach.

"Do you want to stop?" she asked.

He raised her up and impaled her onto him. She cried out, letting her head tip back. "I don't care if we're buried under an avalanche. I don't want to stop."

Ultimately, her body gave out before her will did. They made love once more, and she had begun to doze when Ian shook her awake. They couldn't lie naked in a clearing all night. She had to go home. Groggily, she slipped on her nightgown, robe, and slippers as Ian struggled into his clothing, ruined by dew and dirt. The glow of the St. Elmo's wort was gone now, leaving only crushed plants where their bodies had lain. They were silent as he walked her back toward Cabot Park, though they kept their hands intertwined.

After they had gone halfway there, she kissed him and told him to go back to his caravan. "I can find my way," she said, "and I'd like to be alone for a little while."

He did not argue with her but, after another quick kiss, turned and headed in the direction of Chesterton's farm. She watched him go, perversely wishing he'd insisted on accompanying her. But she had promised herself not to be dishonest with Ian. Especially after the intimacies they had shared tonight.

She could barely assemble any cohesive thoughts as she drifted over fields and through the woods. Her mind and body continued to vibrate with Ian, a tuning fork struck long ago yet still resonant. The moon was beginning to set, but everything was yet bright and silver in its light. It had been both the best and worst night of her life, two sides of the same leaf spinning to the ground. She could not begin to understand the implications of what she had done, didn't want to. Just for now, she wanted only to feel, leave her mind wrapped in its agreeable fog of exhaustion and satiety. She was pleasantly sore between her legs. She could feel her pulse gently throbbing in the sensitive bud nestled in her folds, a continual reminder of the delicious things she and Ian had done together. Why had they resisted for so long? Making love with Ian was unparalleled, exquisite, and she knew he felt the same way about her. It seemed the height of perversity to deny themselves.

On impulse, Sophie decided to cut through a stand of oaks she'd passed a million times but never investigated. It was odd, how often she had walked this route and never given much consideration to these trees. They were young oaks, planted when she was just making her coming out. Perhaps their youth had detracted any interest.

Sophie patted the trunks of the oaks as she passed, greeting them like new friends. Her foot suddenly caught in a root and she went sprawling. She cursed and held her stubbed toe as she sat on the ground. Then she froze.

She wasn't dreaming. There it was. She'd found what she had been looking for.

Snug against the trunk of the tree, as cozy as newlyweds, were bunches of peach-leaved bellflowers. Alive and thriving. With the sessile oak.

Sophie didn't know whether to laugh or cry.

Chapter Fifteen

As Ian slowly walked back to his caravan in the pink dawn carrying two freshly caught brook trout, he mulled over some words of Isaak Walton—his father had given him a copy of *The Compleat Angler* when he was ten—"God never did make a more calm, quiet, innocent recreation than angling." He'd been neither calm, quiet, nor innocent in the past twenty-four hours. Truth be told, his actions had been the precise opposite of Walton's description of fishing. Perhaps that was why, after he and Sophie had parted company in the wee hours, he'd been compelled to seek some measure of meditative stillness. He didn't go back to the caravan. Instead, he found himself sitting on the banks of a country stream with a makeshift fishing pole, recalling as best he could more of Walton while his body and mind rioted in the afterglow of making love with Sophie.

Making love with a woman had never felt so utterly right, as though they had been specifically crafted for each other, fitting together as perfectly as intertwining vines. That perfection worried him a little. He could easily see himself becoming enslaved to Sophie's charms . . . if he wasn't already. He craved her the way an addict craved opium, completely focused on his need for one thing. But addiction wasn't love.

As he approached his caravan, the orange cat appeared beside him, nosing eagerly at the fish and making a series of chirps that nearly made Ian laugh out loud, if he had been able to laugh.

"Take them, you glutton," he said, tossing the fish onto the grass. The cat immediately set upon the fish, happily gorging itself on its unexpected feast. "God knows I've no stomach for a trout breakfast this morning."

He turned back to the wagon. The door was open. He could hear Sophie's off-key singing inside, a sound almost charming. She never sang—and for good reason. It was a wonder the cat didn't join in. Her happiness made him edgy. He prayed that he wasn't the cause, since he would be the one unmaking that happiness in a few moments. Or would he? For several minutes, he contemplated turning around and simply walking away. No one, not even Sophie, need know that he'd been there. He could disappear from Gloucestershire. England was a big enough place, and there were countries he'd never visited. America, for example. All his possessions were in the caravan, but he'd started seven years ago with just as much as he had now. He could do it. He could turn his back. No compromise, no resentment. Only freedom.

He couldn't. He honestly liked Sophie too much. He respected her. The thought cheered and annoyed him at the same time as he peered inside the caravan, his home for the past year. But not for much longer.

Sophie sat in front of her tiny laboratory, dressed in a fresh gown, perched on a chest and checking the contents of one of her many labeled bottles. Witnessing Sophie at work, he realized that the factor that had driven Sophie's suitors away was not merely her interest in science, but that anyone who sought to claim her heart would never possess it utterly. A part would always be withheld for her love for botany. She existed in another world, a world few would ever enter. Only a man with the strongest sense of himself could ever be reconciled to this.

This wasn't a fault, but her strength, a dare for those brave enough to take it. Ian did not want to meet the challenge. He could not.

He braced his hands on the door frame of the caravan and took a deep breath.

Hearing him, Sophie turned, and the look of pure joy on her face sent an immediate burst of answering pleasure spreading through his chest.

"You're so damned beautiful," he rasped.

She laughed. "You say that as if it's a bad thing," she answered, blushing, "but I'll take it all the same. Nothing can trouble me today."

He resisted the impulse to look away. He also resisted the impulse to propel himself forward into the caravan, lunge for Sophie, and throw her onto his bed.

"Sophie," he said, his voice scraping against his throat, "I have to tell you something."

"Yes?" She smiled. "I have news of my own. Who shall go first?"

"You," he said, hoisting himself into the caravan. He slid onto the floor, legs out in front of him.

A gorgeous, heartfelt smile bloomed on her face. "I found it!"

"Found what?"

"The oak and the bellflower," she said triumphantly. She held out a root cutting for his inspection. It was, in fact, two roots interlaced together, the thicker oak and the fine thread of the flower, carefully salvaged by Sophie's precise hand. She waited for him to take the sample from her to have a better look, but he didn't. Puzzled, she gently set it back down.

"I found them on my way home," she continued, still bubbling with excitement. "And I think the secret has to do with the age of the oak. When it's young, it might coexist more peacefully with the bellflower. As it gets older, it could change and produce different chemicals in the soil that make it impossible for something as delicate as the flower to survive."

He only nodded, saying nothing. He could barely hear her over the roaring in his ears.

"We can isolate the chemicals in the roots and determine what makes them flourish together. I know we've found what you're looking for. But it isn't here." She picked up the bottle she had been working with. Sophie pressed a palm to her chest. "It's here."

Ian gave her a questioning look. He could not follow her.

She was wreathed in smiling happiness, more lovely than he deserved, gazing at him with bright, mutable eyes. Sophie glowed, and in the cramped space of the caravan, he felt himself diminish under her power.

"I love you," she said.

Ian's breath snagged, stopped. Ah, God.

"That is my other discovery," she continued, breathless but assured. "I wanted to tell you as soon as I knew. We were looking for the secret to love and I have found it in my own heart. For you. Ian."

He tipped back his head against the wall, looking with sightless eyes at the roof of the caravan. He'd never been able to stand up straight in here. Deep in his gut he felt a cold ember burning, frozen fire sending crystalline flames throughout his body.

He forced himself to speak. "We have to get married."

For a moment, she only stared at him. Then she leapt up from the chest on which she sat, coming within dangerous inches of hitting her head on the roof. A beatific smile filled her face as she threw her arms around Ian's shoulders, sinking beside him.

"That is a magnificent idea," she beamed. She pressed kisses along the line of his jaw, the corner of his mouth, and they felt like the most acute, wonderful torture a man could ever experience. "We will be so happy together. A lifetime of plants and traveling. And love. We've been looking for it so long, but we never looked in the most obvious place." She ran her hands up his neck, threading her fingers into his hair as she pressed her forehead against his temple.

He felt the breath of her astonished laughter warm against his skin. "Someone like me, with years of scientific research and experiments, failing to consider something so basic, so evident, so natural—it's ridiculous."

"Ridiculous," he repeated, his voice hollow in the small space of the wagon.

Sophie pulled back, the barest hint of a frown appearing between her brows as her eyes roamed over his face.

He felt himself ebb beneath her scrutiny. He feared what she would find if she searched too hard, and what she would not find. So he relied on the one thing he knew they shared. Ian pulled her hard against him and kissed her. And was grateful to discover, as he gripped her closely, that none of the passion that burned between them had lessened. She opened her mouth to him, letting him invade her as he struggled to drown out the doubts. He hungered for her, a bodily craving that demanded to be satisfied, but as his hands rose to the hem of her gown, he felt her push him back.

"This isn't right," she said, and she moved across the floor to put distance between them. "It doesn't feel right." Her eyes were wide and confused, like flickering moss and earth in the dim light of the caravan. She snapped her skirts down to cover her legs.

"What's not right?" he panted. He shoved his hair off his face, tried to reach for her again. "We want each other. We are going to become husband and wife. Isn't that enough?"

As she edged farther away, uncertainty guttered in the brightness of her eyes. And a growing awareness. "No," she said slowly. "It isn't."

"Sophie, please," he said, dreading where she was going. He continued to hold out a hand to her, which she ignored, so he let it drop dead to the floor.

She pulled herself up along the wall of the wagon, as though her legs could not hold her weight. Gripping the side of the table where she had been working, she looked down at him. "Once you told me that you would not wed without love, and I thought, when you said that we were going to marry, that meant . . ." Her knuckles whitened on the edge of the desk. The bottles rattled against each other, sounding like the ringing brittleness of bones. "That you love me."

Naked, agonized hope stretched out in her open,

candid gaze. She waited. He could hear the need in her voice, the yearning that threatened to smother them both, a lifetime of expectation that could lead only toward disappointment. Ian was very good at disappointing people, including himself.

It would be easy to lie, to say the words she wanted to hear. He'd woven much more elaborate, complex deceptions at less urging. Trouble was, he couldn't seem to push the words past his lips. He could not tell Sophie something he did not believe.

He'd been silent too long, and she interpreted his silence correctly. "You can't," she said. "Or won't."

"It's not that simple."

Her eyes blazed. "It *is* that simple. And without it," she struggled past a knot in her throat, "I won't marry you."

This was what he had feared, and it felt far worse than he could have ever anticipated. He tried, lamely, to placate her. "I think we have something between us that could make for a good marriage. Better than most."

"It's not enough," she declared hotly. "I want love, Ian. Without it, I might as well have the same marriage as my parents." She pressed a hand to her stomach, looking ill. "I would rather marry Vickerton."

He felt as though she had shot him. "Sophie—"

"At least I wouldn't have to suffer through the torture of loving someone who doesn't love me," she said. Pure sorrow choked her voice. "I would be giving something so precious to someone who doesn't even want it. And you'd come to resent me and my love."

"No."

She shook her head. "You would. It would become

259

a burden to you, as I would. God, I can't imagine anything worse. I can't let that be."

"Sophie, I promise that won't happen." He had no right to make such a vow, but he had to convince her, even as her words rang true.

She gave him a disbelieving stare. "You cannot promise anything. Anyway," she went on, running over him, "how can you marry me? You said you would never marry without love. You left a woman at the altar because you didn't love her. You would be breaking your own commandment."

She was right. In his haste to correct the misdeeds of last night, he had not considered that. It almost amused him. "There are larger social forces at work here," he managed, which was a rather simple way of explaining unbelievably complicated machinations.

"What larger social forces? For God's sake, Ian, you're a *mountebank*." She pounded her fist on the table. Some of the bottles leapt into the air and fell, clinking and rolling across the floorboards. "You have no duty, no obligation to anyone. Your home is this wagon. Your birthright is the road. You have no property or inheritance except a chest full of potions." Her voice grew watery as she sank to the floor. "Don't speak to me of social forces when they have no sway over you. Don't lie to me. I couldn't bear that."

"I'm a viscount."

The words leapt away from him before he could find a more diplomatic way to say them.

Sophie went immediately still. "What?"

And then there was a tumble of words, an inexorable flow that he couldn't stanch, as though he could make it right, make it better through a flood of speech. "Not a viscount, exactly. Right now I'm a baron, Lord Ian Claypool, not Blackpool, but when my father dies I inherit the viscountcy and become Lord Briarleigh. I'm sure the old man would have disinherited me after I left, except I haven't any brothers, and the nearest male relation is a perfectly idiotic simp who lives in London and spends his inheritance in gaming hells. So that keeps me as the heir."

Sophie's face had whitened so much that her freckles stood out as bright fever spots. She tried to open her mouth to speak, but nothing came out. Finally, she managed to breathe, "A viscount."

"A baron and heir to a viscountcy can't sleep with a gentleman's daughter without consequences," Ian said. "A mountebank can slip beneath custom, but a baron can't. I have to marry you, Sophie." He tried to make the prospect sound appealing. "I think it shouldn't be too bad. Pleasant, actually. I won't impede your botany. We enjoy each other's company. And I'll be honest: making love with you was one of the most incredible experiences of my life. I really don't think we have anything to be concerned about. We can even look forward to it."

Before he could stop her, Sophie suddenly darted forward through the open door of the caravan. His hands reached out too late, grasping at the rustling material of her skirts that slid through his fingers as she pushed past him. He had moved to a half-crouch, ready to grab her, when she misjudged the steps outside the wagon and went tumbling to the ground.

He was immediately at her side, offering her assistance, trying to lift her up as she lay in the grass, but he was met with a flurry of swinging fists. She'd tried to hit him before, yet never with the express desire to do real damage. Now she swung at him furiously with grass-stained, skinned hands, her face flushed with hectic color and, God help him, tears coursing down her cheeks. He'd made her cry.

"Damn you!" she cried through choking sobs. "Lying . . . selfish . . . bastard!"

He dodged her blows, though one or two managed to knock into his arms. He had been right. She was stronger than anyone would have suspected. "Sophie—"

She struggled to her feet and kept him at bay with her wild punches. "Be quiet," she hissed. "I won't let you say another word to me. Everything that comes out of your mouth is nothing but lies. Except," she amended bitterly, "that you don't love me. That much is true." She took a few steps away, her hands falling to her sides. "I *trusted* you, Ian."

"Never trust a mountebank."

"But you *aren't* a mountebank," she cried. "Worse, you're a nobleman, a gentleman, but what you did—"

"I only withheld a bit of information—"

"Don't," she warned him. "There is nothing to justify your actions." She took a deep breath, attempting to straighten herself and regain some composure by smoothing out her dirtied skirts. The inherent dignity of the gesture, futile as it was, tore at Ian's heart.

She began to walk home. Ian stretched out his hand to take hold of her arm, but she shied away and fixed him with an icy look.

"You don't understand," he said. "We must be wed. There's no choice in the matter for either of us."

"I am beginning to realize," Sophie countered, clipped and brittle, "that there is always a choice. I have made many bad ones over the course of the past month, but now I intend to rectify that situation. Beginning immediately." She tipped up her chin. "I don't care if I am dragged before the king. I don't care if I am pilloried. I don't care what happens to me, but *I will never marry you.* I could even live with your lies if I knew you loved me, but I know that you don't. I cannot subject myself to that misery."

"You would rather be alone?" he asked in disbelief.

She glared defiantly back at him. "My uncle loved once, and was loved in return. But she was taken from him too early." Admiration thick in her voice, she said, "He has chosen a life of solitude rather than compromise the memory of their devotion."

"He's a fool."

Sophie drew herself up. "He is exemplary."

The sun was shining fully now, filling the field with bright yellow light, but Ian was cold. Cold to the innermost reaches of himself. The pure betrayal on Sophie's lovely face sliced through him like a blade. And he deserved it.

"What if there's a child?" he asked, his throat like gravel.

"If there is, I will raise it on my own. And teach it never to lie to those who deserve honesty." Her voice broke, the tears that had dried welling up again in her eyes. "And I will love that baby. I will give my child all the love its father could not."

She was done. Having said her piece, Sophie left. She did not look back. This time, Ian let her go.

Chapter Sixteen

Blindly, Sophie stumbled toward home. The clear beauty of the summer morning did not register at all as she reeled along the back roads of Sevendowne. The day had started out so wonderfully—what had gone wrong?

The answer was simple: She had trusted Ian Blackpool and given him her love. Ian *Clay*pool, she amended darkly, the future Viscount of Briarleigh. A man who had been deceiving her from the very beginning.

She wondered how much of the man she had come to love was real. The easy humor, the nimble mind, a wealth of small, charming gestures that made him so human and also larger than life—she could not tell what was genuinely Ian and what was his mountebank persona, a costume worn as part of his disguise. Including all of the marvelous things he had said to her, not only about her as a woman but her as a whole person, an entire self containing imperfections and idiosyncrasies.

More than the loss of her virginity, she mourned

the loss of her friend, the one person she felt truly understood and respected her for all that she was. No one had ever given her that before, even Uncle Alforth, though he tried. She valued herself when she was with Ian. She learned to love herself as she came to recognize her love for him. How wonderful it had been. How illusory.

She did not notice where she was going until she saw the turned-up beds of soil in front of an unfinished manor house: Alforth's new estate. She had sketched out some rough plans for the grounds several weeks earlier; nothing remarkable, a combination of French formal style and English provincialism that pleased her uncle. It was a bad time of year to plant flowers, but the gardeners had begun putting in trees and shrubbery. All the workers were gone today; Alforth had given them a week off in deference to the heat. She could be alone here.

Sophie began to stroll through the empty, incomplete garden, examining her handiwork, taking mental notes to give to the gardeners when they returned.

The process should have pleased her, given her a measure of happiness. It didn't. Everything felt hollow and dry, a desiccated, empty seed pod to be crushed under the heel of one's foot.

Sophie sank down onto a stone bench at the back of the estate, staring sightlessly at the mound where a fountain was going to be installed.

"He broke my heart," she said aloud. Even as she said the words, she knew what had happened had not been entirely Ian's fault. Thinking on it now, it was a wonder she had not guessed his identity sooner. He carried a gold watch. His accent and manners were impeccable. The way he carried himself, particularly last night at the Cheltenham ball, showed that he'd had years of formal schooling. He probably *had* attended Oxford, as he'd told Lord Charles.

And he had been candid about his inability to love. He'd told her directly that he could never give it. She'd egotistically believed that his incapability did not apply to her, that she would be the one woman who would change him, the idiotic conviction that she was different, special. She had only proved the oldest truth—love made one foolish. Even a scientist.

Willful ignorance. She'd misled herself just as Ian had withheld the truth from her. Making herself believe that he had been a valet. Scolding him for not taking advantage of life's opportunities. Proffering her heart on a platter like an offering to a saint. Sophie felt ridiculous, humiliated, the creator of her own downfall. Everything about herself was thrown into doubt. She didn't know who she was anymore.

"Damn," she said, dashing a knuckle across her eyes.

"Such language, Sophie," drawled a voice over her shoulder.

Startled, she leapt up from the bench. Lord Charles Vickerton stood behind her, his handsome face bland and unreadable. He had changed from his evening finery and appeared to be the epitome of a country gentleman, as interpreted by the latest fashion journals from Paris.

"I had a premonition that I would not find you at home, Sophie. Somehow I was led to this place." He examined the back of Alforth's manor, approving. "I believe your uncle's new home will be quite charming when it is finished. And the grounds are, of course, delightful."

Sophie could only nod.

"But I did not come here to discuss Alforth Morley's estate," Lord Charles said, turning back to her. He gestured toward the bench. "Please sit, my dear. We have much to discuss."

"I ought to be heading home," she began, but he waved her objections away.

"Indulge your future husband for a moment," he said with a little smile.

Feeling both exhausted and anxious, Sophie did as he asked. Once she had settled herself, he sat beside her. She took a deep breath.

"Lord Charles, about our engagement—" she began.

"Yes, that is precisely the topic I wished to discuss. My parents are still away on the Continent, but I have written them to express my most heartfelt happiness, and our hopes that they will join us for our wedding in December."

He beamed at her, and Sophie felt her heart shrivel into an even smaller husk. Honestly, he wasn't that unpleasant a man. Far from it. Everything about him was polished and sophisticated, calculated to please. He would be conscientious, refined, and, if not precisely the most original thinker in England, certainly he had a measure of brains and could converse with a relative degree of clarity. He would make someone a decent husband. But not her.

"Lord Charles, we cannot marry," she said abruptly.

Instead of appearing shocked or angered by this statement, he merely smiled mildly at her and continued. "December would be best, since my parents will have returned and I know my mother will enjoy planning the ceremony. Perhaps we can have the wedding on Christmas to make the season doubly festive. We can trim the church with holly and ivy. Wouldn't those be enchanting names for our daughters? Holly and Ivy Vickerton. Yes, I believe I like those names very much. Of course, we shall first endeavor to bless the family with a son."

Sophie began to feel a bit desperate, swamped under Vickerton's blithe monologue. "Sir, perhaps you did not hear me," she persisted. "We cannot—"

"I heard you." His voice was clipped, suddenly sharp. "But you are speaking nonsense."

"My family has cruelly misled you," Sophie said. She gazed at him steadily. "And perchance I did, as well. There can be no marriage between us. It was a union I never sought." Her hand crept up to rub her nose as she fought her urge to look away from Lord Charles's impassive face. "When my father accepted your suit yesterday, he did so without my knowledge or consent. I am heartily sorry about the embarrassment we will all suffer when the engagement is publicly withdrawn, but we must, in order to avoid a disastrous mistake that cannot be undone."

"I have made no mistake," Lord Charles insisted with a smile. "Come December, I will take you to wife."

"You aren't listening!" Sophie cried, leaping up. She gasped aloud when Lord Charles's surprisingly strong grip fastened around her arm.

"It is you who are not listening, Sophie," he said, still smiling. "Your family and I have entered into an agreement, a very profitable agreement for both parties, and one which I insist will be honored."

"Profitable?"

He waved dismissively with his free hand. "Some land, a few shipping contracts. Nothing you need concern yourself with. Your parents were willing to trade a certain amount of insolvency for the prestige of a title."

The knowledge that her parents would sell her off in order to gain the cachet of Vickerton's title made Sophie want to retch. She would have, if her stomach had not been completely empty.

"That all means nothing to me," she said. "My mother and father have spent little time concerned with my wishes, and I shall do the same. Whatever you promised them, and however you threaten me, I will not marry you."

Vickerton's lip curled. "You have forced my hand. If you insist on breaking our engagement—"

"There never *was* an engagement."

"Then," he continued harshly, "I will go directly to the magistrate."

"You cannot bring me up on charges," Sophie exclaimed. "Nothing I have done is punishable under the law."

"Perhaps not what *you* have done, but what our friend the mountebank has done."

"Mountebank?"

He looked at her, his eyes flat and cold. "You know who I mean."

Sophie realized he was referring to Ian. "He hasn't broken any laws!"

"He trespassed on private property—several times, including last night at the assembly hall. I finally did recognize him, incidentally," Vickerton added, "only it wasn't from Oxford. He was the same fellow hawking his wares on the day of the fair at Cheltenham. Impersonating a nobleman certainly has to be a punishable offense."

"And what if it isn't?"

"You slept with him, didn't you?" he accused.

She refused to lie, nor would she answer, instead remaining silent.

"So it's true," Vickerton said with distaste. "The mountebank raped a gentleman's daughter."

"It wasn't rape," Sophie cried hotly.

Vickerton shrugged. "You won't even get to testify, so it will be up to the judge to decide what is and isn't rape. Maybe he'll be imprisoned. Maybe transported. Who knows? My family is very influential, and I'm sure we could arrange something suitably punitive for your mountebank."

Sophie began to say that Ian *wasn't* a mountebank, that he was, in fact, a nobleman, but she stopped herself. If Vickerton did manage to find Ian and charge him, eventually the truth would come out and everyone would learn that Ian was the heir to a viscountcy. But the outcome would not be what Lord Charles desired—instead of being punished, and Sophie shamed, Ian would be given a brand-new wife: her. Telling Vickerton the truth would result only in marriage between herself and Ian. She would not allow it. She would not be the loving wife of a man who could not, would not love her back.

Staring at Lord Charles's smug, prideful face, Sophie knew what she had to do.

"I see I have no choice in this matter," she said at last, struggling to keep herself as composed and opaque as possible. "We shall be married."

Vickerton studied her for a moment, trying to read her, but Sophie felt as though she had aged thirty years over the course of the morning, and with age came self-possession. Ian was not the only one who could make someone believe what they wanted to believe. Sophie had gained many skills.

"Excellent," Lord Charles said with a satisfied smile. "I knew you would eventually see reason, Sophie. You're not foolish like most females."

"No," Sophie agreed. "I'm not foolish. Not anymore."

The caravan rumbled up the long, curving drive. Huge, old ash trees lined the gravel-covered path, planted hundreds of years earlier by careful stewards to be enjoyed by future generations. Everything about the estate bespoke an antique lineage, from the formal gardens to the picturesque ruins of a medieval chapel once used for weddings and christenings. The original house had been built during the War of the Roses—the family firmly supporting the Lancastrian Tudors and thus the happy recipient of land and title—but a recent mania for improvement gave birth to a new, modern estate planned by Robert Hooke himself, though many a joke had been made comparing the inhabitants of the estate to the inmates of Hooke's other project, the Bethlehem lunatic asylum. No one was quite sure who the comparisons favored.

The building was palatial, classical, a masterpiece of symmetry and order. Sightseers included it in their travels and happily exclaimed over the estate's size and dignity. Seven years had seen it completely unchanged, which was precisely the effect the owners sought. Continuity above all else. And decorum.

Ian had been unable to provide either. Even now.

Perhaps he was seeking drama. Life as a mountebank had encouraged the showman in him. Instead of driving the gaudy painted caravan discreetly back into the stables, he brought it boldly to the front of the house. Almost immediately, the front door opened and the butler bounded down the stairs.

"Get that thing out of here!" he shouted. "We will not tolerate gypsies of any—" The words died in the butler's throat as he caught sight of the caravan's driver. For several moments he could only open and close his mouth, his eyes staring, all sense of poise and indignation forgotten. And then he turned and ran back into the house.

Ian waited. He sat in the driver's seat, watching as stablehands and servants began to appear in the distance, drawn by the sight of the caravan and the butler's apoplexy. He wondered how many remembered him, and what they did remember. Before he could stop himself, Ian found his eyes roving over the gardens, mentally cataloging the plants and their Latinate names. He'd grown up in these gardens, and they had been as familiar and unremarkable as the second-floor landing, or the turns in the legs on his father's favorite chair. Now he was submerged with names, colors, facts. New eyes gazing upon the mundane and transforming them. Hollyhocks, snapdragons, peonies, poppies, hundreds of roses of every hue and shape. All revealed themselves to him in a profusion of memory and new knowledge.

Abruptly, he turned away, focusing his attention on the open door of the house. An older man appeared. He was hale and distinguished, silver-haired, dressed impeccably but without affectation. He exuded nobility and authority. His face was an echo of Ian's own, viewed through the lens of time. And ashen with shock. He braced himself against the door frame as he stared at the wagon.

"Hello, Father," Ian said.

Chapter Seventeen

"Are you really going to marry him, my dear?"

Sophie looked up to see her uncle standing in the doorway of her room. She had been going through her jewelry box, selecting pieces that would not be missed overmuch but were still valuable. The coral beads. A strand of pearls and matching earbobs. Some rings, never worn, since her hands were usually in the dirt. Sophie had been so absorbed in the task that she had not heard the familiar *step-tap* of Alforth's walk. Nor had she remembered, she realized, to close her door. But she didn't mind his presence. He was the only person in the entire household she could trust.

Still, she had to be on her guard. Ian had taught her that.

"Of course I am," she said in a loud, staged voice. She put her jewelry back and locked the tiny chest. Slipping the key into her pocket, she came forward to take Alforth's arm.

"It's a beautiful day," she continued. "Let's take a

stroll in the gardens." Sophie did not want to tire him, but she had to get away from the listening ears and close confines of the house. Lord Charles had escorted her back to Cabot Park earlier and, after exchanging smug good tidings with her parents, had returned to Cheltenham with a promise to come again the following day. Sophie's mother had ensconced herself with her heaps of correspondence, ready to share the happy news, while her father retreated to the stables to inspect a new litter of hounds. Everyone was doing exactly what they loved to do.

Except Sophie.

Walking sedately with Alforth through the gardens, the blossoms already beginning to wane under the heat of late summer, Sophie felt a measure of peace settle over her. She only felt comfortable indoors when she was working, and her work had been taken from her long ago. Now her laboratory had gone with Ian. She was not sure whether he had left yet, but how could he stay in Sevendowne after this morning? Perhaps he would come for her, demand to see her. No, she did not want that, either, did not want him.

She was completely adrift, lacking any sense of anchor save the assuring continuity of plant life that seemed to tell her, with each step she took, that there was something bigger than herself. She liked feeling small sometimes. Through smallness she came to know herself, to measure her identity against the scale of infinity. Botany was infinite, a giant web interlacing the whole planet and perhaps even extending outward into worlds she could only imagine. Measured against such magnitude, Sophie's unhappiness must dwindle into the finest dandelion seeds borne aloft on the wind.

She led Alforth through the topiary maze until they reached the center. It wasn't a large maze, nor very elaborate, but it afforded some privacy, and Sophie carefully sat her uncle on the stone bench placed conveniently for a weary Theseus.

Alforth took a square of linen from his pocket and mopped his brow. He looked cross, confused, troubled, squinting in the heat. Sophie suddenly wished she had chosen a better spot, but she herself was exhausted, could barely remember the last time she had slept with any degree of success. So she sank down beside her uncle, clasping her hands between her knees, worrying her knuckles.

"I am not marrying Lord Charles," she said, and gave a short laugh. "That seems to be all I say lately: I am not marrying so-and-so. My conversation has grown limited."

Alforth's eyebrow rose. She admitted to herself that she was a changed creature indeed, a new hybrid, the old daisy of Sophie crossed with a showy, reckless rose. What would such a specimen look like? She had no idea, charting its—her—transformation as she went.

She gazed intently at him. "I am going to tell you something, but you must promise me you will do nothing with the information. You cannot act in any capacity. Even if you think it is in my best interest, I have to insist that you *do nothing*."

Alforth eyed her warily. "I don't know. This all seems rather suspect."

"I want to tell you, Uncle A, but I can't. Not without your promise. And I know you never break your promises. You will have to trust me and my judgment."

Alforth debated with himself for a while before finally acquiescing. "Very well, I agree to your conditions. But let it be known that I objected strenuously."

"Objection noted." Then, as briefly as possible, and with as few details as she could manage, Sophie recounted the course of her relationship with Ian and Lord Charles's bargain with her parents. She had to give her uncle his due. He listened well, making choking noises of disbelief or sympathetic anger, and though it was clear he would like nothing more than to carve Ian into Christmas roast, he stayed true to his word. He did not immediately rise and demand Ian's head on a platter, nor did he insist that Sophie marry either of her would-be suitors, though Ian's lineage—if not actions—was impeccable.

"Great God," Alforth said. "I've heard of Briarleigh. A noble estate in Staffordshire, a very old title, and exceptionally wealthy." He frowned, scratching his chin. "Are you sure you want to decline that man's offer? He did you a great injury, which is unforgivable, but there would be some solace in the prestige and fortune of his name."

"I cannot wed him without his love, Uncle A," Sophie answered. She added quietly, "I think you appreciate why."

After several moments, Alforth answered, "Indeed, I do, my dear. But if you do not marry Lord Charles, and you won't have this Briarleigh fellow, what shall we do?" He sighed heavily.

At the use of *we* rather than *you*, Sophie felt some of her earlier misery dissipate. Under the warmth of her uncle's concern, she was never entirely alone, never completely friendless. Alforth might not always be able to protect her—nor did she wish it—but he would do his level best to support her actions. No one else had given her so much encouragement, except Ian.

But Alforth could not help her now. And Ian was no longer a factor she would let herself consider. God, it hurt so much just to think of him. "What *I* am going to do," Sophie declared, "is move on. Start a new life. Far away from my family or . . . old memories." She paused, struggling to subdue a trembling that had begun in her hands. She would not be afraid.

"Where will you go?"

Sophie gave her uncle a bright, cheerful smile that she did not quite feel. "America."

There was some persuasion involved. Alforth was firmly opposed to the idea, especially considering the tensions between the Colonies and England, but Sophie was equally firm in her conviction that she could not break free of her parents on the Continent—there were too many well-connected families traveling who might inform her mother and father of her whereabouts—and India was much too dangerous and unsettled for a female on her own.

When Alforth finally relented, it was on the condition that he accompany his niece.

Alforth suddenly looked to Sophie very much like a man profoundly ensconced in his middle age. In the bright sunlight, the deepness of the furrows around his eyes and between his silver eyebrows became more pronounced. His head sagged forward a little as he chewed on his bottom lip.

"You want to get away," Sophie said, comprehension dawning.

He nodded. "England is a burden to me, my dear.

It always has been. The social conventions. The snobbery. The best men and women of my acquaintance were always those I met in the taproom, honest farmers who were not choked by societal constraints." He sighed. "I hated being a member of the gentry. And I still do. I am happiest when I am gone from England's shores. When I am not at Sevendowne, I am abroad."

"Yet you always come back."

He gazed fondly at his niece. "I have always considered you to be the daughter Violet and I would have had, if illness had not claimed her. Your welfare is very important to me, Sophie."

She was silent, humbled by her uncle.

"I've been reading about America," Alforth continued, "and it seems a perfect place to remake oneself. Why should we not take advantage of such a wonderful opportunity?"

"Uncle A, I don't know."

Alforth was adamant, however, and on this point he would not yield. Sophie found herself secretly relieved that she would not have to undertake so vast a journey on her own.

With the decision made, they had only to plan the necessary steps. Sophie had intended to sell some of her jewelry to buy passage, but Alforth determined that he would send his man ahead to Liverpool under orders of strictest secrecy, where he would purchase two cabins on the next ship bound for Boston.

"And I shall tell Caroline that I have arranged for one last outing for us together, before your marriage," Alforth said. "That shall give us sufficient time to enable your escape." He grinned. "I haven't had an adventure like this in a good long while. I believe I am quite looking forward to it."

"As am I," Sophie concurred, though she could not entirely banish her apprehension. So far away, far from home, far from Ian . . .

Caroline, in good charity with the world, readily agreed to Alforth's proposed trip, and it was not a great effort to pack and set off a few days later. Lord Charles visited once, pleased that his future bride had reconciled herself to her fate, and urged a swift return. It was a visit Sophie gladly endured, aware that she would not have to tolerate his company much longer. With plump pockets, courtesy of her father, Vickerton returned to Cheltenham to await Sophie's return.

She found herself amazed that it should all be over so quickly and with so little fanfare. There were many plans to keep her busy, but she found the whole process bittersweet. She would be parting with her family forever, and they knew nothing of it. Every now and again she would catch herself staring thoughtfully at her father, wondering if he would miss her, trying to picture his face in ten, twenty years or more. Sophie decided she would even miss her mother, though she would never be able to summon her memory without some thread of anger.

The morning after Lord Charles's visit, her parents stood in the drive and waved them off as she and Alforth set out in his carriage, little knowing that their youngest daughter was leaving them for good.

As she gazed for the last time upon Cabot Park, Sophie felt an unexpected sadness burst inside her chest. She was leaving her only home for an uncertain future. But she was making the right decision, she told herself as the last of her house disappeared behind the trees. She was liberating herself from her family, from

Lord Charles. And from the pain Ian had caused her that even now overtook all other emotions. She was ready to begin anew.

"I need to make a stop before Liverpool," she said to her uncle. "There is one more thing I need to do."

Ian stared out the window of the study into the side gardens of the estate. It was the fifth day after his return, and he was reviewing some papers from his London solicitor. He'd spent the past few days visiting tenants and riding over the acres of family property, reinserting himself into the role of son and heir to Briarleigh. Stares and whispers had greeted him at every crofter's cottage, gossip trailing after him like his shadow.

He'd also gone over the books with the steward. It had been unnecessary, since the estate was capably managed, but he felt strongly the need to be active and useful. He missed the sense of purpose being a mountebank had given him, and without Sophie and her botanical research filling his thoughts, he found his days curiously empty.

He watched as a gardener watered an eglantine rosebush, and Ian almost leapt out of his chair to tell the man to keep the leaves dry lest he encourage the growth of disease. Smiling wryly to himself, Ian wondered what everyone would make of him, hale adventurer, pottering around with *rosa rubiginosa* bushes, plucking dead leaves from the ground and fretting about fungal diseases. It would be almost comical, if it didn't make his throat ache to think of it. To think of Sophie. Anything green and growing made him think of her, but roses in particular. He found the bloody flowers arousing. How was that for absurd?

Thus absorbed in his thoughts, he did not notice anyone enter the room until he heard his father's surprised exclamation.

"They didn't say you were in here," he muttered, startled.

Ian glanced up to see William begin to leave the room.

"Wait," he said, standing, "don't go."

Wary, his father stood in the doorway. "I was looking for this," he explained gruffly, holding up a book. He scowled, and Ian could tell that he disliked the faint note of apology in his voice. Remembering himself, that he was master of Briarleigh, and Ian the returning if unrepentant wastrel, he straightened and directed a scowl toward his son that had the reputation of making servants and certain members of Parliament scurry to do his bidding. Until very recently, that same scowl would have given Ian tremors. "What do you want? I've business to attend to." William added, "Unlike you, I honor my responsibilities."

Ian passed a weary hand over his eyes. "Let's not start on this today, Father. That isn't why I asked you to stay."

"I do not think we have much else to discuss."

Every moment with his father had been tense, fraught with words said and unsaid. "How is Alice?" Ian asked.

His father frowned. "Alice?"

"Alice Crowden."

Recognition dawned. His father shut the door. "It took me months to keep her father from suing us for breach of promise. I had to give him a ghastly sum."

"But what about her? Was she all right?"

William crossed his arms over his chest, planting

his feet on the floor. His stance bespoke the nobility of his lineage. "It's a bit late now to develop a conscience, is it not?"

"How is she?" Ian would not be distracted. He did not tell his father about the dozens of letters he had composed, asking for Alice's forgiveness, trying to explain as best he could why he had done something so completely reprehensible, but no words could ever fully articulate the complex knot of emotions that had compelled Ian to abandon his future wife. Ultimately, the letters were never sent, and the best Ian could hope for was that Alice wished him dead, or at the very least had forgotten him.

His father relented. "She's Alice Dunsford now."

Ian blinked in surprise. This was news. "She's married?"

With a rare, tiny smile, William said, "Indeed. A second son of Sir Frederick Dunsford, with a fine living in Somerset. They have two children and are expecting a third come Epiphany."

"Alice married to a clergyman." Ian lowered himself into his chair, musing. She had been full of laughter, merry and convivial, a young lady who loved to dance and sang prettily. He tried to imagine her tied to a sober clergyman. "I hope she is happy."

Grudgingly, his father answered, "Seems the girl has found her calling as a rector's wife, running the parish, her husband, and her children with great good sense." He added with a dismissive wave, "Or so I hear. I do not follow that kind of claptrap."

"Do they love each other?" Ian heard himself ask.

William started, scowled. "How the devil should I know that? And what difference does it make in any event?"

"It makes all the difference."

Slapping his book down on a tabletop, his father glowered. "What is this damned nonsense you are talking about? You abscond to parts unknown for seven years, and when you return you spout romantic gibberish." He took a step forward and pointed an accusing finger at Ian. "*I* was the one who had to clean up your mess. Everyone came to *me* looking for answers, asking me why my son had turned his back on his family and his intended, destroying all our plans, shaming the Briarleigh name. And I had nothing to tell them. No reason to give."

For a moment, the hard veneer of William's facade seemed to give way—he was no longer the imposing figure of paternal disapproval both he and Ian had fashioned him into, tight-jawed and indignant. Instead, briefly, self-doubt and hurt flickered across his aging face, rendering him young, and Ian felt for that ephemeral instant that he was looking at himself.

"I could not tell them anything," his father continued. He seemed almost sorrowful as he lowered himself into a nearby chair. "Because my son, my only child, told me nothing."

Ian had no response to this other than a quick, jerky nod. It was true.

"Why did you leave, Ian?" his father asked in the silence. It was the first time he had asked this question directly, without raising his voice or attempting to cow his son through threats and stormy tirades. "If you did not want Alice, you ought to have told me. We could have found a way to break the engagement."

"I didn't think you would be so understanding," Ian said with a strained, self-deprecating laugh. "If I had come to you two days before the wedding and asked to cry off, would you really have let me do it? Walk away from the whole business?"

After a moment's contemplation, William shook his head. "Most likely, no. In fact, I know I would not."

Ian went to stand by the window and saw that the gardener had moved on. He decided that he would take a greater interest in the grounds of Briarleigh Hall. Though the flowers were pretty enough, he did not think they were planted to their best advantage. He would give the head groundskeeper some suggestions later.

"I needed to travel," he said to the pale shimmer of his father reflected in the glass.

"You went on a Grand Tour," William objected. "What more did you need?"

Ian turned and faced his father. "I had to find out what kind of man I was. To be myself." He glanced around the study, one of the estate's more simple and comfortable spaces, yet still furnished with an abundance of fine Chippendale furniture and walls lined with stern portraits of Elizabethan and Stuart ancestors. "Away from all this. Away from you. From myself as the heir." He gave another self-mocking smile. "To learn whether or not I deserved the things I possessed."

"And what did you learn? Do you deserve them?" The question was partly sarcastic, but there was a hint of seriousness in his father's voice that Ian would not have detected years earlier.

"No." Ian shoved his hands into his pockets. In one of them, he touched the filmy silk of a stocking and rubbed it between his fingers. What was Sophie doing right now? Ian conjured an image of her, bent over her notebook, deeply concentrating as she sketched out the root structure of a wild iris. He could count from memory the freckles dotting the bridge of her nose and spreading across her cheeks. "I certainly don't."

"So why return?" his father asked gruffly. "You could have stopped writing to me, disappeared, and then the title and all the things you claim you do not deserve could have been passed on."

"To Lionel Nethercott?" Ian asked with a wry smile. "The man can barely read."

"He counts on his fingers, too." William's smile echoed his son's, but it soon faded. "And that is why you came back, because you did not want some fool of a cousin inheriting Briarleigh?"

"I came back," Ian said at length, "because I had traveled across the world looking for myself, and I understood finally that the answers were here. At home. There comes a time when a man has to stop running and face the demons that pursue him, see whether or not he can meet the challenge. And," he added softly, "I missed you, Father."

William opened his mouth to speak, but as he did so, a discreet tap sounded at the door. At his command, a footman entered.

"I beg your pardon for the interruption," the servant said deferentially, "but there are visitors wishing to see Master Ian."

Ian rolled his eyes. God, the last thing he wanted was to take tea with some neighborhood gossips waiting to pounce on him. It was a wonder they had stayed away for so long.

"I'm not receiving guests right now, Putnam," Ian said wearily. He wanted to continue this conversation with his father. They had never spoken at such length, not even before he left. "Tell them to come back some other time."

But the footman remained. He coughed discreetly.

"Yes?"

"I do beg your pardon, but they are most insistent."

"Who are these gadflies?" Ian's father demanded.

Putnam handed the viscount a calling card. Frowning, William read it, then handed the card back. "Morley. Never heard of him. Have the man run off."

"Yes, my lord," the footman said with a bow. As he turned to leave, Ian's voice stopped him.

"Is that *Alforth* Morley?"

As Putnam nodded in agreement, Ian's father asked, "You know this man?"

"I should," Ian answered, bolting for the door. "I'm marrying his niece."

Chapter Eighteen

Ian paused outside the door to the drawing room. He took a deep breath and rubbed his palms down the front of his breeches to dry them. He self-consciously smoothed his hair, breathed deeply again, and readied himself to meet Sophie's irate uncle. She must have told Alforth about what had happened between them, about Ian's true identity, about any number of the reprehensible things he had done over the course of the summer. It would not be very difficult to find him, knowing his family name and title. So the old man was probably here to tan his hide and demand he marry his niece.

That was *exactly* what Ian wanted to do. And as he turned the doorknob to let himself into the drawing room, he readied a speech to tell Alforth Morley just that.

The door swung open, Ian stepped inside, and all words fled.

Sophie stood in the middle of the room.

She turned to face him as he entered, serene and

self-possessed in a pale green traveling gown and broad-brimmed hat, and so beautiful that it hurt to look upon her. There was a slight sense of incongruity to see her here, in the gilded rooms of Briarleigh, when in his mind she lived in the green lushness of the forest and hills. Then it seemed so natural, so perfect, that she should be here now, as though his thoughts had summoned her into being, that Ian absorbed the surprise and turned it into unadulterated happiness.

"You've changed your mind," he said, stepping forward.

Out of the corner of his eye, he saw Alforth carefully raise himself out of a chair, and Ian could sense the black waves of hostility pouring off the man.

A sharp, cutting blade of disappointment pierced Ian as he came to stand in front of Sophie. He did not have to hear her answer. He could see it in her carefully composed face, pale underneath her golden freckles, the compressed set of her lips. The flicker of happiness guttered and went out, leaving him in darkness. His hands clenched into fists.

"I came to get something," she said, her voice low and strained, "something that belongs to me."

Ian frowned. This was not what he expected. If she did not mean to accept his proposal and had no diatribe for him—though her uncle surely did—he could not fathom what she was referring to. "I don't have—"

"Ian, will you introduce me to your friends?"

Everyone turned to see William, Lord Briarleigh, enter the room. Sophie curtsied and Alforth bowed, making Ian realize that his father did cut an impressive figure. The Andrewses had money in abundance, but they could not match the sheer aristocratic dignity that came with knowing one's family name was linked with the kings and queens of England. Ian watched as both Sophie and her uncle looked back and forth between his father and himself, mentally comparing the two, searching for a family resemblance, and trying to smother their surprise when they found the son to be a direct link to the father.

A small flare of gratification, petty as it was, rose in Ian. He had not been lying about this. He was not conjuring a patrician fantasy, some wish-fulfillment of a base-born fabulist. *Let them see me in my rightful place.*

Stifling this minuscule sense of self-righteousness, Ian quickly made introductions.

"Andrews," William mused after learning Sophie's name. "The Andrewses of Gloucestershire?"

"The same, my lord," Sophie said.

His father nodded. "A fine family with good connections." He gave a small, relieved smile as he turned to Alforth. "When my son told me just now that he was going to marry your niece—"

"I am not!" Sophie insisted hotly, heedless of interrupting the viscount. Her attempt at composure was now abandoned and she turned burning eyes toward Ian. "How dare you presume—"

Ian's father gazed back and forth between Sophie and Ian with an almost comical expression of confusion. Surely nothing had ever baffled his father before, but this wildflower girl had managed, in one instant, to displace him from his Ptolemaic system. Ian knew exactly how his father felt. His orbits were out of alignment whenever Sophie was around, too.

"Miss Andrews and I have some things to discuss, alone," Ian said. He took hold of her arm and began to lead her to the door.

She struggled against him. "We have nothing to discuss."

"I think our conversation should be held *privately*," Ian insisted through clenched teeth. "Unless you want me to tell my father about everything we've done together," he added softly in her ear. "Who knows? Maybe he'll wish us happy and begin planning the wedding at once."

Snatching her arm away from his grasp, Sophie said to her uncle, "Yes, Ian and I will continue our conversation in private. Please wait for me here, Uncle. I shall be back in five minutes."

They left Alforth and Ian's father in awkward silence in the drawing room. Sophie followed Ian down a corridor before stopping and demanding, "Where are we going?"

He looked around, raking a hand through his hair, disoriented, angry, irritated with himself and with her. She threw him into chaos whenever she was nearby and, as he glanced around at the heavy paneled hallways of Briarleigh, he felt as though her question had several meanings.

"I don't know," he answered crossly. "Tell me why you're here."

She looked both sophisticated and fragile in her hat, tied beneath her chin with slim yellow ribbons. She had to tilt her head back to look into his eyes. It was the perfect angle at which to kiss her. "I've come for my notebook."

He could only repeat blankly, "Notebook?"

She made a noise of impatience. "With all my sketches and notes. I left it in the caravan. It's mine and . . . I want it back." There was a frisson of desperation in her voice, a struggle to maintain mastery over something wild and wounded that threatened to burst forth at any moment.

She was suffering, Ian realized. As much as he.

God, if he could just pull her into his arms, kiss her as he had been longing to do for the last hundred years of his life, perhaps he could erase her doubts, make her forget the impediments that stood between them. The words he could not say.

"Now," she added, squaring her jaw. She put a hand on his chest and held him away. "Alforth and I are running late and need to be back on the road."

Ian stepped back, just noticing that he had been trying to move her up against the wall. "Come with me."

Sophie's resolve was sorely tested when she first saw Ian come into the drawing room of Briarleigh. His handsomeness stretched a tight net of need around her heart—the familiar and exotic planes of his gorgeous face, the taut strength of his lean body. She wanted to throw herself into his arms and tell him that it was all right, she would learn to live without his love if only she could be near him. But she made herself be strong, strong enough to withstand the unbearable temptation he offered as they stood close together in the hallway.

They did not talk as she followed him to the stables. She watched the broad width of his shoulders, the dark fall of his queue that she knew felt both thick and silky in her fingers, the narrow taper of his waist as he moved ahead of her.

She gave a small start to see the familiar, beloved little wagon, so gaudy and cheerful, amid such alien surroundings. To her eyes, the caravan looked a bit melancholy here in the Jacobean splendor of the stables, and far from the life of an itinerant salesman. Strange that she should feel protective of a wagon when her own heart felt as though it had been run over by a hundred heavy mail coaches.

"It's been here ever since I got back," Ian explained tersely as he opened the door.

Sophie peered in cautiously. She felt strange, otherworldly, standing next to the man who figured so prominently in her dreams and gazing at the place that was the site of her happiest moments and worst misery. The caravan was haunted by memories, but she forced herself to stand and stare impassively, as though she could somehow banish it from the hold it had on her soul.

"It's only a wagon, after all," she murmured.

"What's that?" Ian asked. He brushed against her as he stepped inside, and Sophie cursed herself as she darted out of his way. Touching him was agonizing; even the smallest contact sent a torrent of crackling awareness through her body.

"Nothing." She thought she would follow him in, but then dismissed the idea at once. As strong as she wanted to be at this moment, she did not want to delude herself. If she joined Ian inside the caravan, she would close the door behind them and not let him out until he had thoroughly made love to her. And then, damn her, she would beg to be his wife, whether he loved her or not.

"I know that book is here," Ian muttered, half to himself. "Where did I put it?" He shuffled through some papers and books until he found Sophie's notebook. She reached out to take it from him, but he turned, stooping in the half-light of the caravan, and opened it.

Sophie was immediately reminded of their first meeting, when he had looked at her work and she felt as though she was showing a stranger the most intimate and precious part of herself. Little had she known then exactly how intimate they would become. But her love had not been enough for him.

She was about to demand the notebook back when she noticed him jerk away from the pages, his face tense with undisguised pain. Curious, she bent forward to get a better look at what he was staring at and saw the picture she had drawn of him at the beginning of the summer. Sophie grimaced and snatched the book away, snapping the cover shut.

"God, that picture," Ian said hoarsely.

"Never mind it," Sophie choked out. "I was foolish. The girl who drew it is not the woman who stands here now." She moved away from the caravan.

"But," Ian said, his voice thick, "the way you saw me, the way you drew me. No one has ever seen me that way before." He jumped out of the wagon to stand beside her.

Sophie's cheeks flamed, but she could not stop herself now that she had begun. "Though I did not know it then, love made me draw you that way. As if you were the answer to all the questions I've ever asked. The mystery at the heart of every plant."

Ian looked stricken. She tried to take comfort from his unhappiness but could find none.

"I shall not draw you that way anymore," Sophie continued. "You need not worry. I will be going away for a very long time. We will never see each other again, so we won't have to live with the burden of our mistakes."

The muscles in his jaw tightened, and she held her

arms tight around the notebook to keep from running her fingers along the side of his face. She had never met anyone so impossibly masculine, so effortlessly sensual, whose every move called for a host of lyrical comparisons.

"I promise to be faithful to you, Sophie," Ian said, his voice rough, as he reached up and caressed the side of her face with his large, capable hand. She struggled to keep her eyes open, to resist the temptation he was offering her. All it took was the slightest brush of his fingers and she felt herself tremble like a young willow. "As your husband, I will honor our marriage vows. I'll give you all the money and space you need to pursue your botany. You'll have my body, my house—"

"But not your love." He had no rejoinder for that, and she shook her head. "I cannot live like that. I will not. And no matter what you give me, your fidelity, your title, you will always wonder, as you would have wondered with Alice, 'Is there something more?'"

"No—"

"I have something for you," Sophie interrupted, desperate to leave. She reached into her pocket. "You wanted love in a bottle, and I came to bring it to you."

Ian momentarily brightened. "Really?"

"Yes." She pressed a small vial into his hand and swiftly turned to walk away. She had to do this quickly, before her conviction faltered, before she let the last of her youthful innocence dissolve into nothingness.

"It's empty," Ian called out behind her.

She stopped walking but did not turn around. "I know."

And then she was running for the door.

* * *

An empty bottle.

The legacy of the summer now sat in Ian's palm, and he stared at it, then at the vacant space where Sophie had just stood. For several moments, Ian could only look at the small container nestled in his palm. The nothingness inside the bottle was Sophie's last indictment, a bitter coda telling him that the thing he pursued was only a fantasy.

He deserved it.

But he could not let her leave. Not yet.

Ian ran through the stables and across the lawn toward the house, but before he made it back inside, he heard the rattle of coach wheels. Sprinting toward the front drive, he saw Alforth's carriage heading toward the open road. Ian cupped his hands around his mouth and called her name, but either she could not hear him above the din of the carriage or she refused to hear him. He contemplated running back to the stables and saddling his horse to go after her, and then . . .

And then what? The empty bottle still clutched in his hand reminded him that he could never give her the one thing she wanted, and as long as he remained as barren as the bottle, he would always come up lacking.

The gravel crunched as his father came to stand beside him.

"She's the reason you came back," William said.

Ian nodded stiffly. He did not trust himself to speak.

"I thought travel made a man wise," his father added.

Ian's laugh was a harsh bark. "You were mistaken." He looked once more at the bottle, then pitched it into the hedges. "Everyone is mistaken about me."

His father did not follow him back into the stables. Ian walked alone, not realizing where he was going until he was back at the caravan. Strange that he had not come here until today, when there were books and papers and a host of objects that needed clearing out. The wagon embarrassed his father, of course, but William's appeals to destroy it or, at the least, repaint and gut it, were staunchly denied. Ian was not ready to get rid of it yet, just as he had not been ready to break from his past as a mountebank, from his life with Sophie.

Now he sat himself at her little laboratory, looking over the rows of bottles and saw that in her haste to be rid of him, she had left behind a few sheets of notes, still half-buried in the jumble of things he had never summoned the strength to put away. This was where she had sat, where she busied herself every day, going over formulas, distilling chemicals from plants, filling the small space of the wagon with her fresh, sunny smell and her warm, open heart. She was right: He felt as hollow and blank as an empty vial.

He saw the final bottle, its label written in her tiny but clear hand, *Bellflower & Sessile Oak Distillation— 22 August, 1763*, and picked it up. Ian studied its contents, some clear liquid, and understood that what he held in his hand was the last thing she had been working on before everything had fallen apart. Her quest at least had been successful, and now he held the result in his hand. Sophie had thought that perhaps the symbiotic chemical relationship between the two disparate plants might hold the key to what they both sought. Might it? Could it be the answer?

Before he could stop himself, Ian uncorked the bottle and drank.

It tasted like rainwater, slightly musty. He licked his lips, waiting. Nothing. He dropped the bottle back beside its brethren, disappointed, but he did not leave the caravan immediately.

Instead, he stared without seeing at Sophie's remaining notes, and found his hand running back and forth over her handwriting. It was very like her, not overly elaborate nor bold. Small letters linked together, precise, diligent, but the little loops indicated that there was something more to her than mere science. Someone would have to look very close in order to get past the obvious, to discover the hidden treasure—Sophie had a soul that was made for loving.

And then a strange thing happened. As Ian held her notes, as he sat at her laboratory and breathed her in, he felt himself overcome with a liquid, dawning awareness that filled his body as palpably as a beam of light shining through him.

He had seen the sculpted goddesses decorating the temples at Alampur, their lithe bodies curved and alluring, promising physical and spiritual rapture. Sophie, slim and graceful as she walked through the open fields or lay tangled in his arms, made those female figures appear as clumsy and awkward as oxen. The henna *mehndi* decorating the *kuchipudi* dancer's hands became gaudy paint compared to the scattered golden freckles dancing across Sophie's face. Her laughter sounded more beautiful than the famed *ghazal* singers of the North.

Ian remembered a sunrise he had once seen over the Bay of Bengal. He had spent the night learning meditation from one of the most revered yogi in all of India, and with newfound appreciation he had watched the sun come up, turning the water into a shining mirror, foaming and cresting against the shore in a blaze of bright radiance. The world seemed impossibly beautiful to Ian then, everything joined together in an invisible but luminous web, breathing as one, dreaming together. Sitting on a rocky ledge and watching this spectacle unfold before him, Ian had never felt such a profound and deep happiness. Merely naming the emotion he felt diminished it, and so he was content to let it simply be, taking him wherever he needed to go, joining him with the vast fellowship of humanity.

He never thought he would experience anything as powerful as that emotion again. But he was wrong.

Whenever he was with Sophie, the feelings he experienced that morning on the Bay of Bengal faded, diminished, in comparison to the intense, transcendent euphoria she made him feel. She both made the world a better place and also made everything else fall away until there was only her, and she was everything.

Losing her became an unbearable agony, a heavy weight pressing down, a barrenness within himself. He found that he was having difficulty drawing his next breath without her beside him.

Ian braced his arms on the small table, struggling to keep his heart from crashing through his chest. The pain of life with no Sophie in it was physical, acute, unthinkable.

How had he let her leave? What had he been thinking? Something had changed in him that made him burn to get her back—that much he knew.

The answer came to him the way the sun had broken across the waves that morning in India, with a sudden clarity.

He loved her. He had thought it impossible, but it

was true. He loved Sophie, deeply. With all the properties of the earth.

Ian laughed out loud. It was amazing. The most incredible sensation he had ever experienced, this gift of love. Somehow, it had struck him, the proverbial bolt from the blue.

But, no, not out of the blue. His gaze fell on the bottle that had contained the extract of the sessile oak and bellflower, and he realized that Sophie had done it. She had found love in a bottle after all. The roots of the two plants had given him the necessary chemicals he needed to love. The knowledge that a potion had given him the very thing he wanted elated and saddened him at the same time. His theory had been right, and so had hers. They had succeeded. He loved her, thanks to the elixir.

Hands shaking, he scanned the notes Sophie had left behind. He needed to see exactly what she had done, how she had prepared the sample. He could try to replicate it. She could write a paper. They could change the face of the world with one tiny bottle. Sophie was a genius, he had no doubt the love he felt for her proved that. His eyes moved quickly across the page and then, as he read her last notes, he felt his whole body turn cold, then hot.

22 August, 1763: am now preparing solution for extract of campanula persicfolia and quercus petraea. Must first distill and filter water solution before adding plant extracts tomorrow. Success? Must discuss with Ian.

The paper drifted to the floor.

Water. He had drunk distilled water. Nothing more. Which meant . . .

Ian had his horse saddled in less than a minute. He was cantering across the yard when his father came running out of the house.

"Leaving again?" he called after Ian.

"I'll be back," Ian shouted as he kicked his horse into a gallop. "And I'll have my bride with me."

"Thank the Lord for that," William breathed to himself as he waved Godspeed to his son.

Chapter Nineteen

Ian wasn't entirely certain he could catch them. After all, their carriage was being pulled by two horses and he had just the one. But his gelding was bred for speed, and within fifteen minutes, he spied their carriage off the side of the road. Ian smiled to himself. Sophie most likely had asked her uncle to stop so she could collect some fine local specimens for her herbarium. The pounding of his horse's hooves was nearly drowned out by the hammering of his heart as he thought about what he would tell her, how he would win her.

Just tell her the truth, and maybe, God help him, she would forgive him.

Elation withered as he neared the carriage. The driver—Ian recognized him as John Driscoll—sat in the road, cradling a swollen jaw, his expression stunned and uncomprehending. He did not even look up when Ian's horse neared. The doors to the carriage were open, hanging from their hinges like broken wings. Ian slowed his horse and leapt down from the saddle.

No, no. God, no.

Alforth was slumped against the squabs inside, a new bruise turning the side of his face purple. Blood trickled down his chin and dripped onto the snowy white stock around his neck. Ian jumped into the carriage, fumbled for a pulse, and blessedly found it, faint but steady. He tried to breathe a sigh of relief, but it was impossible.

There was no trace of Sophie. She was gone.

"Where is she?"

Gently but persistently, Ian shook Alforth, trying to rouse him as he dabbed at the wound on the older man's face. Sophie's uncle muttered, stirred slightly, struggling to regain consciousness. At least the blood from the bruise had slowed. Under normal circumstances, Ian would have fetched a surgeon immediately. But these were not normal circumstances.

"Alforth, what happened? Where is Sophie?" Ian asked, his voice sharp with urgency.

Eyes blinking slowly open, Alforth mumbled, "They took her. Clubbed Driscoll and took her."

"*Who* took her?"

"McGannon and his men."

The blood drained from Ian's whole body, leaving him colder than he had ever felt in his life. He stilled as his mind raced. He had to get her back. But why the hell had McGannon taken Sophie, when it was him that he wanted? Unless—and this froze Ian with terror—the criminal planned on extracting his revenge on Ian through Sophie. Ian squeezed his eyes shut at the possibility. He would not let anything happen to her, didn't care what it cost, even his own life.

"There's no demand for ransom," Driscoll said, supporting his bruised jaw.

That thought turned Ian's blood into pure ice. No ransom demand meant that McGannon had no plans to return Sophie. He saw her crushed hat in the dirt and swallowed a knot of fear.

Ian vaulted into the saddle. He wheeled his horse around to face Alforth and Driscoll. "Walk to the large hall a mile up this road. They'll tend to you there. And have someone fetch the law."

"But you're unarmed. What will you do?" Alforth asked, now alert and anxious.

"Get her back." With a kick to his horse's flanks, Ian galloped off in pursuit.

Hope had risen in her chest as she sat in the carriage, moving away from Ian and toward Liverpool, when she heard the pounding of hoofbeats. He was coming for her! But then she heard men's voices, shouting, a struggle. The doors to the carriage were almost ripped off their hinges as a face from Sophie's nightmares stared inside.

McGannon. He'd found her at last.

Alforth tried to fight him off, even managing to give one of the henchmen a decent knock, but the blow he'd received to his head sent him careening back against the seat, ghostly pale. Sophie attempted to go to him, terrified that McGannon had killed him, but she felt rough arms around her waist, pulling her from the carriage, away from Alforth. She struggled, trying to grip the door frame as though if she just stayed in the carriage she would be safe, but the hands that held her were too strong. Her fingers were pried back until they almost snapped. Before she could stop it, she found herself slung up onto a waiting horse, McGannon holding her waist in a vise.

She did not bother trying to demand her release, or even offering money or her jewelry in exchange for her life. One look at the savage fury in McGannon's face told her that this was no typical kidnapping: It was revenge.

Cold, murderous rage burned in McGannon's dark eyes. The kind that brooked no quarter, gave no mercy, and said that he had better things to do with her than simply killing her.

Quickly, Sophie assessed the situation, even as fear beyond anything she had ever experienced held her more tightly than her kidnapper's grip. McGannon had a new gang, three men whose indifferent, brutal faces told her that they came from the lowest dregs of society, men who could be called upon to do the most loathsome, foul acts all for the promise of coin. They would be no help to her.

She did not have long to consider her plight. At his signal, McGannon's men mounted and kicked their horses into a run, Sophie and their leader at the head of the pack.

Ian swore. It was taking all the skills he had learned tracking to keep up with McGannon. Soon the sun would set and the trail through the woods would go cold. They had long since passed territory that was familiar to him. He had no faith in the constabulary, if they were even coming. Men like McGannon fell outside their ken.

He thought of Sophie, what she must be going through, and nearly went mad. No, he had to stay focused. For her, to save her life—and his own in the process.

* * *

"Damn it, bitch!"

McGannon called her a dozen other filthy names as Sophie tumbled to the ground. The rest of the gang pulled up tight on their reins as their leader jumped down and grabbed Sophie by the hair. She yelped.

"What the hell do you think you're doing?" McGannon spat, his enraged face inches from her own. He shook her by her hair, forcing tears from her eyes as her scalp burned.

"I fell," Sophie choked.

McGannon snarled as his free hand reached back and slapped her. Lights danced in front of her eyes, and she wanted to ask him to please, please loosen his grip on her hair, but she knew any kind of pleading would only make him more furious. So she struggled to keep silent.

"Bloody clumsy whore," he sneered. "You fall one more time and I give you to my men."

Her eyes involuntarily darted to the members of the gang, who eyed her as avidly as starving dogs would a piece of Sunday joint. "I won't," she promised.

McGannon hauled her to her feet and dragged her back onto the horse. With a shouted command, he and his gang set their sweat-flecked horses back into a run.

In her heart, Sophie tried to make peace with the world, figuring these few hours would be her last, praying she might see Ian once more but knowing that it would be impossible.

And in her hand, she clutched a handful of plants, torn up from the earth when she fell. Plants, she hoped, that would save her life.

Night fell. As Ian wheeled his horse in frustrated circles, he strained to find a trace of the trail left by Mc-

Gannon. He swore out loud. He would not give up looking for her, but his prospects were diminishing.

Peering down from the saddle, Ian thought at first his eyes were deceiving him, showing him something he wanted so desperately to see. Urging his horse forward a few paces, he leaned down and squinted. There it was: a faint, luminescent shimmering, a hazy, unearthly glow in a tiny patch on some dried leaves.

Straightening, Ian stared into the distance and saw—yes—another faintly gleaming smudge up ahead. He dismounted and led his horse to the next glowing spot, where, crouching down, he touched his fingertips to the strange substance. It was sticky, wet. Rubbing the pads of his fingers together, he tested its consistency and then, to be certain, he gave the liquid a careful sniff.

Plant sap. From St. Elmo's wort, the plant that glowed when crushed.

Understanding dawned. Jumping quickly into the saddle, Ian kicked his horse into a run. Sure enough, a few droplets of glowing sap appeared ahead. He was on the right track.

Sophie was leading him toward her. He could only pray he could get to her in time.

It wasn't nearly as flash as the last hideout, just an abandoned gamekeeper's cottage. McGannon had really been keen on that place, the old Roman ruin—it had history, drama, an atmosphere a body might see on the London stage. But it wasn't a secret anymore, not with the law crawling all over the place like lice on a convict's head.

That was another thing McGannon was going to punish that bloody mountebank for, losing his best den. And his men, to boot. They'd woken up with banging headaches and nearly pissed themselves in fright when they realized what had happened. Their confidence in him as the gang's upright man had been shot, and they scattered like a bunch of yellow morts. Which left him without a gang, without a hideout, and the law hot on his heels.

He looked at his prisoner. "Daisy—didn't that mountebank call you Daisy?—I got lots of plans for you and your flash man. Tomorrow we'll deliver our ransom letter to your cove. He'll come looking for you, and that's when I'll get my revenge on the both of you."

McGannon was particularly pleased with himself when he saw the girl begin to shake. She closed her eyes as the men laughed raucously.

"If only I could see the mountebank's face when he finds out we got his bawd," McGannon gloated. "Don't you worry, though. Once he gets our note, he'll be here in a hurry. Then we can have our own little holiday."

"How long we got to wait, Dan?" Southworth asked, standing near the window and peering out into the darkness. "I want to dust it up."

"Me, too," Lincoln chimed in.

McGannon contemplated the doxy as she tried, bless her, not to look scared, but she was plainly quivering with fear.

"Soon, boys," he said with a generous wave of his arm. "Be patient. It'll be worth the wait."

"One way or the other, our mark'll come calling," Southworth said. He looked down at the girl and grinned, looming over her. "So it don't matter what condition the doxy's in, does it?"

"He's got a point," Lincoln added in his fashion.

"I mean," Southworth continued, trailing a finger down the girl's face as she tried to turn away, "we got all night to have some fun, don't we?"

There was a *pop* and Southworth stood up straight with a jerk, then frowned down at the bright red stain spreading across his shoulder.

"What the hell—?" he said, and then toppled to the floor, clutching his shoulder and groaning.

McGannon was on his feet in an instant. Before he had gone two steps, something whizzed into the cottage, landing in the fireplace. There was a loud bang, a bright flash, and suddenly the little room was filled with thick smoke.

"An ambush!" Lincoln shouted.

McGannon knew with fury that the mountebank had tricked him once again.

Sophie's vision and lungs were filled with choking, brackish smoke that poured from the fireplace. As she fought against her bonds, she became aware of a figure close beside her, touching her wrists and ankles. She tried to pull away, or at least hit the man next to her. But then she heard a familiar voice in her ear and could barely keep tears of relief and happiness at bay.

"It's me, Sophie. Stay still so I can cut these ropes."

She calmed herself so he could saw away at the thick bindings. Her hands came free and she quickly bent to help him with her ankles. Ian removed her gag and tied a piece of cloth around the lower part of her face to shield her from the smoke.

Sophie wanted so badly to throw her arms around him, but she knew they could not waste valuable time, so she forced herself to stay focused. "You followed my trail," she said, coughing. She tried to make out the dark shapes of McGannon and the other men as they wheezed and hacked in the dense smoke. "What's in the fireplace?"

"Some dried plants that create a flash when set ablaze together," he explained hurriedly. He too had a kerchief tied around his nose and mouth.

"What happened to the man standing guard outside?"

Sophie fancied she saw him smile beneath his kerchief. "Gave him a good wallop to the head with a tree branch and took his pistol for a souvenir."

McGannon's voice roared out in the haze. "I'll kill you, you filthy whoreson bastard! Lincoln, take him." Ian leapt away from her as the kidnapper's man hurtled forward. The smoke was beginning to clear a bit, but even so, Sophie could not distinguish between Ian and the criminal as they grappled together.

Sophie desperately wanted to help and thought she might be able to throw something at Lincoln to at least stun him and give Ian an opening, but she could not be certain which man she would hit. She crawled on the floor, fumbling for one of the footstools she had seen earlier. Everything eluded her grasp.

A shot rang out and a man screamed. Sophie gasped in horror as one of the two figures fighting in the smoke fell to the ground. She started forward. Please, no. She would go mad if—

"You shot me, McGannon," Lincoln's voice cried. "Right in me arse! You maggoty bastard!"

"Shut up, clod pole," McGannon drawled. "Now I got a clear shot at the mountebank."

"Not before I shoot you first," Sophie said.

Both men turned to her. She clutched the pistol of the fallen Southworth in her hands, aiming it at Mc-Gannon as best she could through the smoky air.

"You don't know how to use that thing, stupid whore! You'll wind up shooting yourself."

Sophie pulled back the hammer. The click silenced McGannon's laughter. "I am a quick scholar," she said, forcing her hands to be steady. "Put your weapon down slowly," she commanded him. "I've never shot a man before, but I think I'd enjoy shooting you."

She darted a quick glance at Ian and saw him eyeing McGannon warily, his body tense and alert in the hazy light. He was slowly, inch by inch, moving toward Dark Dan as the criminal's attention was focused on Sophie. She made herself look back toward McGannon to keep his concentration solely on her.

"All right now, love," McGannon said with oily placation. He kept one hand raised as he began to lower the pistol in his other hand to the table in front of him. "Let's take it easy. Let's not lose our heads. See? I'm putting the gun down, just like you asked."

Sophie doubted that a man bent on revenge would so easily capitulate, and was not surprised when she heard Ian shout, "Sophie, duck!"

Several things happened at once: Sophie dove for the ground, losing her grip on the gun as she heard the awful, loud report of McGannon's pistol and smelled the acrid burn of powder beneath the herbal smoke. The bullet tore into the wooden wall just above her head, showering her with a small rain of splinters. Ian charged McGannon and they both went rolling across the floorboards.

Sophie tried to retrieve the gun that had skittered away from her, but the grappling bodies of Ian and

McGannon blocked her path. The two men fought ferociously, trading the most horrendous blows with a savagery Sophie had never witnessed before.

A grunt near her feet had her looking down. Southworth had managed to rouse himself enough to crawl toward the loose pistol. As his fingers stretched out to the gun, Sophie grabbed a footstool and brought it against his head with all her strength. The footstool smashed apart. With a guttural moan, he collapsed limp to the ground.

But her triumph was short-lived as she turned her attention back to Ian and McGannon. The kidnapper had pinned Ian to the ground; then Ian lodged his foot against McGannon's thigh and pushed him away. Both men leapt to their feet. Bellowing, McGannon hurtled himself toward Ian, but in a blur of motion, Ian kicked McGannon in the chest, sending the kidnapper back to the ground, gasping for breath. Before McGannon could recover himself, Ian swooped around and pinned Dark Dan's arms behind his back. Then McGannon twisted sharply, his eyes rolled back into his head, and he crumpled to the floor, insensate.

Ian rose. His kerchief had been torn off during the fray, revealing a cut by the side of his mouth, which he impatiently wiped at with the cuff of his shirt. And then his arms were around her, enfolding her tightly, and she was pressed to the solid expanse of his chest.

"Well done, Sophie," he said, kissing the crown of her head.

She laughed and cried at the same time, her hands clutching him, grateful beyond measure for his presence, for the very fact of Ian. "And you, too," she managed to say on a half-sob, half-chuckle. "How did you knock him out like that?"

"It's called *kalari payattu*, a fighting technique from India. I learned a bit when I was there. Did those bastards touch you?" he asked, his fingers tender but his voice hard.

"No," Sophie answered quickly. She had never seen such cold fury in his eyes before, and it frightened her a little. "They didn't have time."

"I should kill McGannon," Ian muttered as he bent to retrieve the primed pistol. "But the law will take care of him. His final moments will be at the end of a rope."

"We can tie them up—securely, this time—and take him in for prosecution," Sophie said, shuddering. She moved away to retrieve the ropes she had been bound with earlier.

"What about us?" whimpered Lincoln, cradling his injured bottom.

Ian pocketed the pistols. "You're going with McGannon."

They spent the next few minutes dragging the unconscious guard inside the cottage and bandaging the wounds of the injured. Then they tied everyone together on a lunge line to deliver the criminals to the authorities. It was an awkward business and slow going, but Sophie was far too dazed to feel much of anything beside relief.

"Come on, Sophie," Ian said, his voice tired but exhilarated. She felt his arms go around her again and took immeasurable comfort from them. She breathed him in, alive, warm, and rested her head against his chest. His hands cradled her as tenderly as a rose. "I'm going to take you home."

Chapter Twenty

A crowd of local law enforcers met them as they rode up the front drive of Briarleigh Hall. In the flickering light of torches, at least fifteen men leapt out to immediately take McGannon and his crew prisoner, ready to deliver them to jail and trial.

Ian helped Sophie down from the saddle and supported her weight when her legs proved unable to hold her.

"It's been a long day for you," he murmured in her ear.

She would have given her thanks, but at that moment the front door to the hall opened and Alforth, Driscoll, and Ian's father rushed out.

As quickly as he could manage with his cane, Alforth hurried down the steps to his niece and enfolded her in his embrace. "My dear girl, how I've worried," he said, and she felt on her neck the dampness of his tears. Sophie let go of Ian in order to hold her uncle, brushing her fingers against the bandage on his head.

"How are you?" she asked softly.

Alforth quickly dismissed her concern. "Fine, fine." He sent the viscount a look of gratitude as Briarleigh came down the stairs. "Lord Briarleigh had his personal physician tend to the injury, and I should be right as rain in a week or so."

"Me, too," Driscoll chimed in, though the bandage around his jaw made his words muffled and thick.

Sophie found herself laughing more from relief than at the comical picture he made, but she reached out and took the coachman's hand. "I am glad. Meredith would be most displeased if I let anything happen to her future bridegroom."

Driscoll brightened as best he could from beneath the gauze bandages. "She'll marry me?"

"Oh, my." Sophie gulped. "She hasn't told you?"

"No. I was going to ask, but—"

"Constable! Justice!" a voice cried out. "Come back and arrest that mountebank!"

Sophie turned her attention away from her uncle and coachman to see Lord Charles jumping down from Sophie's parents' carriage, indignant. He pointed at Ian, who came to stand beside Sophie.

Before Ian or Sophie could speak, however, Caroline Andrews's strident voice punctuated the cacophony. As a footman helped her descend from the carriage, she loudly demanded, "What in sweet heaven's name do you mean by running off like that, Sophie? And Alforth, I shall never forgive you for assisting her."

"This is hardly the time . . ." Alforth began.

Sophie put a hand on her uncle's sleeve. "It's all right, Uncle A."

With a frown and a nod, Alforth silenced himself.

"I was leaving," Sophie said to her parents, standing tall and composed, "because you forced me to."

"Forced?" her mother cried. "We never—"

"I shall finish, and then you may speak."

"What about the mountebank?" Lord Charles interjected with a whine.

"Be quiet," Sophie snapped. "No one is talking to you."

Vickerton's response was to turn purple, then red, his mouth opening and closing in impotent fury. Sophie thought she heard Ian's choked laughter, but her attention was focused solely on her parents.

"I didn't mind your indifference. I assumed that was what parents felt for their daughters. But then," she said, her eyes stinging and hot, "you took away the only thing that mattered to me, the only thing that gave my life meaning—to sell me to a title." She felt her throat close as the effects of a tumultuous day and a lifetime of disappointed expectation threatened to engulf her. "I was nothing but a pawn," she added, glancing at Vickerton, "to save your name."

"But she's ruined herself with this *mountebank*," Vickerton insisted. "Destroyed your family name. Though I suppose I could endure her monstrosity so long as I was well paid."

In two strides, Ian had put his fist squarely in Vickerton's face. Lord Charles fell back, shrieking, blood squirting from his nose onto the white lace of his jabot.

"You broke my nose," he screeched. "I'll have you clapped in irons!"

"I doubt that," Ian drawled.

Vickerton tried to laugh scornfully, but it was impossible to do so with a kerchief pressed to his injured, bleeding nose.

Sophie watched as Ian effortlessly summoned every

ounce of nobility he possessed. The effect was stunning. He was magisterial as he regarded her mother, father, and erstwhile suitor.

"I am," he said, "Ian Claypool, Baron Ashford, heir to Viscount Briarleigh."

Everyone gaped. Caroline finally breathed, "Impossible."

"It *is* possible, madam," the viscount said, coming to place a hand on Ian's shoulder. "This man is my son and heir."

While Vickerton goggled, squawking, and Simon Andrews blustered his amazement, Caroline gazed back and forth between the two men, comprehension dawning. Suddenly her face glowed with a smile.

"This is wonderful, Sophie!" she cried, clapping her hands together. "You have netted yourself a viscount's son. I could not have wished for better." She ran forward to clasp Sophie tightly, then stepped back, her nose wrinkled. "But you are filthy. This will not do, not if you are to become a baroness."

Sophie's heart sank. Everyone was leaping to conclusions, assuming that Sophie would gladly become Ian's wife simply because he had a title, when that was the least of her concerns. She could not marry Ian without his love; and yet what, exactly, was she waiting for from him? The words themselves? He had rescued her from McGannon, endangering his own life to save hers. He had offered her the protection of his name, the fidelity of his bed and body. He respected her and her work, encouraged it not only because it meant so much to her but because she was good at it. If what he felt for her was not love, then it came as close as she could hope, and perhaps that would be enough. Better that than the alternative—life without him.

Ian spoke before she did. "Sophie's love of dirt saved lives," he said, tipping his head toward Alforth.

"But if she is to become a member of the peerage, she will shame your family and ours with her bedraggled appearance," Caroline countered.

"She honors all of us just as she is, madam," Ian answered. "But it does not signify. She does not want to marry me."

Caroline looked at Sophie with undisguised horror, the same horror Sophie felt chilling her from the inside out. "You are a fool."

"Sophie is the wisest person I know," Ian said, his voice hard and lethal as he stepped between mother and daughter. "And anyone who says otherwise is the fool."

Sophie's mother gasped, looking to her husband to defend her and finding nothing but a passive shrug. Therein lay the dangers of a subservient husband, Sophie realized: a man who will offer no resistance to you, or anyone else.

"Saying no to me was one of the best things Sophie could have done," Ian continued.

Oh, Lord, he didn't want her anymore. Sophie felt herself begin to shrivel up, knowing that the blame rested solely with her. But she had thought she was acting for the best.

Ian turned to her, and she found herself staring at him, learning his face, trying to know him as thoroughly as she might know a plant, inside and out, so that when the time came, she could recall him perfectly from memory, since that would be all she would have left.

"You were right." He smiled ironically. "If you had accepted my proposal, I would've wondered if there was something I was missing."

"Then we are fortunate that I said no," she said, striving to keep her tears from surfacing. Her heart, exhausted and battered, felt as though it was withering on the vine.

Ian's eyes transfixed her with burning intensity, making the curious faces of their families fade into a pale blur at the back of her awareness. "I spent the past seven years searching for one thing, something I wanted desperately but that scared me to death. I was offered a chance at happiness and threw it away because of stupid fear. I was less afraid of the Thugee or the mounted raiders of Anatolia. It took your rejection and a bottle of plain water to make me realize that the only obstacle preventing me from loving you was me."

"I don't understand," Sophie whispered as her heart began to race. "What bottle of water?"

He made a noise of dismissal. "It was nothing. And everything," he added with a smile. "I drank the water from the bottle thinking it was the sessile oak and bellflower extract you prepared, just after you claimed your notebook."

"So you tricked yourself."

He gave a self-deprecating grin. "It's one of the oldest ploys in the book—the bait and switch. Give your mark one thing when he is expecting another."

"And you were left with the illusion of love where none existed. Well done, Ian," she said. "You are so adept at deception you even fooled yourself."

"Damn it, that's not what I meant," Ian said, rubbing his jaw with his palm.

Stubble had begun to show on his chin, giving him a rakish appearance. At that moment, he was both the baron *and* the mountebank, the dark charmer who had won her heart over the course of the summer and also the strange new nobleman who had offered her marriage.

"I thought I was given the illusion, but instead I got the real thing. I do love you. Completely. Without any tricks of any kind. And I pray," he continued, his voice growing rough as he stared at her as though she were the center of the universe, "that someday you can forgive me for being so damned stupid. Because I will love you for the rest of my life."

He brought the backs of her hands to his mouth, bowed his head, and did not so much kiss her as rest his lips upon her skin in a warm, dry plea.

Sophie swallowed. And swallowed again, gulping for air. She felt the world begin to right, to fix itself in place as she took deep breaths of night air into her lungs. Like Ian's touch, even the simple act of breathing felt exquisite.

"There is usually dirt beneath my fingernails," she managed.

Ian looked up sharply, the beginnings of hope spreading across his beautiful face.

"And I miss meals sometimes when I am working," she added, her voice quavering as her hands trembled. She felt Ian's hands also beginning to shake.

"I know," he said.

"I'd rather be in my laboratory than go to a ball," Sophie continued.

He nodded. "I don't much care for balls."

"Did I mention that I am frequently dirty?"

"Sophie," Ian asked carefully, "are you telling me yes?"

"If your offer still stands," she said with a tremulous smile, "then my answer is yes. I love you, Ian, and I want to be your wife. Will you be my husband?"

His answer was much less complicated than her own. His arms were around her, pulling her hard against him. Their full, lush kiss made her doubt she would ever be able to walk again, much less recall the correct Linnaean names for plants. When they finally pulled apart enough to breathe, eons later, Sophie pressed her flushed cheek against the moving column of his throat.

"I can't be a normal baroness," she said. "Or viscountess."

"I just want you to be Sophie," said Ian, his breath against her hair. "Nothing else matters to me."

Several yards away, everyone watched as Sophie and Ian lost themselves in each other in a flurry of kisses and quiet promises. Caroline and Simon Andrews silently loaded themselves back into their carriage, with Lord Charles following. They all cast a final, doleful look at Sophie before driving away. John Driscoll ambled inside to find a footman and share a toast of whiskey. There was plenty of good news to spread through the servants' quarters.

Lord Briarleigh and Alforth shook hands as they too went back into the hall.

"It seems we are about to become family, Mr. Morley," William said with a grin.

Alforth smiled, thinking of his niece and remembering his own Violet, always young, always beautiful, waiting for him somewhere. They would be together again someday, but there was still a lot of life to be lived, and a distant shore to be explored.

"It does indeed, Lord Briarleigh," he said.

Epilogue

Alforth sat reading in the study at the rear of his new estate. It had been completed the previous fall but had not been completely habitable until only a few months earlier. The estate had no name—the servants had been polled to come up with something suitable and had so far been able to muster only the prosaic sobriquet New Place. And that was what it would be called until something better suggested itself. In keeping with his recent move, Alforth rather fancied this name, and anything more grand seemed to go against the egalitarian flavor of his new American home. Christmas had been a grand affair, with dancing and plenty of ale for everyone. No Boxing Day in America. The servants had their holidays when he did. Easter, no doubt, would be a similarly festive affair.

He liked this room best because Sophie would have

liked it. The study faced the gardens, the gardens she had designed by proxy, and he took immense pleasure in looking up from his book from time to time to admire her handiwork. She would have made a wonderful designer of gardens, but he did not begrudge her the fact that her interests lay elsewhere. No matter. He loved her garden, and so on cool days, when his knee bothered him and he could not go outside, he sat as near to it as he could. He preferred an American winter to any England could offer.

A tap at the door brought his attention around and he called, "Enter." Meredith Driscoll, well into her sixth month of pregnancy, came in bearing a letter on a tray.

"This just arrived for you, sir," she said. "I know you usually wait until later to read your letters, but I couldn't help seeing the direction and thought you would want to have it right away."

"Thank you, Meredith," Alforth said, taking the missive from her. "You know," he added kindly, "you really ought to be resting. I told you and John already that I would continue to pay your wages if you decide to stop working, even after the baby comes. It's the least I can do for you since you and Driscoll came with me to America."

"Oh, no, sir," Meredith said with a blush as she patted her belly. "I like to work. My ma wrote me saying that staying active is good for the baby. Makes him good and healthy. And I like Newport, too. I'd never seen the ocean until we came here, and the sea air is going to be grand for the child."

"I think so, too," Alforth said with a smile, but then he caught sight of the familiar handwriting on

the letter and barely heard when Meredith left the
room, quietly shutting the door behind her.

Putting on his glasses, he read.

7 December 1766
Constantinople

Dear Uncle A,

The journey was long, but at last we are heading
homeward again, hopefully to see you by Easter
at the latest, though it is difficult to arrange passage during these winter months. Everyone
seems inclined to spend the season tucked away
with the comforts of hearth and home. But that
is precisely why we are so eager to come to you.

We have both been exceptionally busy collecting specimens in the Near East—as you well
know there are *hundreds* of plants that no one in
Europe or America even knows about. Ian has no
trouble moving around, but there has been some
struggle finding ways a woman (and a European)
can have access to these plants. We've come up
with quite a few creative solutions, however, and
I will have scores of tales to tell you upon our
homecoming—though I cannot be certain if I
may indeed call it a "homecoming," since I have
never been to your new home. But wherever you
are, regardless of location, is home to me. And
now, at last, I will see America!

Thank you for sending me the final printing
of my little monograph, "Chemical Symbiosis
of the Sessile Oak and Peach-Leaved Bellflower," as well as the clippings. I had no idea it

would be so well received! (Ian claims that I did, in fact, know it would be a success and am being falsely modest, but he does like to tease me.) Word reached us in Cairo that the Royal Society would like me to lead a series of informal salons regarding my research once we return to England. M. Berthiot, whom you may recall kept a correspondence with me when I was known as Mr. Andrew Sophey will be unable to attend, though he has sent word that he commends his "young gentle(wo)man protégé." Ian has promised to watch the baby during these salons, but I should like nothing more than to lecture with little Violet perched on my hip. She has already spoken her first word: *angiosperm*. Well, to me it sounded like angiosperm. Ian believes she was attempting to say *candy*.

This letter serves a dual purpose. The first is to announce our imminent voyage to Rhode Island, and the second is to say that soon Violet will be joined by a sibling. I want to be near you when I deliver this baby, since Lord Briarleigh was good enough to attend us in Venice when Violet was born. He was a very proud grandfather, buying flowers by the cartload for half the populace of the city. I shudder to think what gesture of extravagance he might bestow upon us for this child if he were present for the birth. (And if it is a boy, only the great Shiva knows what William might buy. Perhaps all of Holland.) But most of all, I miss you, dear Uncle A. It has been too long since we have sat comfortably together, as we used to, talking of plans and dreams.

I wonder if I will have anything to speak of, since I feel so perfectly content with my life as it is. How can I dream when my dreams have come true? Truly, Uncle A, I never expected such happiness, and I give thanks every day for the blessings I have received.

With sincerest affection,
I remain,
your niece,
Sophie

After reading the letter once, Alforth read it slowly again, and then a third time, until he was satisfied, for now. He slipped it into his pocket, knowing that he would read it several more times that day, and all the days in between, until Sophie and her husband and child were sitting with him in this very room.

He picked up his book, then set it down again immediately. Musing, thoughtful, he slowly got to his feet and ambled to the window to look out into the garden. Sophie would be very pleased with the way things had turned out. Though he had described the fruition of her efforts for his garden in his letters, he was eager to show her the final outcome. And he had a little surprise for her, too. He stared at that surprise now, smiling to himself. The garden would be in bloom when she arrived, giving her the perfect opportunity to witness her old uncle's botanical efforts.

Planted in the very center of the garden, on a rise and surrounded by neat hedges, stood a single, robust oak. A sessile oak, he had made certain. And come next spring, the oak would be encircled with the light blue blossoms of the bellflower. Both were imported from England, the few remembrances of his old home he wanted near him. The gardener had looked skeptical when Alforth had ordered the tree and the flower to be planted side by side.

But Alforth knew that they would grow beautifully together.

AUTHOR'S NOTE

This book is, at its core, about following your heart, wherever and with whomever it takes you. The botany within it is mostly true, but I have shaped it to serve the story. Science is continually evolving, so perhaps there might truly exist the bioluminescent St. Elmo's Wort, even if it isn't in the wilds of Gloucestershire. And maybe modern botanists will discover the symbiotic relationship between the Sessile Oak and the Peach-Leaved Bellflower if Sophie's lost notes are ever discovered.

Your servant & c.,

Zoe